Memory Whispers

***

Angel Smits

Memory Whispers
Published by ImaJinn Books, a division of ImaJinn

ISBN: 0-9759653-3-6

10 9 8 7 6 5 4 3 2 1

PUBLISHER'S NOTE:
This book is a work of fiction. Names, characters, places and incidents are products of the author's imagination or are used fictitiously. Any resemblance to actual events or locales or persons, living or dead, is entirely coincidental.

Books are available at quantity discounts when used to promote products or services. For information please write to: Marketing Division, ImaJinn Books, P.O. Box 545, Canon City, CO 81215-0545, or call toll free 1-877-625-3592.

Cover design by Patricia Lazarus

ImaJinn Books, a division of ImaJinn
P.O. Box 545, Canon City, CO 81215-0545
Toll Free: 1-877-625-3592
http://www.imajinnbooks.com

He'd been making love to her in her dreams for years, but he wasn't a dream...

"Maybe we *have* met before, Ms. McCoy. Before last night, I mean."

"Maybe. I...I don't know." Faith swallowed against the dryness in her suddenly parched throat.

"You do look familiar," he whispered close to her ear.

She wasn't about to let him know just *how* familiar. A hot flash slipped over her as the thought passed through her mind that this man—or his dream twin—had seen her without her clothes, had actually made love to her only hours earlier.

"Maybe in another life?" he said, and then he laughed.

His words hit her hard. She nearly doubled over from the impact. Could that possibly be where her dreams came from? No, it couldn't be. She looked up at him and his expression looked as startled as she felt.

To escape her own thoughts as much as his presence she turned abruptly and nearly fell over a chair. His warm hand curled around her arm to steady her. "Thank you," she whispered.

He nodded and stepped away,

Relieved by the absence of his disturbing hand, she said, "I'm sure you're curious about the upstairs." She made her way up the steps toward the observation room. Perversely, she wanted to see his reaction. Needed to see it.

"Tell me—who takes care of you?" he asked when they reached the top of the stairs.

"No one. I'm not helpless."

His laugh was soft and deep. "Is that why you run around barefoot in the middle of the night. He leaned closer, his body heat teasing her. "And let strange men give you large sums of money?" He reached up and ran his finger down her heated cheek. "What do you think most men would expect for such a favor?"

"Oh, I don't know..." She backed away from him, her footsteps oddly loud on the carpet runner. "Perhaps this?"

She grabbed the wall hanging and shoved it aside. She lifted her chin and met his stare.

He gasped. Reaching out, he touched the observation room's painted glass. A breath's time later, he spun around and grabbed her. The fabric tumbled back into place.

His fingers bit into her arms as his words slashed through the air. "What the hell are you trying to pull?"

This book is dedicated to my parents, Hugh and Joyce Strong. Thanks for all the traipsing through Cripple Creek in years past. Your interest sparked mine, and I appreciate you always being there for me. I love you both.

One

Cripple Creek, Colorado

Faith McCoy stared at Bennett Avenue from the museum window. It hardly seemed possible she was finally here in Cripple Creek, a town with a history as colorful as the aspen groves that blanketed the surrounding mountains. Below, the wide street was uneven in places. The sidewalks ran at awkward angles much as they must have a hundred years ago. She felt the pull of history, as if she had stepped backward in time.

Thanks to the legalization of gambling, the old buildings that a few years ago had fallen empty and to ruin, were now refurbished and reflected the grandeur of the late eighteen nineties. The spirit of the past mingled with the reality of the present and casinos and businesses crowded the street.

The view soothed her. Beautiful buildings like these were the reason she was here. She'd come to capture the history through her camera lens. From the time she'd first heard about this project she knew she wanted to be a part of it. The buildings provided a new subject for her, and they played into her personal fascination with the past. Hopefully she'd put together a photography collection that would benefit both the Colorado Historical Association as well as her own pathetic bank account.

It was a good town. Solid, with roots. And yet there was something about it. Something that made her feel comfortable and reluctant to return to her house in Boulder. She'd never called any one place home—her father's church work kept the family moving too often for that—but there was an undeniable familiarity to Cripple Creek.

The only major problem she had was the dreams, and they were nothing new. They just seemed more frequent lately.

"If you'll follow me."

The tour guide's voice broke into Faith's thoughts and she turned away from the window. Single file, the small group made their way down the narrow hall. The air, already stifling in the close space, grew thicker and Faith dabbed at the perspiration on her brow.

When the guide turned a corner and stopped, Faith could only stare at the door. Shock snapped through her like lightning, leaving nothing of her emotions but charred remains.

Only this time she was awake.

It was the same door, the door in the dream that haunted her night after night. But it couldn't be. That was just a dream...wasn't it?

She reached out tentatively and grasped the antique doorknob. Fear dampened her palms with perspiration as she turned the time-smoothed metal. The door didn't budge. The lock held solid.

"I'm sorry, Miss. That room isn't part of the tour."

Faith didn't answer. The guide's voice seemed to come from a long way off.

"Miss?" The older woman's voice rose in concern as she tapped Faith's arm. "Are you all right?"

Faith forced her mind back to reality, and she focused on the antique décor of the museum that had once been a brothel. "I...I'm fine." Chills rocked through her as she turned to the guide. "Why isn't this room part of the tour? What's in there?"

A flash of uncertainty and mischief sparked in the older woman's eyes. "Perhaps not *what's* in there, but what was *done* there. It was the observation room," she whispered loud enough for only Faith to hear.

"The what?" Faith whispered back. Her research had referred to such things, but she'd never actually seen one before.

"An observation room." Several other members of the tour moved closer, and the guide shrugged as if in defeat. "One of the girls would go inside, and the gentleman interested in purchasing her for the evening stood outside here."

The guide pushed aside a fabric wall hanging to expose a glass window between the two rooms, which had been painted over from the inside. "The girl disrobed, so he could see what he was buying." She released the wall hanging, and it swished back into place, hiding the window once again. "The corset was a very deceiving device, hiding flaws such as a few extra pounds or too small a bust line," she explained.

Faith shivered. Revulsion slid through her, and she saw similar emotions mirrored on the faces of the others. How could a woman degrade herself like that? A warm flush spread across her cheeks as she recalled her own dreams—or rather nightmares—which frequently included such things as disrobing before a stranger. Her cheeks warmed, and she avoided the others' gazes.

The tour group moved on, but Faith lingered. Images flashed through her mind. Familiar images. Images she'd spent years denying.

A sudden need to find the setting she saw in the shadows of

her mind grew. Would seeing the room banish the dreams? Her hopes rose, but she quickly squelched them. Nothing else had worked. Yet she wanted—she needed—to know more.

She ached to shake the old door until it fell from its hinges. It looked fragile enough. Glancing at the guide's retreating back, Faith pushed on the handle again. The lock remained solidly in place. The group turned the corner, and Faith stood there, the air around her growing heavy and warm with her uncertainty.

She reached into her oversized purse and pulled out a credit card. She'd locked herself out too many times, she decided, as the idea came so easily. Carefully, to avoid damaging the old lock, she slid the card along the frame. A familiar, soft click signaled her success. She'd just peek, just for a second. She had to know if the room inside would match her dreams.

She heard the group head downstairs, and the guide launched into an impassioned speech about how the museum depended on the donations of kind patrons to continue operation. Using the sounds of the woman's voice and the group's footsteps to conceal her actions, Faith pushed the door open. The seldom-used hinges squealed in protest. She quickly slipped inside and closed the door.

She leaned against the wood and gulped in several breaths, fighting to calm her racing heart. Dank, musty air clogged her lungs, and she muffled a reflexive cough with her hand.

Dingy light seeped through the thin layer of paint covering the window. Where she had shivered before, she now trembled.

It *was* the room in her dreams. A room she had never seen in reality before today. The objects were eerily familiar, though they seemed older and were covered in dust.

A tall, wood-framed mirror stood in one corner, its surface surreal through a coat of grime. Beside the mirror sat a tattered fainting couch. Boxes of old papers covered the faded maroon horsehair. Dust cloaked everything.

In the opposite corner sat a trunk. Earlier, the guide had explained how all the girls who had *worked the line* owned them. It made movement from place to place quick and easy. Inside would be all that was left of some girl's life before she *turned out.*

She eyed the trunk's brass fittings. Who'd left this trunk here? Had she been one of the girls who had died here, as the tour guide had mentioned earlier? Was there even anything inside? At the thought, images from her dream flashed through her mind.

A blue dress.

A jeweled comb.

Slowly, she stepped forward to the trunk, leaving telltale footprints in the thick dust. She knelt down. Dare she open it?

She'd heard the tales of the *soiled doves* who had lived in this house nearly a hundred years before. She had cringed as the guide explained about each piece of furniture. The antiques were appealing, but what about the people who had spent their lives lounging on them? Were their stories left out on purpose or by accident?

Either way, the rehearsed script seemed so distant, so impersonal, as Faith knelt before the remnants of one of those lives. No one would know if she took a little peek. Feeling only a slight twinge of guilt, she reached out.

The gentle snap of the latch seemed loud in the tiny room. She froze, waiting to see if anyone came to stop her. No one did, and she pushed up the heavy lid. The cloying scent of ancient mothballs nearly overpowered her.

A gauzy piece of old tissue covered the contents of the trunk. She lifted the paper. Her heart stopped and then pounded against her ribcage. A royal blue gown lay gracefully folded on top. Its bead and crystal bodice winked in the faded light.

Just like the one she wore in her endless dreams.

With growing trepidation, she caressed the soft fabric. The hard beads slid beneath her fingertips.

So beautiful. So familiar. Suddenly, the world that had haunted her dreams for more nights then she cared to count flashed before her. She trembled as the dream played out once again.

She stood facing the mirror. The warm velvet of the dress felt heavy and confining against her body and swept the floor. A long train weighed down the back and flowed behind her as she moved.

The full-length mirror reflected a lovely creature. Long curls that normally fell past her waist were piled on top of her head. A jewel-encrusted comb held her hair in place, allowing a few strands to fall against her cheeks, as if to encourage a masculine hand to brush them away.

Large leg-omutton sleeves helped accentuate the tiny waist that could only be the result of a well-cinched corset. A blush crept over her cheeks as she noticed how she filled and nearly overflowed the low neckline.

The vivid blue of the dress accented the creamy whiteness

of her skin, the copper of her hair and the hazel-green of her eyes. She looked the same, yet the reflection was different. The eyes staring back at her were different—lifeless.

Something moved behind her, and she watched a man appear in the observation window. Shadows and wavy glass distorted his face, denying her a clear view. Dark hair and a mustache dominated his features. Broad shoulders filled his tailored jacket, and a proper white shirt barely disguised the muscles of his chest.

With a deep intake of breath, she stopped her visual journey. Attraction was not important here. He was a client and nothing more. A rich client. He had to be to get past the front door.

In one hand he held a crystal tumbler half full of amber liquor. From here she couldn't tell what it was, but Madame kept nothing but the best. Between the fingers of his other hand rested a thin cigar. He lifted it to his lips and blew two perfect smoke rings into the air. A wicked smile formed on his lips, and she shivered.

Fear warned her that this man had the power to break her.

His gaze devoured her with its implied touch. Hot fire roared in her bloodstream, and she swallowed hard to relieve the pressure. It did little good.

Surprised at the strength of her reactions, her hand flew to her throat. A cameo brooch hung from a blue ribbon. In fascination, she watched the woman in the mirror unpin the brooch. Her own hand mimicked the gesture.

The man stood perfectly still, watching her every move through the window. Her gaze riveted to his reflection, and a new kind of shiver took hold. The room warmed along with her blood.

She reached behind her back and released the row of pearl buttons running the length of the dress one by one. Cool evening air brushed her heated skin as she shrugged the gown off her shoulders.

The rich fabric rustled as it slid over her full breasts, tiny waist and hips. She bent over, giving him a silhouetted view. Slowly, she stepped out of the puddled garment. The tap of her high heels on the floor shattered the tension of the air. She knew he heard nothing.

Carefully, she lifted the dress over her arm. With slow, deliberate steps, she walked to the couch and draped the gown across the back.

A straight wooden chair sat next to the couch, and she lifted her foot to the seat. She unhooked her shoe and slid it off, then removed the other. The black silk stockings caressed her skin, and she slid one finger beneath the garter. She unhooked the stocking and the fabric whispered down her leg. Daring to steal a glance at him, she felt the fire in his eyes, and she removed the other stocking with the same slow, enticing pace. Never once did she break eye contact.

Her breath caught in her chest. She wasn't sure if it was the confines of the corset or the passion emanating from him. She tore her gaze from his and unlaced the corset. It felt so good to be free and unbound even though her ribs ached. Rolling the fabric and whalebone, she slid it into the decorated bag lying on the couch.

She turned to face him then, with only her chemise covering her. Deliberately, slowly, she pulled the jeweled comb from her hair. The heavy copper curls cascaded down, caressing her skin as they fell.

He took a deep swallow of his drink. The lamplight gleamed on his brow, and her gaze traveled the sharp curve of his cheek, resting at last on his mouth. She imagined his taste. Whiskey and man.

Gathering the hem of her chemise, she pulled the garment up and over her head. As she stretched her arms upward, to escape the last of the cloth, she saw him gulp the remainder of his drink.

She stood there totally nude. Longing seized her body. She wanted his hands—the fingers clasping that tumbler so tightly it threatened to shatter—to touch her instead. Suddenly, she knew she'd felt their touch before.

He nodded. A key scraped in the lock. The door swung open. She stood there facing the man without the barrier of the window glass between them.

His shoulders filled the doorway, and the anger in his eyes struck terror in her heart. She clasped her arms self-consciously over her chest, wanting to scurry into hiding. Pride made her stay. She met his gaze with a defiant lift of her chin.

The words falling from his lips rocked the world's foundations. "So, this is what you've become...wife."

Faith jumped. The trunk lid slammed down and caught her finger. She yelped and then clamped her jaw shut, suffering the pain in silence.

The dream faded, and the dusty surroundings came back into focus. She closed her eyes, shutting out the all-too-familiar room. She crossed her arms over her chest, hugging herself, hoping to ease the familiar empty ache the dream always left behind. The ache that magnified the hollowness in her chest and the cold that settled around her heart.

He'd never spoken before. This time he'd left words, but where had they come from? Her imagination? Always before he came to her, then vanished, leaving nothing but emptiness in his wake.

She blinked the tears from her eyes. He'd made her cry too many times.

She heard the sound of voices. The tour group? How long had she been here? Rising unsteadily to her feet, she backed up until she bumped against the closed door.

She scanned the room again. Nothing had changed in the last five minutes, so why did she feel different? She looked back at the trunk. What else was in there? Should she look at the rest of the contents? Or should she run away from the images and their accompanying emotions? The latter won out.

Afraid of answers to her own questions, she turned to escape.

"Why, you silly fool." A soft, feminine voice echoed in the room.

"Hello?" Faith hadn't heard footsteps, and she didn't see anyone.

A giggle slid through the cloying air. Wrenching the door open, she rushed out into the hall, nearly toppling a hat rack sitting outside the door. The hair at the back of her neck stood on end. Chills ran through her.

Get out, her mind screamed. *Leave this place and never come back.* She wanted to. Really wanted to. But she knew she couldn't really leave it all behind. The room and the man would follow in her dreams. Turning, she ran down the stairs, uncaring that her steps might be heard. As she flew toward the front door, she noticed the tour guide standing in the hall talking with a tall black man.

"Upstairs," a woman's voice said, a voice that wasn't the tour guide's.

"No," Faith cried.

"What, dear?" The woman looked at her.

"N...nothing. I'm sorry."

"Come on up and see me."

Faith tore open the entry door and ran from the house. The giggle she had heard upstairs rang in her head. Her breath ripped through her lungs, and her heart slammed against her ribs. At the corner, she stopped and looked back at the house.

It stood as stately and elegant as when she'd entered. The soaring turret, wide verandah and carved gingerbread spoke of a time long past. Dove gray paint added a haughty air, which the peach trim only slightly muted.

Leaning back against a worn brick wall, she closed her eyes and tried to catch her breath. Madness. The dream had sent her near the edge many times. Night after night she awakened, sweating and aching from the potency of the images. Now, the images threatened her waking sanity. She had to fight, but fight what?

The rough brick of the old building bit into her back. She whispered a brief thanks for the slight discomfort. It meant she was awake. Still sane.

She concentrated on her breathing. In. Out. Slowly. The air's sweet scents reminded her she was high in the Rocky Mountains. Her equilibrium returned, and Faith gave in to it.

Opening her eyes, she grasped for the reality around her. The familiar sights of Cripple Creek settled into focus.

Maybe she was just tired. Disrupted sleep and sixteen-hour days could do that. That's why she'd hallucinated back there. Relieved that she'd found a reasonable explanation, she took several more calming breaths. With her confidence firmly back in place, she stepped away from the wall and out onto the sidewalk. As the sun slipped behind the surrounding tall peaks, lights came on in the tiny mountain town.

She turned to look back at the museum again. Suddenly, in one of the house's upper turret windows, a young girl pulled the curtains away from the glass. But there hadn't been anyone upstairs, Faith was sure of it.

Even from this distance, she felt the intensity of the girl's stare, sensed her animosity. Through the old distorted glass she saw the girl's long, black hair hanging in ringlets past her bare shoulders.

A shiver of foreboding snaked up Faith's spine as the girl tipped her head back and laughed.

***

The dream faded. This time the man slipped away without speaking.

"Come back," she whispered, but he didn't hear her. The blackness engulfed him and startled her awake.

Abruptly, Faith sat up in bed. The springs of the hotel's antique brass bed squeaked.

Her heart pounded in her chest and echoed in her brain. *The dream. Damn the dream.* She tried to calm her heart's racing beat by focusing on the ordinary room, on the here and now. She closed her eyes only to see him behind her eyelids. She snapped them open again, anything to chase him away.

Why had the man faded before he spoke? The words he'd said in the observation room only a few short hours ago echoed in her mind. They seemed more real to her than the rest of the dream ever had.

Voices startled her, and she nearly laughed out loud with relief when she realized they weren't disembodied. These were real and coming from outside.

She climbed out of bed to close the wood-framed window. Cool mountain air, heavy with the scent of pine, slipped inside the room. She breathed deeply and fought to slow her thoughts and cool her body.

Frustrated with the dream and her reactions, she stared at the alley below. In the moonlight she made out the silhouettes of two men walking through the night.

They were *trying* to walk anyway. From the zigzag pattern of their path, she realized it was more like one held up the other. The sound of booted feet against the crumbling cobblestones resounded off the surrounding high walls.

Like many of the other old buildings, the hotel's original owner had put much effort into the front and neglected the other three sides. Black lattice fire escapes wove back and forth up the brick walls on each side of the dimly lit alley.

"When are you going to learn?" One man's deep voice broke the night and throbbed in her chest like the bass drum of a passing parade band.

"Hell, learn what? How to punch an idiot harder?"

Faith recognized the voice despite the fact that it was muffled. A security guard at one of the casinos, the Double Barrel Saloon, Johnny Harper was a big bear of a man who'd given her directions the first time she'd visited Cripple Creek. He never hesitated to greet her when they met on the street. His gap-toothed grin and size reminded her of a bedraggled teddy bear.

"Come on, man. I may not always be around to bail your butt out of trouble. What are you going to do then?"

"Hell, I don't know. Find a new friend?" Howling laughter climbed up into the night air, and Johnny doubled over as glee overtook him.

"You know damned well no one else would put up with your behavior." The man with the sober, sexy voice chastised Johnny. Could this be the boss and friend Johnny'd mentioned? Curious, she leaned a little closer to the window.

Together, the two men stumbled toward the bright halo of the old-fashioned street lamp. She caught a glimpse of the man whose voice seemed to echo the beat of her heart. Johnny stopped and sank to the curb as the other man leaned against the lamppost.

He reached into the pocket of his T-shirt and extracted a slim cigar, which he slipped between his lips. The scraping sound of a struck match broke the silence of the alley.

For an instant, flickering flame illuminated his features. Faith gasped. She swallowed the scream bubbling in her throat and ducked back behind the curtains. His head snapped up as the muffled sound seemed to reach his ears. Shadowed eyes stared up into the darkness, and the dream suddenly seemed too real. *He* seemed too real.

She covered her heated cheeks with her hands as if he could see her and tell what she was thinking. The dream returned to taunt her, and the questions she'd asked herself a million times ran through her mind. Where had the dream come from? Why did she know what it felt like to slowly peel away her clothes? She'd never stripped for a man. Sure, she'd had several relationships. A couple had been serious enough to make her think of wedding bells, but never had they progressed to the dream's level of sensual intimacy.

Yet, she knew it all. Knew how it felt to have a man's gaze roam over her body. Knew the heat that crept into her bloodstream and tingled under her skin.

And knew this man's face.

But that couldn't be. The emotions she could blame on reading too many romance novels...but his face? It was a coincidence. Or maybe it was simply that she had seen him before and superimposed his features on the man in her dream. He was handsome enough to catch any woman's eye. And she wasn't immune.

Relief washed over her at the realization. That was it. This man looked similar, yes, but there were differences, like the fact that he didn't wear a thick, dark mustache.

She slipped further into the shadows. Her eyes drank in every inch of him, her imagination filling in the details the shadows hid from her eyes. He was tall, well over Johnny's six feet. The breadth of his shoulders pulled his T-shirt tight over the muscles of his upper arms.

Moonlight and the distorting glow of the streetlight didn't allow her to see the true color of his hair, but she knew the thick dark curls were brown and soft to the touch. She almost felt the smooth, high cheekbones and even planes of his face. The rough texture of his whiskers would tickle the sensitive tips of her fingers.

She tore her mind from that dangerous path. *Stop.* She wasn't here for personal reasons, she reminded herself. She was here to work, that was all.

She'd finished photographing all the buildings on the original subject list. Tomorrow she'd head home. But what about the brothel? It wasn't on the original list—a fact she was sure her father had engineered. The historical association might want the pictures, but Reverend McCoy would never allow his daughter to visit a house of ill repute, even a defunct one. She figured she'd never tell him about today's visit.

Still, the building's clean architectural lines and Victorian air seemed to call to her. It was familiar. Like this man? *Like the voice upstairs?*

She shivered at the memory. No, not like that. Different, as if something from inside her reached out to it.

Her heart pounded in her chest as she continued to stare down at the men. There were no answers in the darkness, just the dregs of her doubts and dreams.

Time and reality faded away, and like a double exposure, she saw him in a great black cape. He blew two perfect smoke rings into the air as he stared up at her window. She blinked and the vision vanished, but the man remained, as did a deep soul-scarring pain that vibrated across the cool night and shivered through her heart.

Two

Cordell Burke saw her through the play of dark and light. Perched on the windowsill, her face partially hidden in the midnight shadows, she seemed familiar.

She turned then, facing him. Their eyes met, and Cord felt as if a fist slammed into his gut.

It was her, the woman who haunted his dreams. There was no mistake. Those long, luscious copper-colored curls. The soft curves of her body. She'd visited his dreams on too many nights. Usually she waited to visit until he was sound asleep, but not tonight. He didn't mind. He enjoyed her visits. The things he dreamed of doing to her...with her...

He blinked several times before rubbing his tired eyes, but she didn't go away. She continued to stare at him. The full moon climbed higher in the sky, and an errant ray slid across her. Heat rushed through his body as he recalled the smooth skin beneath the simple gown. He groaned, the sound echoing through the alley.

Cord wanted her, as he always wanted her. Since that first dream in which she'd seduced him, he'd craved her and only her. He never reacted like this to any other woman—to any *real* woman. She touched something inside him. Warmed him. His arms ached to hold her and protect her. From what, he didn't know, but the need pulsed through him just the same.

She wasn't real. She couldn't be. She was a concoction of the night and his travel-weary mind.

"Cord? Cord!"

Johnny's voice broke into the images that had taken possession of Cord's mind. He looked down at his friend sitting on the curb.

"I don't think I can get up," Johnny said.

Cord sighed. Keeping Johnny out of trouble was turning into a full-time job, a job he didn't want. He'd had enough of that growing up, taking care of his father. Acid memories came back of chasing his father from bar to bar and dragging him home in time to rush off to school. But he forced those thoughts away. Johnny wasn't his father, and Cord was no longer a boy trying to be a man and receiving nothing but pain as payment.

He extended his hand, and Johnny took hold. Cord hauled him to his feet, and the two of them stumbled for an instant before they stood steady.

Cord looked back up at the window. Empty. "Did you see a woman?" He pointed to the darkened opening. "Up in that window?"

"You're hallucinatin', bud. Ain't no woman hanging out a window to look at a couple old drunks." Johnny snickered.

"Speak for yourself. I'm only thirty-four, and I haven't been drinking. You have. Again." He must have imagined her after all. An unwelcome sensation—disappointment?—settled into the pit of his stomach. Slowly, he walked Johnny around the corner and toward The Double Barrel Saloon. Home.

***

Faith had to prove to herself that he wasn't the man from her dreams. She grabbed her jeans and tugged them on, then shoved her nightgown into the waistband. Halfway down the hall she was still pulling on her jacket.

Antique wall lamps dimly lit the hall, and she slowed to keep from tripping. The exit door smacked against the wall as she stepped out into the alley.

Cool night air wrapped around her, and she shivered. Jagged rocks poked the soles of her feet, but she didn't have time to go back and get her shoes.

Noise from the nearby casinos echoed through the deserted air. The streetlight where the men had stood moments earlier cast its glow only a few feet. Patches of light fell through a few windows above, leaving the alley shrouded in a heavy darkness.

They were gone. The alley was empty. Disappointment shot through her.

Crossing to where the men had been, she glanced up to her own window. Had he seen her? What had he thought as he looked at her? Had she imagined the recognition in his eyes?

Don't be ridiculous, she scolded herself. *He hasn't the foggiest idea who I am.* A cool breeze slid between the buildings, and she shivered again.

The bright casinos beckoned. He'd gone that way, and Faith followed. Old-fashioned storefronts splashed light on the uneven sidewalks. It was late, but the town was alive with people and sound.

He'd been with Johnny. The Double Barrel Saloon sat at the end of the block. Like a tempting jewel in a priceless necklace, it dared her to touch. Faith hurried in that direction. Maybe someone there knew where they had gone.

Shivering, Faith rubbed her hands up and down her arms. She stopped and stared through the storefront at the crowd of gamblers. She heard her father's sermons on "dens of sin" repeat in her mind. He definitely wouldn't approve of this place.

She gritted her teeth as she remembered their latest conversation. She'd practically pleaded with him to help her get this job. In a way she felt she owed him some loyalty, but she chafed against that debt.

She'd worked hard to make it on her own. She'd wanted to do this job, but her father's involvement was grating. If only there'd been another way. She stared through the window at a world she'd never experienced before. One that fascinated and scared her at the same time. A world of wealth and risk, of fortunes made and lost, of addictions and failures.

It was drastically different from the safe existence of taking wedding photos and family portraits, a life her father thought she should live.

Just as the brothel hadn't been on the project list, neither were any of the casinos, even those in historic buildings. Her father's hand reaching out to protect her—again? She understood his concern, but wondered if he'd ever let her grow up. She hesitated only an instant longer before stepping inside the casino.

Players pulled the handles of slot machines, the wheels spinning in a myriad of colors and calliope-like music. Music played as coins clanked into the metal tray. A few feet away men sat at half-circle tables. Smoke wafted up from forgotten cigarettes as they stared at their cards.

These weren't carefully contrived photographer poses but reality. There were no smiling brides who turned into weeping barracudas, or babies who smiled except when the camera aimed in their direction. Faith wished for her camera, longing to put to film the expressions of the winners—and the losers. Here she'd control the shot—not brides or mothers.

Clickity-clack. Clickity-clack. A roulette wheel spun and drew her attention. Several people leaned over the edge of the wooden table, and cheers rose in the air as it stopped. "Red eighteen," a man's deep voice boomed over the crowd. A tall, blonde woman screamed in excitement.

A heavy-set man waved a handful of money in the air. "This round's on me." The woman next to him grinned and reminded him that the drinks were free. With a sheepish grin, he ordered the drinks anyway, and everyone laughed. It was all too perfect. Why hadn't she brought her camera?

A waitress in a short dress balanced a tray on one hand as she stopped beside Faith. "Can I get you anything?"

"No. Thanks." The girl sashayed away, and Faith watched her fade into the crowd. All around her people were packed in close. She didn't recognize a soul.

Johnny was nowhere to be seen, nor was the other man. This was ridiculous. She'd never find them. *What am I doing here?* She needed to get up early tomorrow. She should be in bed.

She took a couple of steps backward and bumped into something...someone...hard and warm. Two strong hands on her arms steadied her. She turned and stopped, paralyzed.

Him.

"May I help you?" His words were common, welcoming, but there was nothing common about him. The question in his tone told her he was surprised to see her.

What had she been thinking? Now that she'd found him, what could she say? How did she ask a stranger about the sensual images of her dreams? Heat flushed her cheeks at those memories. "I...uh...I was just leaving."

"But I just saw you walk in." His eyes were full of questions. She didn't have any answers.

"I was, uh, just curious, I guess. It's late."

"The night is young." That deep baritone filled her mind and soul. "Why don't you try your hand?"

"I...I've never gambled before." If she turned and ran would he follow her? Or let her go? She swallowed the longing to find out. Up close he was even handsomer than in the dream. The deep blue of his eyes pulled her in, and she stared, aware of the angles of his cheeks and the soft curve of his lips. He smiled suddenly, and she prayed he couldn't read her thoughts.

"Now's as good a time as any to learn." His big, warm hand cupped her elbow, distracting her. Gently, he guided her to the table, and she leaned against the wooden rail as she'd seen the others do. She stared at the grid of numbers painted on the green felt.

"Name's Cord Burke." His voice rose as the din of the crowd grew. "What's yours?"

She stared a moment. Cord? As in whipcord tight muscles? As in corded abs? She was losing it now. Tearing her gaze from his big, solid body, she looked into his eyes. "Faith McCoy." She automatically reached for her business card then realized she'd left her purse in her room.

"Nice to meet you," he said, his hand engulfing hers in a warm shake.

"I don't have any money with me." Relief washed over her, and she turned to leave, but no such luck. His long, tanned fingers curled around hers, gentle but solid. The hands of a working man used to control and self-assurance. She tried to step back, but he held firm.

"Luke, give us a stack." His voice was too close to her ear. Too close to her heart. She pulled away from his grasp, and he let her go, but she didn't step away. Intrigued, she stayed to watch.

The man behind the wheel slid a stack of green chips across the table with a wooden stick. Cord tossed a chip onto a square in the grid. The wheel spun around before she could think, and her mind spun with it.

"Black four," the man behind the wheel called.

"Looks like you won," Cord said. Laughter built tiny lines around his eyes.

"I did?" She stared at the two stacks placed next to the previous one. She had no clue what the black and green chips were worth, but laughter bubbled in her throat. This was fun.

"Wanna let 'em ride?"

She shook her head, knowing there was no way the same number would come up again. A chuckle escaped his chest, a rich hearty sound, and he scooted half the stack to a red square.

"The lady'll go another round."

The little white ball bounced in and out of several slots before coming to rest on red twenty-three. Faith stared in dismay at the new stack of chips. "Oh, my." She looked over at her gambling partner. He wasn't even looking at the chips. Instead, his gaze nearly burned a hole through her.

She swallowed the tightness in her throat. Had she imagined the flare of awareness in his eyes? Her breath came in shallow gulps as she tried to clear her mind. What was she doing? She glanced at the gamblers around her. Cigarette smoke drifted to the ceiling, and in the distance coins hit metal and bells rang out to form a deafening roar.

Suddenly, Cord Burke's features filled her view. He seemed to be moving closer. Her gaze riveted on his lips. Wide and firm...and warm. She met his gaze, deep and blue, and his eyes lost their distance. She found herself staring into a soul filled with anger and pain.

"What do you want from me?"

His words startled her. She pulled away from him—from his disturbing touch and the realization that she wanted him to lean closer and place his lips on hers.

Tearing her gaze from his, she looked down at the floor—anywhere but into his questioning eyes. Two large, boot-clad feet were planted close to her bare ones. Dark leather boots... threatening and powerful, yet sexy. She suddenly felt very small and out of her element.

She turned and hurried outside, away from him and away from her own uncertainties. The night felt cool in comparison to the warm casino. Sharp edges of the sidewalk and stones poked her feet, but she didn't care. He didn't follow, and she pretended she wasn't disappointed.

That man. Those eyes. That look told her everything she didn't want to know. Recognition and passionate memories stared back at her.

Who was he? And how had he gotten inside her head?

***

The casino overflowed with life as the continuous clank of coins dropping into the slots filled the air around Cord. As he stood staring after her, two jackpots rang out.

Normally, he looked up to see how much he was giving away. Not tonight. Not with her image filling his mind. Not with the feel of her skin against his. Usually, the sounds comforted him, reassured him it was all his.

It was his, all right. His to give away. Even to beautiful damsels in distress with no money and a dream face. Would he never learn? *Stop tryin' to save ever' body.* His father's old line came back to him, and he cringed. Even from the grave the old man grated on his nerves.

Cord's long stride took him across the room to the bar. His thoughts jumbled together, and he had to do something to clear them. "Doug, pour me a couple fingers of whiskey," he demanded.

The younger man stared at him. "But Boss, you don't drink."

"Just pour," he growled. When the tumbler sat in front of him, he stared into the amber liquid. Doug was right. Cord didn't drink. He'd seen too much of the ravages of alcohol, but tonight something deep inside begged for release, for oblivion. Something he refused to analyze.

Vague, distant images swirled in his mind. Images he'd met before but only in the deep of night. Images that had plagued him since he was fifteen.

Purposefully, he brought the dream to mind, making himself face it. The sights and sounds around him faded away.

He stood in the narrow hallway of a house. A whisper of memory tugged at him, but he knew he'd never been here before. The sound of laughter and old-fashioned music drifted up a stairwell to his left, but the hallway itself was silent except for the sound of his own breathing.

There was a window in front of him. Odd place for a window, in an interior wall, looking into another room.

The cool, solid feel of the tumbler against his fingers made him look down. As if he had no control, he lifted the drink to his lips and sipped. The liquid slid down his throat in a smooth burn. Tennessee bourbon. His favorite.

Wait...he didn't have a favorite. He didn't drink.

Confusion and cigar smoke drifted around him, and he noticed the long taper resting between his fingers. Lifting the cigar, he tasted sweet Cuban tobacco and felt the unfamiliar brush of a mustache against his fingers.

Suddenly, the light from an oil lamp filtered through the window glass. A woman stood on the other side. She wore a blue dress, and her hair was curled on top of her head.

"Well, Mr. Cumberland?" A voice startled him. "Does she meet your approval?" He turned to see an older woman, the madam, standing a few feet away. She wore a low cut dress and a secretive smile.

Cumberland? She must have him confused with someone else.

The woman behind the glass unbuttoned her dress, and he couldn't tear his gaze away. Fire heated his blood as she slid the blue fabric down and slipped out of the old-fashioned underwear. She stood there in all her beautiful, naked glory, and he gulped the remainder of his drink.

"Yes," he groaned. If only for a little while. To forget for a short time that she wasn't the woman he really loved. The woman who was no longer his.

Madame reached into her pocket and produced a key, using it to open the door separating him from the beauty behind the glass.

"She's all yours—for tonight." Without another word, she turned and went back down the stairs, the key ring jingling in her pocket.

The beauty behind the glass turned to face him. The full glow of the light washed over her without the distortion of the window between them. How could he not have recognized her? How could the bright gold ring suspended around her neck have slipped past his gaze? He was such a fool. Damn her, and damn all deceitful women.

"So," he said, words that were like a well-rehearsed script. "This is what you've become...wife."

She stood staring at him as if the world crashed in around her. She clasped her arms protectively across her bare breasts. "Wh...what are you doing here?" She backed up and bumped against the wall with a start.

"What does it look like?" He tossed the empty tumbler toward the couch. And missed. The sound of shattering glass rattled around the room. "Looking for what I couldn't get at home. What are you doing here?"

"I couldn't live like you wanted me to, not anymore, not after T...Timmy."

"Don't ever say that name again," he yelled, and she flinched.

"Why not? He was your son, too." Suddenly, tears streamed down her face. She turned to leave. Before she could get through the doorway and away from him, he grabbed hold of her arm. His grip bit into her tender flesh.

The feel of her bare skin against his hand was a spark to dry tinder. Without thinking, without wanting to think, he hauled her into his arms. Trapped between the hard wall and his body, every inch of her pressed against him. God, she felt good. His fingers burrowed in the dark copper curls of her hair, holding her still so his mouth could find hers. The soft fragility of her lips was his undoing. He feasted on them, never wanting to stop.

"You're mine. But rather than live with me, you lower yourself to this?" He pulled back on her hair until her gaze met his. "I'll kill every man who has ever touched you."

"No!" She pulled free from him, leaving several long strands of red hair wrapped around his fingers. "Heaven help us both," she whispered. Turning away, she ran past him and

down the hall as if all the demons in hell were at her heels.

He turned to run after her, surprised when cool liquid splashed across his hand. What the...? He'd thrown the glass, hadn't he? Cord stopped, staring at the tumbler in his hand. The vision faded away, leaving him aching and empty.

Where had the anger come from? Always before he'd hauled her into his arms without a word and the dream ended with that kiss.

A kiss he could still taste.

The sights and sounds of the casino filtered back into focus. He set the glass down, his fingers shaking enough to slosh more of the liquor over his hand. Damn her. Damn the dream.

"Dump it," he ordered Doug as he slid the drink across the bar. He'd sworn off alcohol years ago and cursed himself for even considering it now.

His father's face floated in his mind, bloodshot eyes filled with tears for a woman he'd loved and lost. Cord remembered all too clearly the day he and his father stood on the front porch of their small frame house. Despising his mother and her lover as they drove away, Cord had vowed never to let a woman have that much control over him.

Never.

And Cord Burke refused to break his word—especially to himself.

Three

Faith climbed back into bed and huddled beneath the covers. What was wrong with her, running around town at all hours of the night? What made it worse was the realization that twice today she'd turned tail and run and that left a bad taste in her mouth.

Here in this room she felt safe and let herself relax. Tomorrow she'd get back to her work then head home. Enough of this silliness about dreams and familiar strangers.

She closed her eyes and sank into the oblivion of sleep, but rest eluded her. Even in her dreams, he came back. This time he smiled.

Loving warmth lived in his eyes.

The house was different. Smaller. Outside the window she saw a thick forest of pines and aspen.

His now familiar voice came from the doorway. "There you are." She turned to see his tall frame fill the opening. "I've been looking for you."

She smiled in response to the love on his lips and in his eyes.

"I've got a surprise for you." He stepped closer and pulled his hands from behind his back. The sweet scent of a single wild rose filled the air. In full bloom, the red flower was beautiful, and she noticed he'd removed the thorns.

"I love you." His voice grew soft and husky with emotion. "I'm so happy about the baby."

His lips met hers in a sweet, loving kiss. Strong arms circled her waist, pulling her against the length of his body. The scent of the crushed rose danced on the air between them.

She returned his passion with her own kiss, allowing her fingers to slide over the expanse of his chest and to the nape of his neck. The silky curls of his hair teased her fingertips.

Lifting her in his arms, he walked to the brass bed in the corner. He laid her down on top of the beautiful handmade wedding ring quilt.

"My baby," he whispered as his fingers blazed a trail toward the buttons of her bodice. "The first of many. If it's a boy I want to name him Timothy, after my father."

She sighed, giving in to his touch, relishing the desire racing through her. She opened the buttons of his shirt to reveal hard muscles to her seeking fingers.

Somewhere in the distance a door slammed.

Faith awoke with a start. Cool morning air chilled her sweat-dampened skin. It took several minutes before the blood stopped hammering through her veins, before the dream-induced desires faded.

Memories of last night joined her dream.

What was happening to her? Faith sat up and shoved tangled hair out of her eyes. The dreams had always been strong, but this had been so real. She still felt the warmth of his lips on hers. No real man had ever touched her like that. She wished one had.

Nonsense. Time to get up and get to work. She'd financed this whole trip with the first half of her advance and still had to earn the other half to pay her bills. She had less than two months to get it done and lying in bed all day wasn't an option.

After she'd showered and dressed, she pulled papers from her pack and reviewed her notes and lists. Technically, she was finished with the initial shots and had planned to leave today. If all the photographs developed as she'd designed them, the assignment list was complete so there was no reason for her to stay. The compiling and text were all that remained.

But what about the brothel? And the casinos? It seemed odd that a historical association would commission an incomplete book. Then she reminded herself who was on the governing board. They were only interested in "appropriate" history.

She bit down on her lip in indecision.

Maybe she could convince them if she already had the pictures taken and if she was careful what she put in the text.

The possibilities intrigued and excited her. She wasn't foolish enough to consider turning in a totally different book, but she could put her stamp on this one. The appeal was too strong.

She glanced out the window. The light was perfect today, and for the first time in a long time, her job felt like more than just a job. The enthusiasm was back. She grabbed her camera and headed out the door. A few hours, that's all it would take, and she could spare that.

Outside, the high mountain sun shone bright, and she slid her sunglasses onto her nose and her camera over her shoulder. She headed toward the brothel but stopped at the corner snared by the sight of the Double Barrel Saloon.

It occupied one of the older buildings at the end of the street.

Even from here it was impressive. Someone had paid a pretty penny for the renovations. An air of authenticity clung to its façade with the false front giving the illusion of lofty height. Large, plate glass windows beckoned even the most casual onlooker to peek inside.

Just like last night.

And just like last night, she wondered about the man she'd met. Obviously she'd met him somewhere before but where? The question and lack of an answer nagged at her. He didn't seem like someone she'd have met through her father's church, but it wasn't beyond the realm of possibility. She knew she hadn't met him here in Cripple Creek. On both of her other trips, Johnny had explained that he was out of town, once on vacation, the other on business.

What could Johnny tell her about him? Caught in her uncertainty, she stared, then stopped and aimed her camera. The charm of the building came through the viewfinder. She hoped it showed in the final prints.

The casino was Cord's property. Was he there now? Surely not after working last night. If Johnny were there, maybe he could answer her questions, and she wouldn't have to face the disturbing casino owner. Before she changed her mind, she crossed the street and stepped inside.

There was already activity in the casino. The clank of coins and the gentle whir of slots spinning into action seemed loud in the thin mountain air. She briefly glanced at the silent roulette wheel. Had she really gambled last night, or was that part of the dream, too? She swallowed and mentally shook herself.

Enough with the dreams.

Johnny sat at the bar, and she headed straight toward him. Hunched over a cup of steaming coffee, he looked near death. She tried not to smile. Recalling his state last night, she knew his head had to be killing him.

"Morning, Faith," Johnny whispered, sipping his coffee. "I'd offer you a cup, but I need all the help I can get." A painful smile tugged at the corners of his mouth.

Faith climbed onto the barstool next to him. Laying her camera on the bar's smooth surface, she pulled her sunglasses off. "You don't look so good."

"Don't feel it. Damn." Johnny rubbed his eyes. "Some people get to sleep off a hangover. Not me. My boss makes me come to work anyway. I'll bet alcohol couldn't break through to that black soul."

"I heard that."

The deep voice came from a doorway on the other side of the bar. The bass drum went off in Faith's chest again. No. Not him. Not yet. She hadn't had a chance to question Johnny.

The tall, all-too-familiar man emerged from the doorway. Her dreams took human form and heat sliced through her.

Damp ringlets of dark hair clung to his forehead. As he moved closer, she caught the faint whiff of his clean, masculine scent. The T-shirt he'd worn last night had been replaced with a plaid work shirt that did little to hide the muscles of his arms and chest.

Dark hair peeked out of his open collar and dusted his forearms. A large, white box fit snugly in his arms—just where she'd been in her dreams. As he bent down behind the bar to set the box on the floor, his jeans pulled tight in all the right places. She leaned just a little farther forward...her memories and imagination hadn't lied one little bit.

Oh, my. Faith failed to breathe and tore her gaze away from the appealing sight before she suffocated.

She knew him. The simple way he tilted his head toward her in greeting. His habit of rubbing his chin as he considered her. Every motion was well known to her. A spooky shiver shook her. Where had she met him other than her dreams?

The solid click of his boot heels as he came to stand across from her alerted her to his close proximity. She cast her gaze down to the smooth surface of the bar. Heat rose in her cheeks.

"Friend of yours?" Cord reached across the bar and nudged Johnny, who moaned in protest.

"Faith McCoy, this is my boss, Cord Burke, owner and proprietor of the Double Barrel. Faith's a photographer."

"A...photo journalist actually, and...uh...we met last night," Faith corrected, daring to glance up. Cord's gaze captured hers, and she was trapped, falling into the crystal blue depths of his eyes. Surely he remembered her?

"What brings you to Cripple Creek?" The question sounded innocent enough, though his eyes narrowed as he looked at her.

"Work. I'm finishing a photography collection for the Historical Association. Actually...last night you asked me what I wanted." If the picture she'd already taken turned out, she'd like to use it. Her excitement grew. She saw the muscles of his throat work and rushed on before he said anything. "I want to include your casino in my book." She reached for her bag and pulled out the ever-present release.

"And what do I get for this?"

She blushed under his hard stare. "Free publicity."

He smiled and, for a minute, her thoughts froze. His laughter startled her and burned across her nerves. Doing portraits had taught her one thing—the beauty and art of expressions. For the first time in ages she yearned to capture a single face—his.

"Who else are you including?"

His words startled her, and she forced her mind to think again. "Who?"

"What other buildings?"

"Oh, yes." She hesitated long enough to cause his left eyebrow to raise in question. "The old depot." She recovered quickly. "The jail, the school and the brothel museum for example."

Both eyebrows shot up this time. "Interesting collection."

"All history." She hesitated to explain more. Not everyone would like or understand her ideas. Victorian times were very proper, yet women like those who lived in the brothel still existed. She pushed the image of her father's frown away. "The Historical Association hired me to document the old buildings. That's what I'm doing."

The sound that came from his throat might have been a laugh, but there was no humor on his face. "Are you sure you're working for the same Historical Association that I know? Last I heard they would just as soon erase us from the map." The disbelief in his words matched the directness in his glare. He seemed to dare her to tell him otherwise.

"They may. I don't." She met his glare with one of her own, just as determined. "There were as many—if not more—casinos here then."

"And whatever you decide to do, they'll accept?" He didn't sound as if he believed her.

She didn't blame him. She wasn't sure what they'd do. "I don't know, but I'm willing to try."

Cord crossed his arms over his chest, staring at her as if by looking long enough he could read her thoughts. Only her determination not to let him intimidate her kept her from moving away from him.

"My customers value their privacy. Anonymity is part of the draw. Having Mom, Dad and the kiddies back home seeing them gambling isn't something they want."

She couldn't stop the smile that tugged at her lips. He seemed to actually be considering it. "I won't include anyone who doesn't sign a release."

She held her breath as he looked down at the paperwork and read it.

"The inside or out?" He leaned back against the counter behind the bar.

"Both."

"You're welcome to take all the outside shots you'd like. None inside except after hours."

Why did she feel her hopes fade? He'd given her the okay to use the outside, wasn't that enough? Once again she looked around. While the faces in the room looked different in the daylight, they still held the same intensity and appeal.

"There's more to buildings than wood and stone." She wanted to explain to him what she saw in her mind. He watched her, and she saw emotions in his eyes—desire and questions that echoed her dream. This time she did climb off the barstool.

"I'd like to make the book more than a picture book of architecture. People occupy these buildings, both then and now. The people are what's important."

"I'm not sure the Historical Association will agree with you. Not the group I've met anyway." He grabbed a rag and made circular polishing motions on top of the spotless bar.

"Maybe." She watched him, noticing the long fingers that curled around the white towel. Tanned and strong. She recalled how they felt against her skin last night, curling around her arm in much the same way. Heat grew low in her belly,

"Have we ever met before?" she asked and immediately wished she could take the words back. His hand stopped moving, and he looked up at her.

"Before last night?"

"Yes." What answer did she expect? What answer did she want?

"Not that I can place off hand." He looked away, returning his attention to cleaning the bar. "But a lot of people come in here every day."

"I haven't," she said. Her mind reeled. She'd seen the recognition in his eyes last night. Where had they met? Frustration nagged at her. Then a thought made her stop. If she was familiar to him—what about the observation room? Either her dreams were simply that or this man was tied to her mind. She wanted to know where the dream man came from. "Have you been to the brothel museum, Mr. Burke?"

Faith studied his expression, curious to see any reaction

there. Nothing.

"Can't say as I have, but you've stirred my interest."

He gave her a look that didn't clarify if the sudden interest was in her or the museum or something else entirely. She didn't ask. "You really should see it sometime."

"I doubt there's anything I could learn there that I don't already know." Mocking laughter edged his words.

"History, Mr. Burke. History." She met his gaze, though her first instinct was to avoid his nerve-shattering stare.

"Could be interesting." His hand stopped moving as he met her gaze.

Her heart pounded and dampness pooled in her palms. He unnerved her with a simple glance so easily. Too easily. "I really need to get to work. I'll leave the release, and you can let me know."

Cord grabbed a pen from under the bar, and after a couple changes allowing her outside use only, he scrawled his name on the line at the bottom of the page. He pushed the paper across the bar toward her. "Let Johnny know if you need anything." He turned and disappeared into the storeroom.

She watched him go. Would he vanish? She wanted to wait and see if he returned and mentally chided herself for her foolishness. The curiosity and desire she felt toward Cord Burke were too strong, too similar to those in her dreams. Until she analyzed them and figured out what was going on, she had no business indulging in them.

"I'll see you later," she said to Johnny as she shoved the paper into her bag. Grabbing her camera and sunglasses from the bar, she walked to the door and out into the bright sunshine.

She wasn't any closer to solving the mystery of who he was or where they'd met. Disappointed, she headed to the other place she might find answers.

The brothel.

***

Cord returned with another box in time to watch Faith leave. He'd dreamed of her too many times to believe she was real now. She didn't vanish, but she didn't come back either.

"Don't you go scaring her away." Johnny's words shattered Cord's thoughts as he glared at Cord. "She's the best thing to walk through that door in ages."

"I won't scare her. I'll probably never see her again. Man, you're grumpy in the morning." Cord pulled bottles from the box and shoved them under the counter.

Cord wasn't in any better mood than Johnny. He'd had another dream last night, a new twist this time. They'd been lovers—happy lovers. He'd actually given her a rose, for God's sake. Cord Burke had never given a woman a rose in his entire life. From his experience there weren't many women who deserved such treatment.

The contented feeling the dream gave him didn't sit comfortably. He'd actually cared—something he'd seldom let himself do. Seeing this woman, who looked like the one in his dreams, stirred the unwanted emotional embers to life.

"When did you meet her?" Cord couldn't keep from asking, and immediately regretted it when he saw the twinkle of curiosity in Johnny's eye.

"Couple months ago. When she first came up here. Took her out to dinner." Johnny paused, taking a deep gulp of his coffee. He grimaced as he swallowed.

"You turning into a lady's man while I'm gone?" Cord teased, enjoying the scowl on Johnny's face.

"Aw, shut up Cord. I saw the way you were looking at her. Your mind's in the same place mine's been most of my life. The gutter." Johnny chuckled then moaned as if regretting it.

Cord stared at the door. His thoughts about her were vivid all right, but he doubted Johnny had the same ones. He certainly hoped not.

"I can handle it until the next shift. Why don't you go on?" Johnny offered, in an effort that obviously cost him as he grimaced again.

"And where am I supposed to go?"

"Oh, I don't know." Johnny rolled his eyes. "Maybe on a tour of the museum?"

Johnny stood, impressing Cord with his resilience. It was all show, but he wasn't going to pass up the offer. His interest was piqued. What could possibly be in that museum that interested her? Cord pulled off the bar apron covering the front of his jeans, and he leaped over the bar and strode toward the front door.

He saw her at the other end of the street, leisurely making her way toward the museum. There was no missing her bright head of hair. The sun seemed to love playing in it, just as the moonlight had last night. She turned around a corner, disappearing from sight. He quickened his pace, half convinced he'd never see her again.

***

Click...whir...the familiar sound of the film advancing filled Faith's ears. She aimed the telephoto lens at the brothel again and snapped off several more shots. Antique glass windows reflected the sunlight in a distorted, ethereal way. Gray paint turned white. Window shades partially drawn gave the illusion of slumber and the rigid line of the veranda formed a grim, unsmiling visage.

Perched atop a crumbling brick wall, the only remnant of yet another deteriorating old building, Faith lowered her camera. She glared at the house, willing it to reproduce itself on the film as she envisioned. Good shots would go a long way toward convincing the board—and her father—that it belonged in the book.

She jumped down from her makeshift seat and headed toward the front door. The little museum was crowded with tourists. A sign on the door informed her that in fifteen minutes it would close for the lunch hour.

The polished hinges squeaked softly. They'd been imported from Belgium. Why that fact stuck in her head from the tour yesterday she didn't know, but she looked up at them. A sense of dejâ vu slipped over her. She shivered and shook it off. Of course this was familiar, she'd taken the tour yesterday. A tiny bell jingled at the top of the door as she entered.

Faith held back while a group prepared to leave. Several people handed the guide a dollar or two, which was graciously accepted. The tiny lady pocketed the bills nearly as quickly as they met her palm.

"Excuse me," she said to the woman.

"Yes?"

"I'm looking for the director." Faith plastered her broadest smile on her lips.

"That would be me. I'm Opal Drysdale." The woman took her hand and returned the smile. "And you are?"

"Faith McCoy." She reached into her oversized purse and pulled out her business card. "I'm doing a pictorial book for the Historical Association of the old buildings."

"Oh, yes." Opal moved to sit behind the antique desk where she pulled out a modern-looking strong box. "I heard about it. I didn't know they'd made a final decision." After putting the box away, Opal straightened. "Were you here before? Yesterday, on the tour?"

"Uh, yes." Faith shifted from foot to foot. "I wanted to get a feel for things before we talked."

"I didn't think they'd be interested in us." A pleased smile formed on her lips and lit her entire face.

"I'm still compiling the list." The woman would obviously be disappointed to learn the museum had been left off the original list, and she didn't want to disappoint her. "Since you know about the project, I hope you're interested."

"Yes." The older woman picked up a ball of yarn and a pair of knitting needles. "But, I can't permit flash photos." Opal pointed one knitting needle at Faith's camera. "The light damages the old fabrics."

"The new films don't need a flash." Faith looked down at her camera, hiding her excitement. She'd already taken several exterior shots, but now she wanted to shoot the inside. All the inside. The room upstairs had stirred up too many feelings. Cord's face came to mind, and she forced the image away. She had to see the room and trunk again. Perhaps after all these years she could solve the riddle of the dream. She swallowed her apprehension. Would the laughter come back? She forced those thoughts away, too.

This wasn't the time to let Opal know there was more to her request than the photos for the book. Her search for answers to the dream was too private.

Opal's chuckle interrupted her musing. "A brothel." She gestured to the room around her as if it were a much-loved friend. "Hardly the normal Victorian image, as I'm sure the committee mentioned."

"I realize that." Faith responded to the laughter in Opal's eyes with a smile of her own. "But it is a new twist."

"That it is." For a moment Opal sat silent. "I'm more than willing to share whatever information I can about the girls and the building."

"I'd like that." Faith's mind spun with ideas. Where should she start shooting? The other buildings she'd photographed had been beautiful, but none evoked this same personal reaction. In the months she'd been working on this book, searching for answers to only half-asked questions, none of her subjects had drawn her as this one did.

"One more thing." She met Opal's gaze. "The observation room. I want it included." The air hung still and quiet between them.

"I'm not sure." Opal's eyes grew distant. "The key's been missing for quite some time."

Faith felt her cheeks grow warm. "Surely such an old lock

would be easy to open." Had she even bothered to relock it yesterday?

"I suppose," Opal said. "I'll have to contact the owner. I can't promise anything. I'll let you know tomorrow."

Elation soared through Faith. She quickly put a clamp on the emotion. Seeing the room again wouldn't necessarily give her the right to go through the old trunk, which is what she really wanted to do. "Sure. Thank you, Ms. Drysdale."

The older woman smiled a reassuring smile. "Call me Opal. Everyone does."

"I hope we can work together, Opal. I'm sure the book could use your expertise."

"What makes you think anyone will be interested in this old brothel?" Opal peered over her glasses at Faith.

"For the same reason you continue to give tours. It's a forbidden fantasy."

Opal chuckled. "That's one way of looking at it. We don't get as many visitors since they legalized gambling."

Faith saw the sadness in Opal's eyes. Had the legalization of gambling in this small mining town harmed the museum? Could the casinos really save the town?

If not, would they let this place die? History lived here. So many stories—some Faith wasn't sure she wanted to hear—hung in the air.

Faith's enthusiasm rose. "Let's see what we can do about that, okay?"

***

Cord pulled the museum's front door open and stepped inside. His guard went up, and he didn't know why. The hairs on the back of his neck tingled.

No one came to greet him. He paced the small foyer for a moment or two, glancing first up the stairs and then down a short, dark hallway. Still no one. He thought about leaving but refused to back away.

A soft sound came from down the hallway. An open doorway allowed faint light to fall onto the old-fashioned carpet, and he followed its trail.

Faith knelt in the center of the room, her copper curls tumbling down her back. Black jeans cupped her bottom as she crouched, aiming her camera at a chair. The sound of the shutter going off seemed loud in the silent house. A jolt of recognition shot through him as she grabbed a handful of her lovely curls and flung them over her shoulder. The gesture was expected.

Familiar.

"I didn't know chairs were part of the business." He smiled when she jumped. A soft snapping sound filled the silence as the shutter went off again.

"Don't sneak up on me like that." Faith knew irritation tinged her voice. The sudden, wild beating of her heart didn't help. "I thought you were working," she said.

"One of the benefits of being your own boss. Johnny is handling it." He looked around the room. "Pretty fancy place."

She stood silent, waiting for a spark of recognition in his voice. Disappointment filled her when he showed no reaction. This wasn't the place to be alone with him. "Opal, you've got a customer," she called. The woman failed to materialize from around the corner.

"Opal?" Faith walked back to where the older woman had been sitting. The chair was empty. Odd, there had been no other visitors since she'd arrived. "I don't know where she went. I'm sure she'll be right back."

"Why don't you give me the tour?" He looked down at her in silent challenge. "You could tell me more about your work."

She didn't want to be alone with him. "I don't think that's a good idea."

"Oh, I do." He slowly walked toward her.

He stood too close. Surely he was the one sucking up all the air in the room. His eyes were close enough for her to see the deep blue color. Hastily, she stepped away. "I don't really know that much about the history without my notes."

"That's okay. I'm not exactly a history kind of guy. Just give me the abridged tour."

His thumbs slid into his belt loops, stretching his shirt tight across his chest. She had enough difficulty concentrating, now this. Did he have the slightest inkling of what he was doing to her?

"Th...this is the parlor." She turned away from him and gestured to the room behind her. "That chair is from France, imported over a hundred years ago. All the furnishings and fixtures are original to the house." She found herself relying on Opal's well-rehearsed speech she'd heard yesterday.

"So, what? They had nice furnishings. Tell me about the people who *lived* here. Isn't that what you said you were interested in, the people?" He didn't bother to look at the antiques she'd described. He stared directly at her.

"Yes." She edged toward the door to the dining room. The

look in his eyes made her feel like prey being sighted through a scope.

"So who lived here?"

"Uh, ladies."

"Ladies of the evening?" he teased.

"Yes." She quickly turned and walked through the door to the dining room. "This room was used for formal dinners. As you can see there are doors that close it off from the rest of the house. There's an outer door in that wall used by prominent gentlemen who came here for thousand dollar dinners, including the governor. They didn't want to be seen by others who might be in the house." Faith knew she babbled, but his stare and close, warm body made her nervous.

"Where is the stairway up to the girls' rooms?"

"Excuse me?"

"You're not going to convince me that they came here only to eat dinner." His words were filled with laughter.

"No. I'm sure they didn't." She gulped back the images forming in her mind. "I guess you'll have to ask Opal when she shows up. I never really thought about it."

"Never thought about it? What'd you think they did?" There was more than laughter in his voice now. He was taunting her.

"Very funny. Do you want a tour or not?"

"Yes. Please proceed." He bowed slightly at the waist and gestured for her to go into the next room, which was the salon.

"The wallpaper in this room was also imported from France. In 1890 it cost a hundred and fifty dollars a foot. There's supposed to be real gold in it." She had wanted to touch it, and with Opal's watchful eye absent, she did. It felt the same as modern wallpaper, and she found herself disappointed.

"Expecting something?" he whispered, and she jumped again.

She hadn't realized how close he'd come. But once he'd spoken, she was surprised she hadn't noticed. He stood so close that she heard the air moving smoothly in and out of his lungs. The rugged scent of his cologne wound around her, and she breathed deeply, savoring the spicy tang. She'd seen him, felt him, and touched him in her dreams, but he had never had a scent.

"Maybe we *have* met before, Ms. McCoy. Before last night, I mean."

"Maybe. I...I don't know." Faith swallowed against the dryness in her suddenly parched throat.

"You do look familiar," he whispered close to her ear.

She wasn't about to let him know just *how* familiar. A hot flash slipped over her as the thought passed through her mind that this man—or his dream twin—had seen her without her clothes, had actually made love to her only hours earlier. She struggled with her sanity and moved away from him. Looking through the viewfinder of her camera, she effectively hid from him.

"Maybe in another life?" he said, and then he laughed.

His words hit her hard. She nearly doubled over from the impact. Could that possibly be where her dreams came from? No, it couldn't be. She looked up at him and his expression looked as startled as she felt.

To escape her own thoughts as much as his presence she turned abruptly and nearly fell over a chair. His warm hand curled around her arm to steady her. "Thank you," she whispered.

He nodded and stepped away,

Relieved by the absence of his disturbing hand, she said, "I'm sure you're curious about the upstairs." She made her way up the steps toward the observation room. Perversely, she wanted to see his reaction. Needed to see it.

The smell of polish and time sifted through the air. She took a deep breath and stepped up, instinctively reaching to move her skirts aside. Silly, she was wearing jeans. Where had that idea come from?

Even before she reached it, she knew the sixth step would creak. It made the expected noise, and she shivered. Reaching the landing, she stopped and looked back at him. Shadows shifted around her, and she curled her fingers around the wooden rail. For an instant, she thought she saw a beautiful woman standing in the foyer—a woman dressed in old-fashioned clothes. A big, black man appeared and nodded as he flashed a subservient smile.

Faith stumbled. Cord's strong hand steadied her again, and the shadows vanished. She looked up and met his frown. The faint scent of an unfamiliar perfume hung in the air between them. She shook her head and closed her eyes, letting the momentary darkness soothe her frayed nerves. He hadn't seen them, had he? He'd been looking at her, not down at the foyer.

"Careful," he whispered when she opened her eyes and pulled away.

"I...I'm fine."

"Could have fooled me." This time he didn't step away, and his breath fanned across her skin. "Tell me—who takes care of you?"

"No one. I'm not helpless."

His laugh was soft and deep. "Is that why you run around barefoot in the middle of the night?"

So he had noticed.

He leaned closer, his body heat teasing her. "And let strange men give you large sums of money?"

She recalled the chips on the roulette table. Slowly his meaning soaked in. She narrowed her eyes at the inference.

"I told you I wasn't there to gamble," she whispered in denial.

"Ah, so you did." He reached up and ran his finger down her heated cheek. "What do you think most men would expect for such a favor?"

Stunned she stood there, her blood boiling with anger and something else, which she chose to deny, ignited by that finger.

Her breath caught in her chest and then came out in a rush. She fought the longing this man inspired in her and moved past him. Somehow, she had to regain control of her mind and the situation.

"Oh, I don't know..." She backed away from him, her footsteps oddly loud on the carpet runner. "Perhaps this?"

She grabbed the wall hanging and shoved it aside. She lifted her chin and met his stare.

He gasped. Reaching out, he touched the painted glass. A breath's time later, he spun around and grabbed her. The fabric tumbled back into place.

His fingers bit into her arms as his words slashed through the air. "What the hell are you trying to pull?"

Four

Cord stared into her wide, frightened eyes. He knew his fingers pinched her arms, but he couldn't seem to let go. She was real. The room was real. What else was real?

"It's familiar to you, isn't it?" she whispered, breaking through the haze that cloaked his mind. Abruptly, he released her, and she nearly stumbled.

"Hell, yes. What else did Johnny tell you?" Cord's voice rose.

"No...nothing. It's a dream, isn't it?"

"Of course it is. Johnny knew that. This is a sick joke."

"I'm her, aren't I?"

Her words startled him, even though they echoed the thoughts he'd had last night when he'd seen her in that window. "That's crazy. It's only a dream."

"Yes. Only a dream." Faith backed up and leaned against the wall. For an instant she closed her eyes, and then she opened them again to stare at him. "A dream where I stand on the other side of that glass in a blue dress—at least in the beginning." Her eyes grew distant, as if she really could see the dream—his dream.

"And you stand here." She pointed to an eerily familiar place on the carpet. "Smoking a cigar, drinking and watching."

Cord's gaze followed the pink blush up her cheeks, feeling his body warm with the memory of the dream. He stepped back before he reached out and touched her. Would she vanish if he did? A shiver slid up his spine.

He'd told Johnny about the dream but not in this much detail. "And what am I watching?" She closed her eyes again, and he whispered, "You, strip?"

Her eyelids flew open, and the shock in her eyes told him more than he wanted to know. Was it possible for two people to have the same dream? How?

"And you called me your wife."

Silence was the only answer. The fear in her eyes reached out to him. What was she afraid of—him or the dream—or something else?

Before he came up with an answer, an elderly woman stepped from one of the rooms down the hall.

"Faith? Is that you?" The safe, friendly voice broke into

the trance holding them captive.

It took several seconds for Faith to answer. "Yes, Opal. It's me."

"Hello." Opal turned to face him and smiled.

"This is Cord Burke." Faith's voice wavered only a little.

"I own the Double Barrel." He extended his hand wanting to find someone or something normal in this strange place. She took it and gently shook.

"Nice to meet you. Come see what I found." Opal beckoned and turned into a room at the end of the hall.

Frowning, Faith followed. Cord fell into step behind her. His silence set her nerves on edge and his angry reaction fell right in line with the dream man's reaction. She shivered, wanting to question him more and yet afraid of what he'd reveal.

Opal waved them into the room. Startled, Faith stepped back, bumping into Cord's broad chest. In the corner sat the brass bed from last night's dream. She'd been through this house yesterday, yet she didn't remember seeing it. What was going on? Cord remained silent behind her.

"I know you snuck into the observation room yesterday," Opal admonished, with only a trace of a smile in her voice. "The owner won't be very happy, but I have to admit I'm kind of thankful. All these years, I've been curious about what was in there. Look what I found in the trunk." With an intentional flourish, Opal unfurled an old, handmade quilt. "It's the wedding ring pattern. And so wonderfully preserved."

The bright colors on the white background mocked Faith's very existence. It was the quilt in last night's dream. As the fabric drifted through the air, a piece of paper flew upwards then landed at Faith's feet. An old-fashioned photograph lay silently on the polished wood floor.

A little boy's cherubic face stared up at her. His eyes held a strong hint of mischief. Faith felt herself falling into those eyes, seeing the trusting love of a child. She'd always enjoyed the magic of photography, but in all the years she'd been snapping pictures, she had never been able to capture such a strong sense of the subject.

She bent down and picked up the picture. The thick paper protected the fragile image, and she held the edges carefully. Turning it over, she saw the ornate feminine script. *Timmy Cumberland, 1898. Age 4.* The words formed an echo inside her head. She tried to turn back to Cord. Even his anger would provide a stabilizing presence. She couldn't reach him. He seemed too far away.

Blackness surrounded her. From a long way off she heard a child's cry. *"Mama! Where are you, Mama?"*

***

Faith crumpled like a wilted flower into a heap at Cord's feet. Her camera thumped against the wooden floor as her bright hair fanned out across the toes of his boots.

"Faith?" He knelt down, nudging her shoulder. She didn't respond. Gently, he slid his arms beneath her and lifted her off the floor. Something had frightened her—badly. Seeing that quilt, he understood. Something strange was going on here.

He carried her to the bed, uncaring that it was an antique, and lowered her to it. He felt as if he had stepped back into the dream. Had the quilt startled her? Had she possibly dreamed of it, too?

"What did she pick up?" he asked Opal.

The older woman lifted the photo from where it had fallen from Faith's hand. "It's a picture. Cute little guy." Opal handed it to him.

He took it and seeing nothing unusual, turned it over. *Timmy Cumberland.* He'd spoken of a baby named Timmy in his dream last night, and in the recurring dream the woman who opened the door called him Mr. Cumberland.

Dread formed in his gut as realization showered over him. He stared at Faith, lying there on the bed. Her copper hair and pale complexion appealed to him, but what reached deep into his soul was her familiarity.

"Faith?" He gently shook her shoulder again. She lay silent and unmoving. Concern and confusion filled his mind. A distant image played in his thoughts, of her lying in this same bed her eyes closed in sleep. He'd wake her with a kiss. The image seemed so real. Leaning closer, he could almost feel her...taste her...

"Timmy." The single, whispered word escaped from between her pale lips, and Cord straightened guiltily. Her eyes fluttered open, disoriented and filled with pain. Her skin remained pale, but her eyes grew more alert and wary. She turned those distraught eyes to him, and he felt that familiar tug—that trap he so easily fell into. She was a damsel in distress and his shining armor awaited.

No. He didn't have time for this. He fought battles only for

Cord Burke and the Double Barrel these days.

"Why don't you get her a cool glass of water, dear?" Opal appeared at his side. "Just go through the door across the hall."

Glad to escape, Cord strode from the room. The tiny bathroom felt claustrophobic. It smelled of thick perfume, as if the scent permeated the very walls. He filled a glass and then grabbed a washcloth. He heard laughter, and some of the tension rolled off his shoulders. She must be awake.

He picked up her camera from the hall floor and stepped into the room in time to hear Faith reassure Opal that she was fine and didn't need a doctor. When he saw her, he wasn't so sure about that.

Faith leaned back against the pillows, her eyes closed, her skin pale. Opal sat beside her on the bed, a frown creasing her brow.

"Thank you." Opal took the cloth and pressed it against Faith's brow. She barely opened her eyes.

"Did you dream about that quilt last night?" Cord leaned against the doorframe, trying to appear casual. What answer did he want to hear? He hadn't a clue.

Faith opened her eyes. With a gentle tilt of his head, he indicated for her to look down. She recoiled from the quilt and hastily pushed herself into a sitting position. She nodded vigorously. He stepped over to the side of the bed.

"And did I talk to you about naming a baby Timothy?" He carefully laid her camera on the bed.

"Y...yes. I don't understand." Fear and confusion shimmered in her eyes.

"Me, either."

Faith swung her legs over the edge of the bed and took the cup from Opal's hand. Apparently realizing Faith would be okay, Opal moved over to an antique rocker near the bed and sat down.

"We need your help." Cord turned toward Opal. "I don't know how to explain any of this, but I've had recurring dreams about this place." He looked at Faith to see her reaction.

Faith nodded, avoiding his gaze. She sat the cup down on a nearby table. "Me, too. Since I was a teenager. I think that's part of why I've always been interested in the Victorian era."

Opal looked back and forth between them, confusion clouding her eyes and creasing her brow. "Do you dream about just this place?"

"No." Faith stared down at the quilt, bunching it in her fists.

She'd grabbed it in the same way in last night's passionate dream...

Cord moved over to the window, away from her and the familiar longings she stirred in his blood. "Faith—or a woman who looks just like her—is in all of them." His mind saw the long-watched images. The power of the dreams reached out to him.

"I see a man in mine. A man who looks just like Cord, except for a mustache." Faith avoided his gaze, looking instead at Opal.

"It's nice to know I wasn't hallucinating." Cord stared out the window. "I wasn't too sure last night." Thick, black clouds scudded across the sky.

A typical late afternoon rain would fall soon. The same gloom hovering in the sky settled over him. Thunder clapped in a promise of havoc to come. "We need information." Cord turned his back to the window. "About this house. About the observation room. Anything would be of help."

"I'm not sure." Opal clasped and unclasped her hands, all the while staring at them. "This all sounds a little strange."

"Opal." Faith leaned toward the woman. "I know it sounds crazy. I can't explain it. We need to find out what's going on."

After a long silence, Opal nodded, though the wariness didn't leave her face. "I can tell you about the girls who lived here and about the history. I don't know much else. And I don't know anything about the observation room."

"Why not?" Faith struggled to stand, holding the headboard for support.

"The owner has always been adamant about that room remaining sealed. He's going to be upset about it being opened —if he ever finds out." Opal glanced away.

"Who is the owner?" Cord walked back to stand beside the bed.

"He's a very old gentleman, must be a hundred years old. He lives in Denver someplace. His name is Tim Gibson."

Cord met Faith's surprised gaze. A current of recognition slammed through the air. Was the name a coincidence or was he the little boy in the picture?

"Can you give us his phone number?" Cord asked.

"The only phone number I have is his daughter's. I do have his address where I send the monthly bookkeeping."

"It's a start." Faith stepped away from the bed. Cord reached out a hand to steady her. Their eyes met, and reality faded away.

She quickly moved back, and disappointment shot through him.

"We'll figure this out." He offered to ease the fear he saw in her face.

"Will we?" Doubt tinged her voice. "How?"

"First we talk to Gibson. Then we start putting pieces together."

"I'll get that address for you." Opal left them alone.

"Why do I get the feeling I don't want to know the answers?" Faith paced away from him.

"I don't think they'll be very happy ones." Cord stood silent. He reached down to the quilt, brushing its softness as he scooped the picture into his hand. "I have a feeling this little guy has a lot to do with it all. How about you?" He extended the picture out to her.

"J...just before I fainted, did you hear anything?" Faith took the picture, feathering her finger over the little face.

"No. Like what?"

"A child's voice. I thought I heard a child cry 'Mama'." She looked up at Cord. Tears formed in her eyes. "It sounded so sad."

The pain in her eyes tore a hole in Cord's soul. He reached out to comfort her, but she moved away.

"I don't want to face this. I don't want to hurt. Those people hurt."

"What if those people were us?" He watched her shake her head in denial, but the lack of surprise on her face told him the thought had crossed her mind. "When I mentioned another life downstairs, I was joking. Now I'm not so sure."

"Yes, you are. That's a mythical belief made up by people who can't face reality, or who don't have a belief in God."

"If God can send you here once, why can't he do it again?"

"I'm not going to stand here and discuss religion, or the lack thereof, Mr. Burke." Faith backed away from him. "I have work to do." She grabbed her camera and hugged it to her as she left the room without a backward glance.

Cord felt the pounding of each of her footsteps on the stairs. He thought about following her, but to do what? Images of the dream woman in his arms forced their way into his mind. He closed his eyes, not sure which face he saw, which body he wanted to hold.

What was happening was too odd, too unreal to actually allow into his life. But did he really have a choice? The woman he'd met only a short while ago had become a part of him. This stranger was as familiar to him as any lover had ever been.

"Here's that address." Opal's return interrupted his thoughts. "Is there anything else I can do? Where's Faith?"

"She's working. She went downstairs, I think." Cord fit his most winning smile on his face. "I know your boss doesn't want anyone to see that room, but could I, please?"

"There's really no sense in denying you. You'll probably do like Faith did and break in," Opal grumbled good-naturedly.

"Probably." Cord chuckled. "Shall we save us both some trouble?"

Opal smiled in defeat and gestured for him to follow her. "I couldn't re-lock it anyway."

Cord pushed the wooden door open and felt an icy chill slip out and caress his skin. The air smelled dank and musty. It reeked of mothballs and dust. His heart pounded in his chest. Down to every minute detail, including the mirror in the corner, it was the room from his dreams.

Footprints marred the smooth surface of the dust-covered floor. Two sets to and from an old, battered trunk. One Faith's. The other Opal's. His boots thudded loudly as he followed their path.

Kneeling on one knee, Cord reached out to open the lid. The scarred wood and metal felt cold against his fingers. Suddenly, blinding heat shot through his skull. Cradling his head in his hands, he struggled against the pain.

What the...?

As quickly as it came, the pain vanished. His sight cleared, and he found himself staring at the contents inside the open trunk. He didn't remember opening it.

Tough Cordell Burke had to admit he was shaken. He gulped back his apprehension.

The blue dress was there. Gently reaching out, he touched the beadwork. Beautiful. Sensual to his touch. He could almost remember...

Forcing his mind back to the present, he slid the dress aside. It was a futile attempt to banish the memory of it hugging Faith's body—a body that was more than dream material.

"That's where I found that lovely quilt." He'd nearly forgotten Opal's presence. "The picture must have been wrapped in it." She hovered in the doorway uncertainly, twisting her fingers.

"It's all old. When was this put in here?"

"From the style of the dress? I'd guess around 1900. But it could be later. It took longer for dresses to go out of fashion then."

Cord rummaged through the contents of the trunk looking at each item for a clue, any clue. There were several boxes of jewelry, a couple of corsets and a pair of beaded shoes. In a lower corner a red box sat beckoning him with its brightness.

He reached for it. As his fingers connected with the smooth, painted surface, the image of a similar box resting in his hands flashed through his mind.

He hesitated before lifting the box. Setting it on the edge of the trunk, he opened the lid. His heart stopped. A yellowed newspaper article sat on the top of the box's contents. Big bold letters proclaimed, *"Murder In Poverty Gulch"* and in smaller letters, "*Local Couple Sought For Questioning."*

Cord unfolded the worn pages and stared at his own picture.

Five

Faith admitted she was shaken. Downstairs, she returned to the parlor where Cord had first interrupted her. It couldn't have been more than an hour ago, and yet she felt as if years had passed. A dull ache formed behind her eyes, and she rubbed the bridge of her nose to ease some of the tension.

Focus. She had to finish her work so she could get out of here and go home. This book was too important to her self-esteem and her bank account.

She took several deep breaths before turning to her camera. The fall didn't appear to have caused any damage.

Overhead, she heard footsteps, heavy footsteps. What were Cord and Opal up to? What he'd suggested wasn't possible. It just wasn't. All her life she'd been taught about right and wrong, about heaven and hell, about life and death. There was no such thing as second chances. God didn't send you back—did he?

No, he didn't. She was sure of it.

So, why did she remember bits and pieces of what seemed like someone else's life? The throbbing in her head increased. And why did Cord have the same thoughts?

Crouching, she focused on the Victrolla that sat in the corner. She brought it into focus, snapping off several pictures from different angles. One item at a time. The mantlepiece around the fireplace was next. The intricate carvings shadowed well—

"The dreams aren't going to go away." Cord's voice came from the doorway.

Faith closed her eyes, hoping he'd be gone when she opened them again. He wasn't and neither was the fear that he was right. He stepped into the room, blocking any escape. The room suddenly felt small and cramped.

Faith stared at Cord and then hid behind her camera again. "I don't want any more to do with this."

Reaching out, Cord grabbed her wrist and hauled her close. "You can't run away from this," he said.

"Why not?"

"Come with me." He didn't release her wrist but pulled her toward the stairs.

"No."

He stopped, and she saw his shoulders lift as he took a breath. The eyes that turned to bore into hers were determined.

"Yes."

He didn't wait for her answer. The fingers circling her wrist were strong and warm. Heat shot up her arm—warm, sensual heat. She wasn't sure what bothered her the most, his touch or the fear of where they were going.

"Let go of me and I'll follow. You'll probably knock me down the stairs."

"Don't tempt me." He released her and she followed him upstairs.

Cord stopped outside the observation room. His big hand dwarfed the small doorknob as he pushed the door open. The musty scent reached out to her.

"I'm not going in there with you." What would happen? She'd seen too many horror movies and had too many dreams. What if she heard the voice again? Would he? If the dream came back, would he be angry? Would he pull her close and kiss her? She shivered—afraid of both options.

"I'm not carrying that two ton trunk out here." He stepped into the room, but she remained in the doorway.

Cord knelt beside the trunk. The contents had been jostled. Carefully, Cord pulled out a red box. He didn't say a word just moved past her and into the light, cradling the box between his palms.

"What...what is that?" She leaned against the doorframe, hoping to appear nonchalant, but knowing she needed the support.

"I found this."

He didn't say anything more, but simply flipped the lid of the box open. Her gasp filled the hall.

The faded and worn newspaper looked ready to crumble to dust any second, yet the headline blared loudly in her mind. She watched as he carefully opened the ancient folds. The walls spun as she saw her own image reproduced on the page.

She wore an ornate dress with a hat nearly three times the size of her head. Long plumes added height to the outlandish hat.

Cord continued to unfold the page, and she saw an accurate photo of him beside hers. He wore an old fashioned dark business suit. A bowler hat sat rakishly across his brow.

"How...? No, I don't want to know." She moved away from him and walked to a small window at the end of the hall but didn't leave. She stared out the window to the street below. It looked so normal. So peaceful.

"There's a story here. Want me to read it?" At her silence, he read aloud. *"Mr. and Mrs. Rafe Cumberland are being sought in last evening's suspicious death of Miss Delta DeLange of Poverty Gulch. This reporter has information indicating Mrs. Maria Cumberland works at the same Parlor House in which Miss DeLange worked and was killed. Listen to this," Cord paused. "The Cumberland's son, Timothy disappeared several months ago, and that incident has never been explained. There is much supposition by all as to what this inquisition will reveal about both crimes.*

"Do you think you can walk away now?" Cord's voice was soft, yet it filled the entire room.

"I don't understand." Faith turned to face him, leaning back against the cool glass. "This is all crazy."

"I agree." Cord stepped closer, setting the article on a side table. "Are you okay?"

"No...I don't think so." She glanced back at the picture in the newspaper article. "I'll never be her."

He paused only a moment. "What if you already are?"

"I'm not."

"What makes you so sure?"

She hesitated, cringing at the possibilities of other lives. She closed her eyes, her father's voice ringing in her ears. His beliefs were strong, beliefs he'd drilled into her.

She'd always tried to be a good girl, but she never quite made it. Even when others saw her as good, she knew in her mind that it was never quite enough. The thought of being a prostitute in some dim past made her stomach clench and churn.

"We're going through everything in the trunk," Cord's words shattered her thoughts.

"You go right ahead. I'm finishing my work, and then I'm leaving." She refused to look at him. Everything she'd ever believed in seemed threatened. What if she learned she was that woman? Could she handle it? Could she face her father? And if she ran away would she always wonder?

Cord walked into the bedroom and returned with Timmy Cumberland's picture. "What about this?" Suddenly, all of her dream-visions came back. The sensual horror of removing her clothes before a man. The scent of a crushed wild rose. The sound of a little boy's voice calling for his mother.

They were so real. Too real. Cord's big, strong hands reached for her shoulders, and she finally looked up at him.

"Is that all there is? Dreams?" he whispered as he bent down to place his lips on hers.

Startled, she knew she should push him away, but she didn't—she couldn't. She needed him, needed his solid reality. For a long time his image had been kissing and loving her in the shadowy world of her mind. While it left her hot and wanting, those dreams were nothing compared to this.

His mouth demanded a response from hers, and the insistent tip of his tongue prodded her lips until they parted. She could deny him nothing and relished the warmth reaching to her soul. His arms slid around her and pulled her against the length of his body. She clung to him. He was comfort. He was heat. He was a dream and more.

A steady beat echoed in her ears that she thought at first must be her heart. Slowly, she realized someone was coming up the stairs. Cord seemed to hear it at the same time. He pulled away, ending the contact and leaving her chilled at his absence.

Opal smiled from the landing. "I'm closing up now. Do you have more work to do?"

"Yes." Faith swallowed, trying to calm her heart. "Could I stay just a little while? I think I can finish up tonight."

"Sure. I need to run to the store. I'll be back to lock up."

"I'll wait for you."

Opal's footsteps vanished as Faith stood there. She didn't immediately turn around to face Cord. She took the time to catch her own breath, uncertain if she was glad for the interruption or not.

Acting as if nothing had happened—as if his lips hadn't left their brand on hers—she finally turned back to face him.

"Well? Are you ready for this?" Cord moved into the doorway, his hand outstretched toward the observation room.

He was right. There was no escape. She had to know one way or the other who she really was. She sought his glance, needing to see the strength she knew he possessed. "No, but let's do it anyway."

He stepped into the room first. She tentatively stepped inside. The light was soft, and she didn't have a flash, but... "Wait." She waved him away and snapped off a couple shots. "Okay."

He knelt again, and she knelt beside him. The room didn't transform, nor did he grow angry. No voices came out of the air, and she breathed a sigh of relief. He didn't try to pull her close again, either, and she ignored her disappointment. They found a plaque attached to the trunk's lid with *Maria Cumberland* engraved on it. In a jewelry box, Faith found a wedding band. She held the box out to Cord.

He reached out and gently fingered the simple gold band. "That's the ring you...she...wears in my dream. I suppose she took it off when she started working the line."

"I don't understand. I can't figure any of this out." She stood, holding the ring box in her palm. She went back to the hall and picked up the picture of Timmy. Closing her eyes, she willed images to come to her, but there was nothing except darkness behind her eyelids.

Warm, strong arms slipped around her almost naturally, and Cord let her rest against him. Gently he rocked her back and forth, soothing the tension within her.

It felt right to be here in his embrace, to lean into his strength. He seemed to understand the emotions warring within her. "They weren't very happy, were they?" she said.

Faith's throat hurt from the tears she held back. She had never been one to share her tears. Years as an only child and the minister's daughter, of being expected to be strong in the face of other's pain, had built a strong shell around her heart.

"No." Cord's voice was soft and gravelly. "I don't think they were." He rested his chin on the top of her head.

She didn't want to care, didn't want to know their anguish. It was too real to her right now. A twinge of sorrow shot through her heart. She closed her eyes, but not before the tears slid past her lashes and down her cheeks.

She felt him shiver against her, and she tightened her grip. Something told her to never let him go.

From somewhere in the distance, the rumble of thunder echoed across the wide valley in which the town sat. The clouds moved across the sky at an alarming rate, full of dark, angry rain. Within minutes it was nearly as dark as night, and the streetlights flashed on. The overhead lights flickered.

"Damn." Cord lifted his head and loosened his hold on her. "If there's a power outage I'll be needed at the casino."

"I'll be fine, if you need to go." Faith wiped her cheeks with her fingers, and stepped away from Cord's arms, missing their warmth immediately.

"Are you sure?"

"Yeah." She forced a smile onto her lips, and Cord smiled in return. He leaned down to give her a parting kiss, and a bolt of white lightning struck outside. Thunder reverberated through the building, ringing in their ears. The bitter taste of ozone tingled on her tongue.

"I'll check on you later. We'll look through the trunk then," Cord assured her. He left, his footsteps loud on the stairs. She heard the back door close behind him.

She leaned against the window frame and watched as he hurried up the street. Wind stirred up wild dervishes in the dirt and fingered through his hair. She wanted to go with him. Shaking her head, she turned back to the room.

The past seemed to have taken over. So much for her plans to leave town quickly.

The silence of the brothel unnerved her. Outside, the storm raged, beating on the window as if trying to get in. Faith shivered and rubbed her arms in search of warmth.

Earlier she'd tried to find a way to look through the trunk, but now here it sat like a gift ready to be torn open. So, why didn't it feel like Christmas?

Curiosity mounted inside her. Cord had found the box and the ring. What else did the trunk hold?

She took a step and then stopped. Then she took another step. The seconds ticked by filled with the erratic beating of the rain on the window and her heart against her ribs.

She didn't have time for this. She had a book to finish. Work to do. *This is ridiculous.* It's just a bunch of antiques and she loved antiques. Damned trunk...the trunk! Her thoughts tumbled over each other, almost too fast to catch.

Inspiration sparked, and a smile broke out on her lips. She could shoot some of the items for the book. *Yes.* What a wonderful addition. She hurried back to the observation room.

The dress seemed to wink at her in the dim light from the hall. She ran her fingers over the delicate beading. She'd never owned anything so lovely in this life, and she wasn't sure if she had in another.

She lifted the dress, unable to resist holding it against her. The waist was impossibly tiny, but otherwise it looked the right size. As she took a couple steps, the light caught on something in the trunk, and she bent to see what it was.

The jeweled comb. It lay nestled beneath the shoes. Reaching out, she pushed the shoes aside and lifted the comb, examining it more closely.

Precious stones were imbedded in the heavy metal, and from the weight of it, Faith could only surmise it must be gold. Turning it over, she was surprised to find the rough feel of engraving beneath her fingers. She tilted it better in the light to read. *Our wedding Dec. 25, 1888. You fill all my dreams. Rafe.*

The metal comb fell from her fingers and landed on the floor with a thud.

Faith McCoy had never known what it was like to really fall in love, and yet in an instant, love wrapped itself around her and pulled her into its warmth. Closing her eyes, she saw Cord as she had seen him over the last couple days. His image fused with the man she had dreamed of and been mentally intimate with for years. The kiss they had shared only moments ago merged with the dream lovemaking.

Shaking her head, Faith banished the thoughts. Daydreaming was a foolish waste of time and in this case could be dangerous. She set to work instead. She made several trips back and forth between the observation room and the bedroom down the hall. Laying the dress out across the bed, she lovingly caressed the soft velvet.

From the trunk she lifted a pair of buttonhook shoes and grimaced. There were some modern conveniences she deeply appreciated, like the worn pumps in her suitcase. Her fingers encountered the softness of silk, and she lifted black stockings until they dangled in her fingers. She swallowed the heat rising in her throat. Beneath the stockings lay a lacy black garter belt. Maria had obviously known her business.

A shiver shot through her. Simply looking at the sheer stockings was enough to make her wonder. How would a man's hand feel through them? How would Cord's fingers feel...?

Stop it. With the comb, the shoes and the stockings in hand, she returned to the bed. The picture formed in her mind exactly as she wanted it laid out.

Wantonly the dress reclined on the bed, falling suggestively over the edge. The stockings peeked from beneath the velvet, hinting at intimacy. A single garter hooked the top. The comb nestled on the pillow, and the shoes she cast aside on the floor, almost carelessly.

Everything covered the bed artfully, and she stepped back. Grabbing her camera, she lifted it and looked through the viewfinder. Flat. She tried several angles. From above, crouching on the floor. As she continued to snap off shots, she knew she was wasting film. Her frustration grew.

Finally, she tossed the camera onto the bed and plopped down onto the chair. "What am I missing?" She often talked to herself when she worked as it helped her focus.

She also paced. Standing, she moved back and forth. She wanted depth and layers and life in the picture. She needed the essence of the woman it represented.

The article still lay open where Cord had left it on the table. She stared at her picture—at Maria Cumberland's picture. If only she could find a photo of Maria. The old newspaper photo wouldn't reproduce well, and the odds of finding the original were astronomical. She didn't have time to do that kind of research.

If only she could take a picture of her dream.

She stopped pacing. Her palms itched like they always did when an image struck. She barely resisted the urge to pick up her Nikon and hug it.

Perfect. She'd take a picture of her dream.

Did she dare? It was one thing to add the buildings to the book, but to add a photo of a person? The words she'd spoke to Cord earlier about how people had lived here came to mind. She'd meant them then and realized their importance now. Those people deserved to be acknowledged, no matter who they were. She'd always been taught to accept people.

Her father's shock at her idea was easy to predict. The image challenged and intrigued her. She couldn't resist.

Grabbing the dress, she held it up to her again. Almost a perfect fit. She'd never get into a corset, but she checked the seams at the waist in particular and was glad when she found extra fabric. Historically women hadn't had the luxury of malls, and extra fabric was often left in to allow for size changes. At least she'd learned something in the last few months as she'd traipsed through these old buildings.

She hurried downstairs and retrieved her purse. She ran upstairs, pulling her travel sewing kit out. She paused, the enormity of what she intended to do hitting her. She didn't want to damage the dress, but would it rip if she didn't remove the stitches? Uncertainty and excitement drove her. Carefully, finding the garment solidly sewn, she snipped a couple stitches. It was enough to loosen the waist without hurting the integrity of the dress. Now she was sure it would fit.

For the first time in what seemed like forever, Faith laughed. She had been looking for a special twist for this book. Having found it, her enthusiasm nearly bubbled over.

With a modern hand, she reapplied her day-worn makeup. The dress seemed to beckon to her. Carefully, in case she had misjudged the size, she slipped it on.

The velvet against her skin brought warm images and a blush. Instead of the stranger behind the glass, she envisioned Cord staring at her. The taste of his lips returned, and an ache formed low in her belly. Would his eyes flame with the same heat the dream man's had?

It didn't really matter. He'd never see her in the dress. She dismissed the stab of disappointment with a shake of her head.

In the dream she had no trouble with the myriad of buttons running the length of the back of the dress. Reality was a different matter entirely. She struggled, unsure if she was going to be able to accomplish the task of buttoning them all. Finally she had them done, and stood before the small mirror on the wall.

She had expected a resemblance, but this was unreal. She *was* Maria Cumberland. No. This was temporary. Pretend.

Picking up the comb, she studied her reflection. She closed her eyes and conjured up the style of her hair in the dream. As in the case with the buttons, it took her several attempts to get all her bright copper curls to stay up on her head. The comb held them in place.

Would the curls really waft down if she pulled the comb out? She stared at her reflection for only a minute, afraid the dream would return.

She wished for her tripod. The small table in the bedroom would have to do, so she pulled it down the hall and set it up just outside the door of the observation room. She fumbled with filters and lenses until she found the one she wanted. Everything arranged, she stopped in the doorway.

It would be much easier with an assistant, but there was no way she was letting anyone see her in this dress. She might look like Maria Cumberland, but she definitely was *not* her.

She stepped inside the observation room. Realizing she'd been holding her breath, she let it out with a shudder. The dust on the mirror only enhanced the image. For a long minute she stared at her reflection. It was eerie. She almost changed her mind.

But she couldn't pass up this chance. Trying several poses, she finally set the camera's timer. She stood before the mirror. The shutter clicked off the first shot. Suddenly, she remembered the cameo brooch.

Turning carefully so she wouldn't trip over the dress's train, she went back to the trunk. Kneeling, she searched through the jewelry box. It wasn't there, and she sat back as a sharp stab of disappointment shot through her.

"It's mine," a voice whispered behind her. Faith spun around to find only the empty room.

"Who's there?" Faith heard the break in her own voice.

"Mine."

"Who's there?"

Laughter echoed through the room and through Faith's brain with ringing familiarity. It was the same laughter she had heard the first day she'd come here. A laugh filled with wicked joy.

Six

What a stupid idea it had been to put on the dress, and even stupider to come here. As soon as Faith slipped through the doors of the Double Barrel Saloon, she realized her mistake, but she was too frightened by the prospect of hearing that voice again to be alone. She shivered just thinking about it. Only one person would understand.

She surveyed the crowd, trying to find Cord. From the doorway she could see across the room. Heads swiveled as she stepped further into the large, noisy casino. Voices lowered, and for a long moment, she held their attention. Ignoring the looks, she headed for the bar.

The young man behind the carved wood served cheer with a smile that lit his entire face. Odds were he'd know where Cord was.

As if feeling her gaze, he looked up. His gaze swept up and down the length of her body and she blushed. She'd never worn anything like this before. She swallowed her discomfort.

Something akin to mischief sparked in his eyes and he grinned. Lifting his arm, he beckoned for her to sit at the bar. Sitting on the tall barstool, she sat at eye level with him.

"What can I get for the lady?" He leaned across the polished wood surface, bringing his face close.

"A...a Vodka Collins?" She hadn't had hard liquor since college. The bartender stared at her, an eyebrow arched in surprise. She knew the dress suggested she sip Dom Perignon, but she didn't feel much like celebrating. Normally, she'd order a glass of wine. Not tonight. Tonight she needed something stronger to bolster her shaky nerves.

With no reaction other than that raised eyebrow, he fixed her drink, sliding it across the bar on the crisp, custom-printed napkin.

Faith took a deep swallow. She coughed, and her eyes watered. She finished the rest of the drink more slowly. Its warmth barely touched the chill inside her.

"Another?"

She looked at him and shook her head. Her eyes were damp with liquor-induced tears. Before she could ask where Cord was, he looked as if something behind her startled him, and he backed away.

"What the hell...?"

She turned around at the booming sound of Cord's voice. He'd just stepped out of the cashier's cage. In only a few steps he was beside her, their eyes level from her perch on the high stool.

Where the bartender's gaze had been appreciative, Cord's was a visual caress. He looked down. "Barefoot again?"

She swallowed hard as his hands circled her waist and set her on her feet. Grasping her wrist, he pulled her behind him. When she stumbled on the hem of the long dress, he barely slowed his pace. He held tight to her hand as he carved a path through the crowd.

Faith saw a door partially hidden behind a set of potted plants. A brass plaque had the single word *Private* emblazoned across it. Cord headed toward it. After he unlocked it, he pulled her inside. Then he slammed the door and turned the key behind them.

She stopped and stared. A huge window covered nearly one entire wall of his office. Outside the window, the night- darkened silhouette of the surrounding mountains dominated the view. A few stars shone beyond the shadows of the growing Cripple Creek skyline. The effect was stunning.

"You want to explain what's going on?" he said, interrupting her thoughts.

Unsure what to say now, she looked around the room with growing trepidation. This was obviously his domain. Books and ledgers lay scattered across the desktop. Shipping boxes stood stacked in the corner. But what caught her attention most was the decor. The dark, somber colors echoed his strength. The filled bookshelves reflected his intelligence. The emerald green carpet made her think of a forest, lush and deep.

Lightheaded from the unaccustomed alcohol, Faith reached out and fingered the filigreed wallpaper. It reminded her of the brothel. Images filled her mind. Images she'd fought these past few days. Of men and women. Together.

Heat infused her cheeks and drifted to other parts of her body. She turned to look at the incredibly beautiful man glowering at her in confusion. "This room fits you. Except I'm not sure which you it fits."

"I could say the same about you and that damned dress. What possessed you to put it on?" He motioned her toward a leather chair, which she didn't take.

Pulling out the desk chair, he sat down and propped his feet on the desktop, ankles crossed. He didn't seem to notice the mess of scattered papers.

"I know it was probably stupid, but I had a great idea for a shot..." She'd go back for her camera when Opal was there to keep her company. Slowly, she walked around the room, surveying and studying each item, seeking more information about the man who had created it. "I had to get out of there."

"I told you I'd come back as soon as I could."

"I couldn't stay there. N...not alone." She shivered at the remembrance of that cold, sinister laughter.

"Why not?"

"I..." She couldn't tell him yet. He'd think she was crazy, probably already did. She stood beside the floor-to-ceiling bookcase and found herself looking at a brass statue of a stallion on one shelf. His hind legs were firmly planted in a mound of brass while his mane flew in an imaginary breeze. The tiny front hooves pawed at the air. Wild. Just like the fire she saw in Cord's soul.

Her fingers ran down the smooth back of the horse, feeling its sensual pull. Being here, in this dress, alone with him, reminded her of that first dream. Maria had known the ancient art of seduction, had learned how to please a man.

For the first time, Faith tasted the power of a woman over a man. Even from here she felt the vibrations emanating from him—his interest and desire reaching out across the air. Turning, she leaned back against the bookshelves, feeling the solid wood behind her and the wildness of the horse prancing through her blood.

She met his gaze with one of her own—a gaze she knew told him she was captured by Maria's spirit. "Tell me more about your dream."

Cord stared at her, shock obvious in his eyes. "Is that why you wore the dress? To relive the dream?" His feet slipped off the desk, and he strolled around to stand before her. "Or maybe to find out what happens next?"

He stood so close. The longing she'd experienced earlier intensified with the memory of his warm lips. He'd locked the door when they'd come in. No one would interrupt.

"I have to know." She was lost in his eyes, drowning in his pull. "Do you see the same images I do?" Was that whispery voice really hers?

Stepping back, Cord put space between them and sat on the corner of his desk. "Okay." He ran his fingers through his hair. "I'm in that upstairs hallway of the museum. I'm standing on the outside of that window. It's not a museum then, and I can hear the music downstairs." His eyes met and captured hers. "You're wearing that dress, with your hair just as it is now."

He stood and took a step forward. "But you know that, don't you? That's why you know exactly what happens between us... them."

"No...No I don't. I know I...*she* takes off her clothes." The rising desire in Cord's eyes told her his dream matched hers. "But that's where it stops."

"Mine has a bit more." He took another step. "A woman appears beside me. She has the key and opens the door."

"Who is she?" Faith reached out, urgently touching his arm. "What does she look like? Does she laugh?"

"What's going on?" His gaze burned through her.

"You'll think I'm crazy." She paced in front of him.

"I seriously doubt anything you could say at this point will shock me. Did you find something else in the trunk after I left?" He grabbed her arm to stop her pacing.

"Well, this for one." She reached up and pulled the comb from her hair. The curls she had struggled with came tumbling down around her face and shoulders. She wanted to show him the inscription, and she didn't think about what her actions might cause. Their eyes met, and the heated longing of the dream played itself out in her mind.

Forcing her mind to clear, she extended the comb to him. "Look at the back." His warm fingers closed around both the hard metal and her hand. She quickly pulled away, retreating several steps. Her fingers tingled. Anticipation built in the air between them. If they weren't careful, someone could get burned.

"It's heavy." He looked at the comb, inspecting its several jewels.

"I think it's real gold," she said.

"I'd bet it is."

"There's an inscription."

He turned the comb over and read the words she'd found earlier. "The only thing missing is the brooch," he whispered as his gaze flicked to the empty neckline of her dress.

Faith's hands trembled as she touched the empty spot on her throat. "I...I looked for it." She turned and paced again. "But a woman's voice said, 'It's mine.'"

"A voice?" His left eyebrow lifted, and he stared at her.

"I knew you'd think I was crazy, but it's not the first time

I've heard it. There's, well, laughter, too." How did she describe the laughter to him? Or the shivers it sent through her? He was already looking at her as if she'd lost her mind.

A sudden blast of wind slammed against the window, and Faith jumped. It howled around the building, and the lights flickered for a moment. There'd been so many storms lately. Was there a connection? That was ridiculous. It was impossible.

Still, what if there was?

"Have you noticed an odd change in the weather lately?" She moved closer to that gorgeous window, gazing through its height to the sky beyond. Dark, scudding clouds gobbled up the stars.

"Yeah. It's been odd. You're starting to lose me here, lady. What's going on?"

"You asked me if I believed in another life. Now it's my turn. Do you believe in ghosts?" She looked over her shoulder at him, wondering if she'd lost her sanity.

"In what?"

"You heard me." She moved to face him. Only an inch separated them. The wind increased in intensity. She stepped back and it lessened. "Go along with me for a minute," she whispered, running her fingers over the rough stubble of his jaw.

Loud thunder clapped around them, and while she heard it, it disappeared in the storm going on in her heart. Cord's hands encircled her waist, pulling her into his arms. She should have warned him this was only a test. But she hadn't, and now she was paying for it.

What a delicious price. His lips claimed and consumed hers, seeking the passion their dreams had only hinted at. The heat of his hands was everywhere, devouring the velvet and her. Fever leaped through her, matched by his rising desire.

The world vanished except for the feel of his lips as they plundered hers. She ached and knew he could ease the throbbing deep inside her. Her lips parted, and his warm, moist tongue took the offered advantage. Her sigh of contentment drowned in the fury of the storm around them and created a tempest between them.

A tempest that caught Cord up, too. He knew the woman was up to something, but he didn't have the foggiest notion what. At the moment he didn't really care. He wanted her, and what had been a dream before became blessed reality. He needed to see if she was the same as in his dream. His fingers traveled up over the tight bodice to the full swell of her breasts.

The softness of the fabric, combined with the warm smoothness of her skin, drove him to distraction. The fabric, barely covering her rounded breasts, teased him. Cord wanted to tear the cloth away. He was sure he'd drown in his own passion.

His lips left hers, blazing a trail down her chin and neck. The hard tip of her nipple pushed against the velvet. She leaned back, and the dark circle peeked out above the low neckline. His moan of pleasure drowned in the thunder.

Cord drove Faith to the brink of insanity with his touch. His kisses dampened the fabric, and it clung to her, hot and wet. She expected steam to rise around them. His mouth found her hardened nipple, and she gasped. Warning bells rang out—warning bells the storm smothered.

He intended to make love to her, here and now, and Faith knew there was nothing she could do to stop him. Nothing she *wanted* to do to stop him.

From the dream, they knew where the buttons were on the back of the dress. Her shyness gone, Faith turned in his embrace, presenting the long row of buttons to him. She grasped her long hair and pulled it over one shoulder. Glancing over the other, she begged him with her eyes to make her dreams real.

His fingers trembled, but Cord managed to slip the pearl buttons through the tiny loops. Soon the expanse of her bare back was visible to him. He slipped his hands inside the loosened bodice. Her skin was both silk and satin, and his fingers greedily sought to touch it all. Slipping his hands across her back and around her sides, he cupped the full weight of her breasts in his palms.

Faith leaned against Cord, reveling in the feel of his shirt against her back and the heat his fingers created against her bare skin. Warmth rose inside her and escaped in a flush where her thighs met. She wanted him there, wanted him filling her. The way he held her made it impossible to move. Entrapment in the delicious vise of his arms only enhanced the ache inside.

Cord nuzzled her hair, pushing it aside until he found the tender skin at the back of her neck. Gently, he nibbled there and Faith's legs trembled. Soon they'd give out and she'd fall to the floor. The hot surge of his breath sent goose bumps over her sensitized skin.

"I want you," he breathed against her as his fingers tightened.

Cord caught her weight as her knees gave way, and shivers shook her as she felt the hard edge of his arousal. Carefully, he turned her into his embrace. The hem of the skirt wrapped around her feet and she stumbled, bringing her closer.

He slid his arms beneath her knees and set her on top of the desk. Ledgers and papers flew to the floor.

His touch smoldered and burned through her as he brought his lips to hers. Their bodies were close. Her fingers fumbled with the buttons of his shirt. She pulled and the buttons gave. She parted the fabric and leaned against his bare skin.

His hands burned a trail up and down the ridge of her back and teased the sensitive area below her waist. He stepped away, still keeping his lips on hers and pulled the bodice over her shoulders and down her arms. Her breasts fit so well into the palm of his hands. For several long moments he worked the same magic as before. Gathering her against him, an inferno erupted as his heated flesh met hers.

A loud roar from the wind battered at the window in rhythm with her pounding heart. Suddenly, the storm burst through. The sound of shattering glass filled the room and shards rained down on them.

Cord pulled her close, shielding her as much as possible, but still several pieces cut across her shoulders and back. She clung to him, sure the room would fall around them at any moment.

In the distance they heard thumps. After a few seconds, Cord realized someone was pounding on the door he'd locked earlier. "Just a minute," he yelled, and the sound ceased. A voice came through the roar of the wind, but she couldn't make out the words.

Rain soaked everything. Cord set her on her feet. He pulled up the front of her dress. Gathering her close against his side, Cord helped her walk into the adjoining bathroom. The walls muffled the roar of the storm.

"I need to unlock the door for Johnny. I'll be right back." He left her alone.

The bathroom was tiny and quaint. And cold. She shivered and wrapped her arms around herself. What was happening between them? She'd never been this wanton—and yet the feelings he created in her were so wonderful and warm. She closed her eyes, reliving Cord's touch, his kisses, his heat.

Once again the familiarity of it shook her. She'd known things...she'd expected certain feelings...as if she'd done this before. Which she hadn't. She heard all the words her father had said, all the lectures on what constituted good behavior. But how could something so wonderful be so wrong?

Opening her eyes, Faith caught sight of herself in the mirror. She looked wan and bedraggled with her damp hair hanging in her face. Numerous cuts scattered across her shoulders and back. Tiny rivulets of blood ran down her chest, soaking into the delicate fabric. A stab of guilt shot through her that she'd damaged the beautiful dress.

Suddenly, all the cuts stung. She reached for a washcloth that hung on the rack beside the sink. She soaked it in warm water then applied it to her skin, hoping to stem some of the bleeding. She slowly peeled the wet fabric away from her skin.

"I won." The familiar but unwelcome voice echoed malevolently in the tiny bathroom. Shivers of a different sort skittered up Faith's spine.

"Who are you?"

"He's mine, too. Don't you understand?"

Faith looked up at the mirror and saw her own reflection again. And then she saw her. The woman stood only inches behind her. When Faith turned, there was no one there. Slowly, she returned her gaze to the mirror. The woman was still there. A scream tore from Faith's throat.

The reflection wore old-fashioned pantalets and a camisole cut low over her breasts. Her ebony hair was coiled high atop her head, much like Faith's had been earlier. At her throat, which she was busy caressing, was Maria's brooch pinned to a strand of black velvet ribbon. A sinister laugh echoed in the room and inside Faith's head.

"It's all mine now, Maria. And I'm not giving up."

Cord tore open the door, and the image of the woman vanished, leaving Cord in its wake.

"Are you all right?" He stared at the blood sliding down her skin. "I heard you scream." He stepped toward her, taking her shoulders gently between his hands. "We need to get you to the doctor. It looks like there's some glass in there."

"She was here." Her voice was weak and frightened. Faith stood stiff, unable to move.

"Who?" He didn't look like he really wanted to know the answer.

"Her. The ghost I told you about. She was wearing the brooch."

"You've had quite a shock." He spoke through clenched

teeth.

"I'm not making this up." She grabbed his arm. His eyes met hers.

"I know." He gently steadied her and stared at her for a long minute. Nearly too long before speaking again. "Doc's clinic isn't far. We can talk later." The command in his voice calmed and soothed her. "Can you pull the dress up?"

She shook her head. The tight bodice would pull painfully against her skin.

"Here, step out of it." He helped her pull the soaked dress downward. When he came to the garters and stockings, he stopped. Looking up at her, the fire rekindled. She saw him swallow hard. "I have a change of clothing in the office. It'll be a bit big, but it'll get you to the doc." He beat a hasty retreat, as if not trusting himself to be alone with her.

The sounds of hammering came through the door, and she wondered what was going on. The wind raged softer. She shivered and clutched the damp dress in front of her, as much for warmth as to hide from Cord's heated gaze when he returned.

"Here. It's not the best, but it'll do." Cord handed her a white shirt, like the one he wore and a pair of black sweat pants. "I'd like to stay and help...out...uh...I...I'll wait out here." He tore his gaze away from her. The passion between them had only been interrupted.

Faith slipped out of the stockings and pulled on the sweat pants. They were warm against her chilled legs. Then she pulled on the shirt. The fabric rubbed against the cuts, but it was big enough that the pain was bearable. Red stains quickly appeared on the pristine fabric.

Afraid to look in the mirror—and just as afraid not to—Faith turned to find only her own reflection in the glass. She saw the pain and disappointment in her eyes. That disappointment upset her nearly as much as the window's menace.

She'd wanted Cord's touch, wanted him to love her, right there on that desk. Was she more Maria than she wanted to be? What did Cord think? Did he see her as Faith...or a harlot? Shaking her head, she thrust her thoughts away.

"No," she whispered to the bedraggled woman staring back at her. "I'm not crazy." Saying the words aloud helped, but not enough to convince her someone wasn't trying to control her very existence.

With a determination she didn't feel in her heart, Faith pulled the door open. Cord and Johnny had nailed boards over the broken window. They both turned and looked at her. She gave a defiant lift of her chin and clung to her pride—what was left of it.

"I...I want to leave the dress here. We can take it back to Opal tomorrow." She sought any normal topic of conversation. She looked at the disaster the papers and ledgers made on the floor. Anyone would believe the wind had caused such a mess. She and Cord knew better. She blushed with the memories.

"There." Johnny stepped back from the window. "That ought to do it. Hey, kiddo, you okay?" His voice was filled with genuine concern for her.

"I think so."

"Call Doc James and tell him we'll meet him at the clinic. She has some pretty deep cuts," Cord said.

"Sure thing." Johnny nodded and left without another word.

"Can you wear a jacket?" As she shook her head, Cord gently took her elbow, steadying her. He wanted her to look at him, she was sure of it. She adamantly examined the top button of his shirt.

"Faith?" She refused to meet his gaze. Gently, as if to avoid hurting her, he tilted her chin and placed a warm and loving kiss on her brow.

Before she could speak, and before the sweet, protective feelings melted away, he led her out through the casino.

The incident had disrupted the gamblers for only a few minutes. Normality reigned, and they continued betting. Only a few heads turned as Cord and Faith headed toward the side door near the bar and slipped into the night.

Only the bartender noticed the red rose that suddenly appeared on the bar. He tossed it into the trash beneath the bar. Wicked laughter faded into the noise of the slot machines as they rang out jackpot after jackpot.

Seven

Cord held tight to Faith's elbow as they hurried through the rain to his jeep. With each soggy step his concern for her grew.

The cuts were a physical threat, but what worried him more was her mental state. He didn't think she was crazy. Hell, after all the things he'd seen in his life, nothing really surprised him. What he feared was the toll this seemed to be taking on her. He'd seen men stronger than her crack. His grip tightened, and he urged her into a quicker pace.

He kept telling himself that he couldn't make her his concern. He really couldn't. Yet he felt himself reach out to her, his mind working to find answers to ease her fear. The urge to pull her close and protect her overwhelmed and surprised him.

Was that sucking sound he heard caused by his feet pulling from the muddy puddles, or was it his resolve to keep his distance from her going under?

***

The doctor's office was little more than a converted storefront. Faith only vaguely registered the "For Sale" sign in the window. Like everyone else in town, the doctor apparently hoped to make an extra dollar or two by selling his property to a casino.

Cord ushered Faith in as soon as the doctor opened the door. Johnny had called ahead explaining the situation, just as Cord had asked.

"What about you?" The doctor looked Cord over from head to toe.

"I'm fine. She was nearest the window."

Faith was grateful Cord didn't mention she'd been practically nude, while he'd had his shirt for protection. Seemingly pleased with the answer, the old man nodded and led her into the examination room. She blinked in the bright florescent light.

Cord stayed in the ramshackle waiting room, and through the open door, Faith watched him, comforted by his presence. He paced at first, then sat down to read a dog-eared sports magazine. Even then, his eyes flicked back and forth as if keeping tabs on her.

Dr. Raymond James, an elderly man, walked with a heavy, shuffling step across the examination room. He closed the door with a solid click and spoke with an age-worn voice. Time had not been kind to this man, and Faith wondered why he still practiced medicine in this remote little town. The familiar desire to hold her camera and capture him itched in her fingers.

Decorations were at a bare minimum in the office. She suspected it was more from lack of time than desire. She'd noticed stacks of patient files in the front office when they'd passed it. Here in the examination room, everything was utilitarian and every space judiciously used. The doctor spared no room for frivolity.

He set about his work with the same no-nonsense attitude, gathering modern, clean instruments from the neatly arranged drawers. Despite his age, his hand was steady and sure.

Only two of the cuts required stitches, but both of them were located close to major veins. "You're a lucky young lady. Another inch or two..." He shook his head. "These old windows are so fragile."

Tired and weak from the loss of blood and frazzled nerves, Faith didn't answer him.

"All this renovation, they should replace 'em, not keep 'em," he grumbled as he took another stitch in the deep cut just below her collarbone. He spent several minutes pulling out slivers of glass. "You know, you look awfully familiar. You from around here?"

"No. I'm just working here for a short time." She sucked in her breath as his needle pierced her skin again. The anesthetic he'd given her had been only partially effective.

"Sorry," he mumbled, but he didn't stop his work. He carefully sponged just ahead of a trickle of blood. "You still look real familiar. You got relatives here?"

"No. None."

"Humph. I never forget a face, which is good, because I've dealt with a lot of people."

"How long have you been here?"

"I was born over in Victor. My Daddy was a hard-rock miner, one of the last. He died in one of the district's last cave-ins."

"How awful." She knew that many of the area's mines had closed decades ago, which would have made him very young when his father died. "I'm sorry."

"Don't be. He died doing what he loved. He always said he'd go under the ground and save Mama the trouble of buryin' him." The doctor chuckled at his father's morbid joke. "Why, he's practically a legend around these parts."

"You must know a great deal about the people who've lived here."

"Yes, I do." He set aside the needle, and bandaged the stitched areas. "I know just about every tale ever told in the district."

"Do you know much about the old brothel?"

"Well..." A crimson blush crept over his wrinkled cheeks. "Can't say I know any more, or any less than any other man."

She felt a smile pull at her lips. "I'm working on a photo book of the old buildings, including the brothel. We found a trunk with an old dress and some items in it." She watched the old man's brow pucker in concentration. "There was a picture of a little boy. I got the impression some tragedy was involved."

"Hmm. Let me think a minute." He stood and walked to the sink to rinse his utensils before putting them aside to be sterilized. The sound of water rushing into the metal sink seemed loud in the small room.

Suddenly, he spun around. The startled look in his eyes surprised her. "Timmy. Timmy Cumberland." He turned back and shut off the water. He was silent for several moments, leaning his hands on the sink's edge. His arms straight and stiff, he gazed down into the swirling water.

"What do you remember?" She gently prodded. "I'd really like to know."

"It's a very sad story."

"Please, tell me." A shudder of fear raced through her, but she controlled it.

"My mother used to tell me about Timmy. Lots of the mothers told their kids about it, as a warning." His eyes were distant and his voice softened. "Back in the boom days, Timmy's mother came to town shopping. The boy got into trouble and disappeared." He halted, his brow gathered as if he wished he didn't remember.

"A few weeks later they found his body at the bottom of a mineshaft. His parents never were the same."

Strobe like flashes went off in Faith's mind. A child's face, animated in laughter. The heart-rending scream of *"Mama"* through the darkness. Pain and grief tore a hole in her heart. She was afraid to ask, but knew she had to. "What happened?"

"Tore 'em up pretty good. He was their only child. It was pretty hard on them."

"Weren't people back then more prepared to lose a child?"

The doctor pinned her with a dark stare. "You ever had a child?" When she shook her head, he shoved his hands into his pockets. "I've seen plenty of folks lose kids, and I'm sure it hasn't changed. Even then they had the 'it doesn't happen to me attitude.'

You're never prepared for it."

Somehow she thought she understood.

"The mother was a beautiful woman. I remember seeing an old picture of her. That's who you remind me of."

"And the father?"

"He fell apart. Drank pretty heavily. About six months later he died, too. No one knows for sure if it was murder or suicide. Died in the brothel. She was the last one to see him alive. Gunshot wound clean through his left temple. Some say she killed him. Some say he killed himself."

Bile rose in Faith's throat. Gruesome images flashed through her mind too faint to catch, yet strong enough to stab her with pain. "I don't feel so good."

"There's a bathroom through that door." He pointed across the room.

"Excuse me," she mumbled and hopped down from the examination table and rushed into the bathroom. Slamming the door, she retched in solitude, longing for the illness to pass and the almost memories to fade away. The man in her dream merged with Cord, who had touched her so tenderly only a short while ago. It was suddenly all too clear. All too real.

How could anyone survive so much painful loss in one lifetime? It hurt Faith's heart just thinking about it.

She slumped against the wall and let the tremors take her. Hot, scalding tears ran down her cheeks.

A soft tap came at the door "Faith, you okay?" Cord's voice sounded distant, muffled.

She didn't—couldn't—answer. He wrenched the door open. The hall light silhouetted his tall figure in the doorway, disguising his features. Faith started in fear, and a small cry escaped her throat as he hunkered down beside her. Gently, he touched her forehead, carefully avoiding the tiny cuts. Reaching out, he pulled her to him. His fingers slid over her hair, comforting and kind. "You okay?" he repeated.

She pulled away, looking up at him. "I don't know."

"What happened?"

"The doctor. He told me about Timmy...about you, I mean him...Rafe Cumberland." She stared at his left temple, recalling the doctor's description of Rafe's fatal wound.

Confusion filled his eyes, and Cord stood. He pulled her to her feet and helped her bathe her face with cool water and rinse her mouth. Turning into his arms, she clung to his strength and reality, not caring that the cuts stung as she snuggled against his shirt. “Don’t let go. Please.”

Carefully, Cord guided her down the hall. The doctor closed the examination room door as they passed.

“Send the bill to the Double Barrel. I’ll take care of it,” Cord said.

“Some people have difficulty with anesthetics. If your stomach hasn’t settled by mornin’, give me a call. If you want to know more about the Cumberland’s, there was plenty of coverage in the papers, though you’ll probably have to go to Denver to the archives to find ‘em.”

“Thanks.” Cord guided Faith out into the night, his fingers tight around hers.

The solid, constant click of his boot heels on the pavement snapped through the quiet night all the way to the jeep. The storm had passed, leaving the air sweet and clean. Soft sounds of trickling water came from the distance. Cord slipped his arm around Faith. His warmth seeped into her.

“Want to talk? What did he say about the Cumberlands?”

Faith shook her head, and her drying curls bounced around her shoulders. She didn’t want to talk about the tragedy echoing through nearly a hundred years to hurt her.

The doctor’s words rattled around her head like an accusation. *She was the last one to see him alive. Some say she killed him...* Had the images she’d seen really been part of the past? Some odd memory left over from an unfinished life?

If what Cord had spoken of earlier was true, then the images she had seen of Rafe Cumberland may have been his last moments alive.

***

The quiet and warmth of her hotel room was a welcome contrast to the cool night. Only Cord’s presence disturbed her peace.

She grabbed and tossed whatever object came in contact with her hand into her suitcase. There was no rhyme or reason to her hasty actions, just a means to getting packed and out of here.

“You’re leaving.” It wasn’t a question. Cord simply stated the obvious to break the tension in the room.

“I’m not prepared for this...” She waved her hand vaguely. She couldn’t meet his eyes—they’d been her downfall from the beginning. Instead she concentrated on packing.

“And I am?” He reached out and stopped her with a warm, strong hand. Still, she wouldn’t look at him. “Running won’t help. The dreams will still be there.”

"You don't know that." She pulled from his grasp and headed for the bathroom. She gathered up her toiletries in one sweeping action.

She was surprised to find tears lurking in her eyes as she unceremoniously dumped it all into her suitcase. Wiping a tear off her cheek, she flinched as she encountered a tender spot where the glass had cut her skin.

"Will you give the dress back to Opal tomorrow?" She finally looked up at him. He stood only a few feet away, and yet a gulf yawned between them.

"Sure. I'll take care of everything."

"Thanks." She stood, intent on finishing as quickly as possible. "I just want to get back to my own life. Look, I got what I came for. All my shots are done, including the brothel." That reminded her, she had to pick up her camera on the way out of town. Would the back door still be open? She didn't remember locking it.

"Where does that leave us?" he whispered, moving closer to her.

"Us? What us?" His body heat reached out to her. He stood close. Too close. It took all her strength not to reach out to him. Closing her eyes, she fought her own desires, but her mind betrayed her. Images of him played behind her closed eyelids, reminders of the passion they'd shared only a short while ago.

She opened her eyes and met his stare. The blue light in his eyes had fanned to a brilliant flame of passion.

"There can't be any *us*." She backed away, afraid she'd be unable to resist him much longer.

"Whether we like it or not, we're in this together. No one else has the dreams."

"You don't know that for sure."

He shook his head. "Yeah, I do. There's got to be a reason why this is happening."

What he said made sense, but it also scared her. What could the reason be? She didn't have a clue, and the beliefs she'd clung to all her life were little help now. "I came too close tonight—"

"Too close to what?"

"To dying." And to giving into desires I didn't know I had, she added to herself. She wasn't sure what bothered her more.

"We'll be more careful. I'll protect you—"

"From what?" She almost laughed at the blank stare he gave her. "You don't even know the answer to that. You can't take care of everything." She grabbed her suitcase and headed for the door.

"When I dream, I won't be able to forget that you're real." His frustration showed in the depth of his voice. She stopped in her tracks yet reached for the doorknob, curling her fingers around it.

Cord's words hit her heart like tiny missiles, leaving destruction and pain in their wake. Before she could move, he was beside her, threading his fingers through her hair. His lips gently found each of the tiny cuts on her cheeks and neck, soothing away the hurt.

"Will you be able to dream about me and believe this is only a figment of your imagination?"

His lips captured hers before she could speak, but her answer was clear enough as she dropped the suitcase and wound her arms around his neck. She'd never forget he was anything but a real, hot-blooded man.

She tried to break the embrace. She needed to leave, but her resistance vanished. He pulled her tight, wrapping his arms around her and encasing her in a velvet cocoon of caring.

A flash of lightning lit the room. A loud clap of thunder followed on its tail. Faith knew she should have expected it. Cord lifted his head, and she buried her face against the strong wall of his chest.

"Damn you," Cord yelled into the room. "Who the hell are you? What do you want from us?"

There was no answer except the howl of the wind. Cord and Faith instinctively moved away from each other as another peal of thunder rumbled through the sky.

Faith grabbed the suitcase again, and she had the door open and was halfway down the hall before he caught up with her. He grasped her arm and pulled her abruptly to a halt.

"We're not finished yet."

"Oh, yes we are." She glared at him, hoping to banish her feelings for him from her heart. "Every time you touch me, my life nearly gets wiped off the slate. I don't know if we were reincarnated, or if this is some cruel joke, but I want to live my life to its natural end." Her voice broke and she turned, running down the stairs before she lost her resolve.

***

Cord stood in the rain, letting the water wash over him as he watched Faith go. He fisted his hands to relieve the urge to reach out and haul her back. She pulled her car away from the curb, and the red taillights created an eerie glow in the gloom as she disappeared around the corner and out of town.

In his experience women didn't stick around. Why had he thought Faith would be different? His mother had never had time for him when he was a kid, and that hadn't changed now that he was an adult. The legion of "girlfriends" and "aunts" who had invariably left had taught both he and his father all to well about the staying power of women.

Only this time Cord found himself wishing Faith would stay. *Hell.* He didn't need this. He stalked back to the casino, his casino, the one place he knew he mattered.

***

Outside the night was cold, the skies vacant of stars. The moon seemed to have vanished. The streets were empty, the cool night having chased most of the gamblers indoors. She didn't have any trouble reaching the museum.

The parking lot was empty. No lights shone in the front windows. Everything looked empty and deserted.

She couldn't go back in there alone. She couldn't even remember if she'd closed, much less locked, the back door as she'd promised Opal. The very thought of going inside made her heart race and her stomach clench.

She didn't know how long she sat there staring at the empty house. A knock on her window startled her and she nearly jumped out of her skin. A squeal escaped her. She turned to find a tall man standing outside. His dark skin blended into the night, but his smile, bright and warm, belied any threat he presented.

She rolled the window down a few inches. The puff cloud of his breath carried his words inside. "Do you need something?"

"No." She shook her head. "I left my camera in the museum earlier. I thought someone might be here."

His smile widened—if that were possible. "I'm the maintenance man here."

Vaguely, she recalled seeing Opal talking with a man when she'd first toured the museum.

"I'll get your camera. Do you know where you left it?"

"Upstairs. In the room with the brass bed." She realized a few of her other things were there, too. "I'll go with you, if it's okay."

She dreaded going inside the house again. Afraid of the voices, of the images, of her own feelings of confusion and inadequacy in regards to the brothel and its history. Oddly enough the old man's presence comforted her and she followed him up the walk.

Together they stepped into the empty museum. The old man flipped a light switch and several lamps came on. It seemed almost homey with the muted glow.

The upstairs still looked dark, and then he flipped another switch and its shadows vanished as well.

"I told Opal I'd check that back door," he told her. "Go ahead and grab your stuff. We'll go back out the front." He disappeared down the hall, and Faith hastily went upstairs. She grabbed her camera and clothes, barely giving a thought to the pictures she'd taken. She put the furniture back and hurried downstairs.

He was waiting for her.

"Thanks." She stepped off the last step. "I need to get back down the mountain. I hated to wait to get these," she explained, realizing she was babbling. Again. She walked toward him. "I'm Faith McCoy. Thanks for your help."

He clasped her hand and held it. A frown creased his brow. "You look familiar. Have we met?"She started to shake her head then stopped. "I was here yesterday. I think I saw you then."

"Oh, yes. Maybe." He released her fingers, and she realized she'd enjoyed the human warmth of his grip. She liked him.

A cold breeze hurried them down the walk, and she hastily climbed into her car. At the edge of the lot, he raised a hand and waved, and then he disappeared into the darkened night.

She sat there for several long minutes after he'd gone, the purr of the engine and the white shafts of her headlight beams the only respite from the night.

Putting the car into gear, she took a deep breath. She felt as if she stood on a precipice, ready to fall off into something frightening and unknown. Something she wanted no part of.

Determined, she headed toward the highway and out of town. The winding mountain road was difficult enough by day. By night, and after several days of rainstorms, it was treacherous. Faith drove slowly around the hairpin turns, her knuckles white on the steering wheel. She should have waited for morning, but if she had, would she have been able to leave Cord?

"Mama."

The cry came from out of the darkness. Startled, Faith slammed on the brakes. The small car went into a slide. Wet gravel ground beneath her tires.

The car finally came to a halt on the shoulder of the road. Faith's fingers gripped the steering wheel. Sweat beaded on her forehead, and her heart thumped hard in her chest. The headlight beams reached out over the edge of a ravine and disappeared into the night.

Leaning back, she closed her eyes and fought the delayed panic mounting in her mind.

"Mama, don't go."

The soft, pleading voice surrounded her, seeping through the car and into her brain. She clasped her hands over her ears, but the childish voice penetrated to her heart.

"No, you can't follow me," she whispered to the night. Frantically, she shoved the car door open, drinking in deep gulps of the cold, pine-scented air.

Could this unearthly thing follow her? She'd understood the truth in Cord's words when he'd said the dreams wouldn't go away. She was sure she'd manage to live through that. But what if the voices—and the laughter—followed her? Was she up to that?

The night air grew cooler as she stood there. A breeze whispered through the pines, and she watched their branches sway with the wind. The branches danced and then parted, as if a great hand pulled at them.

Shadows formed, and she backed up until the steel frame of the car supported her. She should turn and run, but her feet refused to move. Her gaze was riveted to the spot in the tree branches where figures swirled and slowly took shape.

She recognized the brass bed she'd come to realize was Rafe and Maria's marriage bed. The quilt lay rumpled and askew across the mattress. Cord—no he had a mustache—it must be Rafe, looked right at her.

His long fingers reached out and grasped the quilt, pulling it up over his waist, a smile of satisfaction on his face.

"Mama! Mama!" the tiny voice echoed from somewhere outside the vision, and Faith heard the patter of running feet in the distance. "Look, Mama." Timmy Cumberland's excited face appeared beside Rafe, looking up at her expectantly. He thrust a stuffed bear toward her. The bear's big black eyes sparkled in the light. "Santa came, Mama. He really did."

"Now, what makes you think Santa left him?" Rafe leaned back against the brass headboard and laughed.

"'Cause he ate the cookies we left. The note said they were for Santa." His excitement grew as he thought of the wondrous stranger, Santa Claus, actually being in his home.

Faith heard her own voice joining theirs. "Come show me your gift."

Timmy jumped onto the big bed, and Faith could almost

feel his warm little body pressing against hers.

In an instant he nodded off, forgetting he was too excited to sleep and that the bear he held so close was a new friend. She looked down at him. Soft eyelashes rested upon his cheeks. His hair was nearly as dark as those lashes. A stray lock curled and fell across his brow. He'd be a heartbreaker someday, chasing all the pretty girls.

But she knew he'd never grow to manhood.

A sob broke from Faith's throat. Suddenly, an icy breeze whipped through the fantasy bedroom, stealing the stuffed bear from Timmy's arms. He started awake. Tears rolled down his cheeks, and his sad eyes turned to Faith. "Mama, I'm scared."

"Don't worry, Mama won't let anything happen to you," she heard herself promise. Her voice echoed through the night until it diminished with the growing breeze.

The scene melted away. The dancing tree branches fell back into place. Faith trembled, unable to move, afraid the vision would return—and just as afraid that it wouldn't.

As the daughter of a minister, she had spent half her life in the pews, listening to her father speak of the ways of the world. He'd spoken of spirits, but never quite like this.

He'd also spoken of the afterlife, but that too had been drastically different than what she had witnessed over the last few days. Tipping her head back, she stared at the stars, wondering about heaven and hell and any worlds in between. The quiet, still night held no answers.

"I have to go," she cried, explaining to the voice, to the vision, to the wind. "I can't stay."

She expected to hear a childish voice ask her why, and when the sound didn't come, disappointment slipped through her.

There were answers. She had to find them and knew of only one person who might know how to help her. First she had to get away from here, away from the distraction of Cord, away from the frightening images in Cripple Creek. Away from the painful memories of Rafe and Timmy Cumberland.

So why did that knowledge hurt so much?

Eight

The smell of old books and paper permeated the air. The quiet of the library had always comforted her, and Faith relished its warmth.

As she strolled through the stacks, she'd thought about how she should have called her father this morning to update him on her work. She needed to pave the way for the changes she planned to make to the book. But she hadn't called.

She'd crossed a line in Cripple Creek—an invisible line, but definitely one her father wouldn't understand. She didn't even know where to begin to explain. Instead, she'd called and left a message for her friend Clarissa Elgin and headed for the library. She'd relied on research in the past, so surely she'd find answers here.

Like neat little soldiers, the books lined the shelves, a contradiction to the variety of topics represented: apparitions, astrology, ghosts, paranormal.

"You won't find what you're looking for in any book," a soft, female voice said behind her. Startled, Faith dropped a book on her toe. Grimacing, she bent to pick it up.

She straightened to replace the book and then turned to face her friend. Clarissa leaned on the edge of the shelves, a smile on her face. Only she could wear the bright orange dress hanging loose around her trim figure and look so good. A matching scarf pulled thick blonde hair away from her face. Gold bracelets matched the chains gathered around her neck. A large black amulet hung between her breasts, pushing the fabric close to the tanned skin at the low neckline.

"Hi." Clarissa smiled, and her whole face lit with animation. "I got your message." She waved her hand in a clatter of metal bracelets. "Cryptic meeting place."

"Funny." Faith's composure returned, and she pushed the book back into the empty slot. Casting a quizzical glance at Clarissa, Faith reached out and hugged her friend. The simple gesture felt good and reassuring.

They pulled apart, but Clarissa didn't let go. "Are you okay?" Clarissa leaned back, peering into Faith's eyes, a frown on her face. "Those cuts..." her voice trailed off.

Uncomfortable with the close scrutiny, Faith moved away examining book titles.

"Oh, heavens. It was real." The color drained out of Clarissa's face. "He's still not safe."

Clarissa's voice stopped Faith dead in her tracks. "What's that supposed to mean?"

"The danger hasn't gone away." Clarissa walked quickly toward Faith and laid a hand on her arm. "I saw him. Who is he? Whatever or whoever is trying to hurt you is also trying to hurt him. The window was just the beginning of things to come."

"How do you know...?" Faith felt the color drain from her own face. Her breath caught in her throat.

"You know I've had visions all my life." Clarissa let go of Faith's arm and rummaged through a dilapidated purse, which at one time must have been white. "But never about people I know."

Clarissa didn't look anymore like a psychic was supposed to look than she had the day they'd first met. There was no dark hair, no craggy features, no secretive Gypsy air. Just Clarissa with her bright hair and warm smile. And a mind too filled with horror. She and Faith had been friends for years and never once had she been close to one of Clarissa's visions. The fact that she was now seemed to scare them both. "Are you sure?"

"You know I don't ask for these damned visions. They've been quiet until lately." She paused to take a breath. "I know most people don't believe me, but I always thought you did."

Her words were loud in the small library. Several heads peeked around book stacks to see what was going on. At least no one mouthed, "Shhh."

Clarissa glared at her. Faith knew Clarissa hated people who didn't believe her, something she'd encountered too many times.

"That isn't what I meant. Come on." Faith grabbed Clarissa's arm and walked to a small grouping of chairs by the windows. The view was beautiful as the midday sun glinted off the distant snow-capped Rockies. Clarissa stopped beside the chairs and stared back at Faith, waiting for her direction.

Faith pulled out a chair and sat, motioning her friend to one of the wide chairs in the grouping. Sitting, Clarissa pulled her feet up underneath her skirt. She looked like a rag doll, her wide skirt and vivid curls strewn across the chair. Faith sat stiffly facing her.

"I see things in my dreams, remember? Sometimes, like this time, I get a vision during waking hours. Usually around sundown or just before a storm. Last night I dreamed about you. I saw you here by these books, and then I saw you up in the mountains someplace. There was a man with you."

"Wh...what did he look like?"

"Drop dead gorgeous." Clarissa smiled at her. "About six foot two? Dark curly hair? Eyes like ice chips with fire inside? Am I ringing any bells?"

"Yes."

"He's in danger."

Faith felt panic grip her chest like a cold hard fist and leaned forward. "How do you know that?"

"In my dream I saw a huge yawning cavern. At the end of the dream, it was looming over him. He was looking for someone—or something."

This was too weird. Faith wrung her hands and sat forward in the seat. "I don't understand any of this, Clarissa. I don't know what to do." Faith stood and stalked a few paces away. "I don't want anything to do with it. I just want things to go back to normal."

"Normal? What's normal? What does the name Timmy mean to you?"

Faith spun around and met Clarissa's eyes. There was no gloating stare, no taunts. Faith recognized genuine concern. Something told her this was as real as the other events in her dreams. Dangerously real.

She wanted to run, wanted to leave everything behind. Even as the thought raced across her mind, she knew it would do no good. She'd run away from Cripple Creek and Cord, but she couldn't run from her memories of the feelings the past days events had created. There were several questions she wanted—needed—answered.

Faith looked around at the crowded library. "We can't talk here."

"I'll treat you to a triple mocha," Clarissa offered, and Faith smiled. It had been several weeks since she'd had time to stop in at Clarissa's coffeeshop, the Angry Bean.

"You're on." Faith searched through her purse for her car keys. "Can I drive you?" she offered, recalling Clarissa's habit of walking whenever possible. The shop wasn't far away.

"I'm parked right out front. I'll meet you there."

Faith saw something resembling relief flash through Clarissa's eyes. There were numerous questions she intended to ask her friend—as soon as she had a strong cup of coffee between her trembling fingers.

Clarissa walked to a vivid red, late-model sports car. Faith was impressed. Psychic work or the coffee shop must be doing well. Clarissa climbed behind the wheel. She sped out of the parking lot before Faith could get her car door open.

The Angry Bean was small, and a stand of pine trees hid it from casual passersby. Slipping around the side of the building, Faith found the heavy wooden door open to the warm sun. She stepped into the dark interior, blinking several times before seeing Clarissa seated beside the window. A large mug sat before her. Steam wafted towards the slowly moving ceiling fans.

Faith slid into the wooden seat. The waitress set a large mug of chocolate-laced coffee in front of her before she finally looked up. "Where do we go from here?" she asked.

"That depends on you." Clarissa took a deep swallow of coffee.

"Me?"

"Yes. Do you believe me? I can't force you to; I can only tell you what I see."

Heavy silence hung between them. They each took a few sips of coffee. The restaurant was quiet. The lunch crowd hadn't yet put in an appearance.

"Okay. You know I believe you. I'm just afraid of what's in that brain of yours." Faith took a deep breath. "What have I got to lose? Tell me, what did you see?"

Clarissa smiled and stared at Faith for a long moment as if trying to gauge her emotions. "Many lives tangled together. A great deal of time is involved. Last night in the dream, the man was searching in darkness. I wish I could have heard his voice. He spoke, and his expression held a great deal of pain." Frustration filled Clarissa's voice.

"Where was he?"

"I'm not sure. It's an unfamiliar place. Can I ask you some questions? Perhaps I can get some clues from your answers. I've seen other images over the past couple weeks, and I think they might be connected to you."

Words escaped her, and Faith swallowed against the sudden dryness in her throat. She wrapped both hands around the warm mug. She didn't really know if she wanted to hear about Clarissa's dreams, yet she knew she had to.

"There are mountains around the man."

"Yes. He's up in Cripple Creek."

"That explains the image of lots of money and machines. I also see a blue dress, a red wooden box and…Wait I've been keeping track."

While Clarissa reached into her old purse again, Faith drank deeply of her coffee. She wished something stronger than chocolate laced it.

"Here it is." Clarissa pulled a tattered notebook from her purse. She quickly flipped through the pages. The sound of the crackling paper seemed loud in the quiet, empty restaurant.

"A brooch. I had a dream about it last week. Pretty thing, I drew a sketch of it. Does this look familiar to you?" She turned the book around for Faith to see.

Maria's brooch. This was too real. "Oh, God," she murmured, rubbing her suddenly pounding temples. "You're not kidding, are you?"

Clarissa smiled. "You know I do sometimes. Adds to the image and all." Her smile faded, and her expression grew serious. "But not this time." She reached across the table and covered Faith's hand with hers. "You've helped me in the past. It's my turn to help you."

"I don't want to need your help."

"You need it. She's not going to leave you alone."

"She?" This wasn't getting any better.

"The voice. She's from the past, and she's here to hurt you—or him. What's his name?"

"Cord." Speaking his name aloud brought forth images Faith wanted to forget. Images she had hoped would stay behind in the tiny mountain town. Images of Cord making love to her. Even so far away, his memory wreaked havoc with her body. It would feel so good to have his strong, warm arms around her right now.

"I don't know why, but I got the idea it was a different name." This time Clarissa looked confused.

"How about Rafe?"

"Yeah." She nodded. "That's it. Who is that?"

"It's him...sort of. I think he was reincarnated. I think maybe I was, too." She felt strange admitting this to anyone, even someone who had a connection to the world of the unusual.

Clarissa sat up straighter, interest sparkling in her eyes. "Really? How fascinating. What makes you think that?"

"We've both had dreams, actually the same dreams, for years. We recently met and found the room we've been dreaming about. I know it's a little odd." Faith ducked her head, sipping her coffee, trying not to feel like a fool.

"It's not so odd," Clarissa assured her.

Faith sensed the sincerity in her friend's voice. For the first time since they'd left the library, she felt safe and smiled.

"What do you know about the people you think you were?"

"Not enough." The grainy photo image of Rafe Cumberland leaped into her mind, reminding her of the doctor's suggestion to visit the state archives. She'd thought about going this afternoon. "Have you ever been to the archives in Denver?"

Clarissa shook her head, causing her long hair to glisten in the sunbeam falling through the skylight. "No. Where are they?"

"Downtown, near the capitol."

"Are you planning to visit?"

"I'd thought of going this afternoon."

"Can I tag along?"

Relief settled over Faith. She'd secretly dreaded facing what she'd find—or not find. Having Clarissa along might bolster her courage. Faith glanced at her watch.

"We could leave now."

"Works for me."

Clearing their dishes, Clarissa gave instructions to her waitress before they headed for the door.

***

The Colorado State Archives building was modern, but the inside was as old as time. A guard sat at the front door, as if the state feared the history might suddenly vanish. His head swiveled toward them when they entered.

Clarissa stopped as Faith pushed open the door. "Oh, my. Talk about sudden impact. There are a lot of lives here."

"You feel something?"

"Overwhelmed. This could be more difficult than I expected. Images are crowding in."

A light sheen of perspiration stood out on Clarissa's brow, and lines of strain bracketed her lips. "Here." Faith led the way to a large table. "Sit down, and I'll get what we need."

A young man sat behind a wide desk, carefully turning the pages of an old book with white-gloved fingers. He looked up as she approached. "May I help you?"

"Yes." She smiled at him. "I'm looking for information about Cripple Creek." She recalled the date on the newspaper Cord had read to her.

"The late 1800s is quite a way back. I'll get what I can for you. That sounds like about the time of the fires." He slipped into another room. It seemed an eternity before he returned.

Faith glanced back at Clarissa. Her eyelids drooped and her skin had grown pale. She tried to perk up each time Faith glanced her way, but Faith could see it was an effort. An antique grandfather clock bonged loudly in the corner.

"That's weird. I wonder if anyone knows we're coming up on the anniversary of that first fire?" The man plopped a heavy book on the counter and grinned. "A few years ago a history professor reconstructed the history. He found the old timers and put this together."

The book was the length and width of a newspaper page and about three inches thick. Flipping open the front cover, Faith found the book consisted of actual newspapers bound in the single volume.

"Thank you," she breathed. The man hefted the book off the counter and took it to the table. Clarissa slumped in her chair.

"If you need anything else, let me know." The young man stepped away. "Call me when you're done." He moved back behind the counter and returned to his work.

Slowly, carefully, Faith and Clarissa flipped the timeworn pages. The paper was weathered and fragile despite the obvious preservation process. Nothing triggered any images for Clarissa and nothing familiar showed up.

Disappointed, Faith turned the last few pages. Suddenly a full copy of the article that had been in the red box in the trunk faced them.

Faith's heart pounded in her chest. She wasn't sure if it came from the excitement of finally finding something, or the joy at seeing Cord's image again. It had barely been twenty-four hours, but she missed him. That was silly, since she'd only known him a couple of days. Why did it seem like a lifetime?

Clarissa's audible gasp startled Faith out of her reverie. Paler than before, Clarissa's fingers clasped tightly around the edges of the book. "I see her. She's begging for her life. I can feel rage. No! No!" Clarissa cried out. Her face turned ghost-white.

The image faded as quickly as it had come, but Clarissa's composure didn't return. She looked at Faith, a deep pain in her eyes. "Turn the page."

Faith stood, leaning across the wide book for a better look, then did as Clarissa suggested. It was her turn to gasp. A picture of a young girl filled a quarter of the page. Her beauty was transmitted over time, even through the grainy black and white picture. The girl in the mirror.

Young Girl Murdered. The headline screamed in Faith's head.

"Who...who is she?" Faith recognized the face but didn't really want to know her name. But running away wouldn't change the facts.

"Delta DeLange. She's the one who's trying to hurt you. The one who broke the window."

"But how...Why?"

Clarissa hesitated, shivering. "Revenge." She closed her eyes. "The sheriff's looking for him. I can see them in the brothel." Her eyes snapped open. "Rafe Cumberland murdered her."

Nine

"What?" Faith didn't care that her voice echoed through the cavernous building. She dropped into the chair next to Clarissa with a thud. "That can't be true. Cord would never." She shook her head vehemently, waving her hands in the air, as if trying to erase Clarissa's words.

"Not Cord. Rafe." Clarissa grabbed Faith's flailing arms. Their gazes clashed, and Clarissa managed to break through Faith's confusion. "They are not the same person."

"Aren't they? At least a little bit?"

"Maybe a little." Clarissa paused. "Let's get out of here." Struggling, she picked up the heavy tome and took it over to the counter. Faith met her at the exit. Their footsteps rang out in the silence. Outside, the sun slipped toward the horizon, plunging the city into a late afternoon glow.

Clarissa broke the silence first. "Who were you?"

"What?" Faith struggled to recover. "Oh, in the past?" Faith laughed nervously. "Maria Cumberland. Rafe's wife—and a prostitute." It was all really absurd. She'd never been married and didn't know what a hooker's life was like.

"So, are you Maria right now?"

"No. At least I don't feel like it. I feel like Faith McCoy, but I share a lot of interesting dreams with Maria." They reached Faith's car.

"For her they weren't dreams." Clarissa pulled open the passenger door and climbed in. "They were the fabric of her life. You didn't share that life."

"I know that. But it's so confusing." Faith settled in the seat beside her.

"And Cord is not Rafe." The click of their seat belts and the roar of the engine were loud in the silent parking garage.

"The other night, when I was in Cripple Creek, I put on a dress of Maria's." Faith stared out the window without really seeing anything.

"And...?"

"I felt like her. I don't know how to explain this, but I knew her. I understood her."

"I gather you don't like that."

"No, I don't. I...I grew up in a very strict household."

"Being a prostitute isn't quite what you pictured in your

life?" Clarissa's eyebrows rose as Faith turned in her seat.

"Not hardly." Faith rubbed the strain from her eyes, not sure which was worse, the sun's glare or the visions in her mind.

"That's why you can't believe Cord and Rafe are different?"

"Sort of." Faith shook her head, trying to clear her confusion. How easy it would be to listen and believe in Clarissa's words, but Faith couldn't. Rafe and Cord were too intricately intertwined in her mind. The man watching her through yesterday's window of the observation room was one and the same as the modern man she'd left behind in Cripple Creek.

Traffic grew heavy as they headed out of the city. The mass of downtown commuters made it necessary for Faith to concentrate on her driving, and she was thankful for the distraction. Clarissa sat quietly, her head back against the seat, presumably listening to the soft music coming from the speakers.

Cars filled the parking lot at the Angry Bean. Faith pulled into the only empty space, right next to Clarissa's car. Several long seconds passed.

"Thank you." Faith ran her finger around the steering wheel. "At least you don't think I'm crazy."

"No more so than I am. Think about what I said." Clarissa stepped out of the car, then turned back to face Faith. "Call me if you need me. If I have any more visions, I'll get in touch." Clarissa headed into the little coffee shop without glancing back.

As Faith headed home through the shadowed city, she thought about all she'd learned today. Rafe a killer? Why did that knowledge make her heart ache? The man who had been so gentle in her dreams, the image that had made love to her, had committed murder?

But how?

And why?

***

Faith tossed and turned most of the night. Her unanswered questions made sleep difficult and elusive. Somewhere near dawn she finally fell into a fitful slumber. She awoke to a hungry and demanding cat pacing across the bed. "Mornin', Singe," she grumbled and pulled the pillow over her head. The gentle thud-thud-thud of the cat's paw on the other side of the pillow told her she wouldn't get any more sleep.

"All right." Tossing the pillow aside, she looked at Singe as he sat next to her. He methodically licked his left paw as if he had all the time in the world.

"Miserable feline. Who pays the rent around here anyway?" A soft meow was her only answer.

A short time later, Faith drank her coffee, and Singe lapped up the saucer of milk she gave him in their morning ritual. Faith stared at the phone. She was only a phone call away from hearing Cord's voice—his real voice. She'd heard the dream one in her sleep. The dreams were different this time, just flashes. Bits and pieces of voices and darkness.

If she called him, what reason would she give? She'd left Cripple Creek and him behind. He was a stranger and likely to remain that way. A stranger with a dangerous kiss.

"It's just you and me, Singe." She rubbed the cat's thick fur, letting his soft purring soothe her. She almost wished she could go back to sleep. Almost. The thought of the dreams coming back deterred her.

"We've got work to do." She should bury herself in her darkroom, but her mind raced. That work would have to wait. Too many questions plagued her.

Though her newspaper years had been few, she'd made some contacts. An article she'd written a couple years back about land deeds came in handy. It took only a couple phone calls for her to locate Timothy Gibson, the brothel museum's owner.

Her fingers trembled as she dialed the number. After several seconds a young girl's voice identified the household. In a few moments Tim Gibson's daughter, Lorenia Watson came on the line.

"Is Mr. Gibson available?" Faith asked.

"No, my father isn't feeling well enough to take calls.

"I..." Disappointed, she forced a light business tone into her voice. "I'm Faith McCoy, the journalist who requested permission to photograph the house in Cripple Creek."

"Ah, Ms. McCoy. Opal mentioned you. Is there a problem?" Her voice was distant.

"Everything's fine. I just have some questions the curator was unable to answer. I was hoping Mr. Gibson might be able to help me."

"Questions? What about?" Lorenia didn't sound receptive to allowing Faith to talk with her father.

"I want to get the complete history of the house, including something about the current owner. The book could be important to the future of the museum. Even Opal seems concerned about the lack of visitors lately."

There was a long pause. "I don't know, Ms. McCoy. My father's a frail, old man."

"I only have some simple questions. It's important to me and could be very important to the book."

"Very well." Another long silence filled the line. "Can you be here around two this afternoon?"

"Yes."

"I'll warn you, Ms. McCoy. I don't want him upset. He may be old, and I may be old myself, but he's still my father."

"I understand." Faith's breath rushed through her lungs. She grabbed a stubby pencil from the cup by the phone and wrote the directions on the back of her utility bill. It didn't sound hard to find.

Lorenia Watson said good-bye. The line went silent in Faith's hand, and she stared at the receiver until an obnoxious buzzing startled her.

Two hours. Two hours to prepare for what could be the most difficult and important interview of her life. She tried to focus on the tasks at hand.

Did she really want to hear what he had to say? Did she have a choice?

***

Timothy Gibson's home was actually a "cottage" at one of Denver's posh retirement communities. A millionaire's cottage on the south side of town. The community bordered the area where many of the old Cripple Creek millionaires had once lived.

Faith drove up to the gate and took several calming breaths. A uniformed guard came to greet her, and he checked her name on his clipboard. When he was satisfied with her I.D., he returned to the little cubicle and pushed a button. The large wrought iron gates swung open. Faith drove through the gates, her palms damp on the steering wheel. They clanged shut behind her, trapping her inside. She shuddered and forced her mind to look at the beautiful area around her.

The driveway wound between tall, aged pines. A lush, green golf course stretched to the right. The old, rather formidable main building of Prescott Estates came into view. Built to look like a large medieval castle, signs indicated that the office, clubhouse and central hub of the complex were inside. Two turrets shot upwards into the sky. As she slowed her car to look at it, she envisioned armor-clad guards walking back and forth between the parapets.

Outbuildings dotted the wooded area behind the castle. She followed the main road until it turned into a paved path. Large, wrought iron numbers labeled the fifth building on the right as number eighteen.

An attractively dressed, older woman stood on the front door's threshold. Her artfully coiffured hair blazed white in the sun. A hesitant smile settled on her lips, and Faith's tension diminished.

"Hello, Ms. McCoy. You're very prompt. I'm Lorenia Watson, Tim Gibson's daughter."

"Hello, it's nice to meet you." Faith returned the woman's smile and followed her into the hall.

Faith looked around with interest. The air of old money permeated the room, accompanied by a homeyness that pleased her. Her shoes echoed against hardwood floors as she followed Lorenia.

To the right a curved staircase led upstairs. Down a short hall, she saw the kitchen. On either side stood a set of double doors. Lorenia opened the doors on the left that led to a spacious living room.

The furnishings were old, and while well preserved, they showed definite signs of use. Lorenia settled on a wide couch, indicating a matching chair for Faith.

"This is a lovely complex." Faith perched on the edge of her chair. "I've never been here before."

"Few people ever get inside those gates. Father is the last of a dying breed. Cripple Creek's elite are fading away. In May he'll be a hundred and two years old." As if to distance her mind from the thought, she reached to a waiting tea service and filled two cups.

"Quite a milestone," Faith said.

"Perhaps. My father had a difficult life. I must warn you, I'm against this meeting." She offered Faith the cup. For several moments only the gentle clink of the spoon in Lorenia's teacup broke the silence.

"May I ask why? Perhaps I can avoid upsetting him. Is that your concern?"

"Indeed, it is my concern." Lorenia leaned back in her seat. "But after your call, I started to wonder if perhaps this isn't fate. You want to talk to him about the house. And that very topic is the cause of much of the unhappiness in my father's life. Perhaps by talking with you he can come to peace with his memories."

The pressure of fixing an old man's life weighed heavy on Faith's shoulders. She had enough to carry already. She couldn't take on more, but she saw no other way. "I can't promise anything."

"I don't expect you to, dear." Lorenia smiled, sipping her tea and watching Faith over the delicate, china rim. "Perhaps I can help you some, and then the time with my father won't be as long. He's very fragile these days."

"I can understand that." Faith tasted her tea also, buying time to calm her heart. She was so close to the answers. Would they be what she wanted? What she needed? What did Tim Gibson know about the Cumberlands? "I'd like to know how he acquired the house."

"He inherited it from my grandmother. Are you going to take notes?" She indicated the notebook in Faith's lap.

"Oh, yes." She felt like a cub reporter on her first assignment. "Your grandmother?"

"Yes. She was the owner, proprietor and I assume one of the participants in the business of the brothel." The older woman shuddered, her cup rattled as it touched the saucer. "He never really knew her, but he knew what she was and what she had done to him."

"Done to him?"

"After their daughter turned into a street walker, my great-grandparents raised him. They were very strict, even for their time. It wasn't a happy childhood. When he was eleven he ran away."

"I'm sorry." Faith's heart hurt for the child he had been. She felt a twinge of disappointment. He wasn't the little boy in the vision. Intellectually she knew that, but she'd hoped, just a little, that maybe the boy in the dreams and the boy the doctor said had died weren't the same. That he really hadn't died. She forced her thoughts away from her emotions. "How did he survive?"

"He worked in Denver's rail yards. When he met my mother, he was as poor as they come." Her eyes grew distant, a proud smile hovering on her lips. "Mother was a beautiful woman. It was love at first sight and lasted over fifty years. He found with my mother the love and respect that his mother had denied him."

"How did he know about his mother? Did he visit her?"

"Heavens, no. She sent money each month. His grandparents wouldn't allow them to see each other. They never let him forget what she'd become. They preached to him about her evil ways. He only saw her once, just before she died. She was quite elderly."

"Is he anything like her?" Faith saw the defiance in Lorenia's eyes.

"Somewhat, I'm sure," she admitted. "His stubborn streak runs deep, and he has an ornery side that loves to play jokes on people. But he's a God-fearing man. Until his recent illness, he faithfully attended church and was deacon for years."

Faith sat silent, staring at the scribbles that would eventually pass for her notes. There weren't any answers here. "What was your grandmother's name?"

"Most of those women had a stage name of sorts. Her real name was Annie Gibson but she was known as Delta DeLange."

Faith's heart fell to the floor. That couldn't be. Delta died young. Rafe had killed her. Hadn't he? Faith rubbed her forehead, trying to ease the confusion forming there.

"Are you all right? Can I get you something?" Lorenia reached out and laid a hand on Faith's arm.

"No, I'm fine. Just the beginnings of a headache. I'm sure it will pass." When had she become such a good liar? Faith forced her mind to focus on the notes on the page. They didn't make sense.

"H...how long did the house operate as a business?"

"Until the twenties. My grandmother closed it, and she became somewhat of a recluse until her death. She spent her time taking care of the house. It was in beautiful condition when she died. When Father inherited it, he created the museum."

"Why is the observation room sealed off?"

"I don't exactly know." Lorenia was silent for a moment. "I went with Father to see the house after her death. Father found me looking into that room and grew angry. He said Grandmother had told him the truth, and that he'd sworn no one would ever go through what she had. He locked the room that day. As we were going back to the hotel, I saw him throw the key down the sewer grate."

"I still don't understand why." Faith's confusion grew.

"It was my grandmother's wish." As if that explained everything, Lorenia picked up her teacup again.

Faith was even more confused. Laying down her pen and notebook, she looked over at Lorenia Watson. "I'd really like to see your father now."

The older woman paused, then taking a drink of her tea as if it were fortifying whiskey, she nodded. She stood and motioned for Faith to follow.

A makeshift hospital room had been created in a small room off the kitchen. One entire wall of thick glass overlooked the eleventh green. Sunshine warmed and cheered the room.

The tiny figure of a man lay in the sterile, white bed. His eyes were closed. Faith couldn't tell if he was awake—or even alive. His hair was sparse, but what there was gleamed white as spring snow. His skin, thin and filled with tiny blue veins, had a gray cast.

As their footsteps echoed on the floor, his eyes slid open. He pinned Faith with a surprisingly alert stare.

"Papa?" Lorenia spoke. "This is Ms. McCoy. I told you about her coming to visit today?"

He motioned for them to come over by the bed. "Sit down, Ms. McCoy." His voice was raspy but strong. She sat in the chair beside the bed. "Why don't you see what Miriam is fixing for dinner?" he urged his daughter, who dutifully turned and left them alone.

"So, Ms. McCoy. You're interested in my brothel. Why?"

His directness bothered her. She had imagined a semi-senile old man who would have little to tell her. She suddenly wasn't sure she wanted to know any answers.

"I'm fascinated with the Victorian Era," she said. "There's a magic about that time that we've forgotten these days."

"And?" he prompted.

From the gleam in his eye, Faith realized he knew. Knew why she was here. Knew there was more to this than the answers for a book. "Don't glamorize those women's lives, Ms. McCoy. They were hookers. Nothing more, nothing less. They lived terrible lives."

Faith hesitated. She didn't want to upset him; she had promised his daughter she wouldn't. His gaze turned to hers, filled with curiosity and understanding. She hoped he would believe her. "The fact they were bad or good doesn't diminish their place in history." She met his gaze with a defiant lift of her chin.

He leaned forward, an angry frown adding creases to his

brow. "Now tell me the truth. Why are you here?"

She swallowed. What did she have to lose? She'd already finished photographing the house. "I have dreams. I've had them for as long as I can remember. I'm in that room—the observation room." She watched a scowl settle on his brow. "I'm un...undressing before a man." Heat bloomed in his cheeks. "At the end the man informs me he is my husband. He's very angry."

"I can understand his anger." He relaxed against the pillows, watching her closely.

"A couple days ago, I met a man. He looks just like the one in my dream. He has the same dreams." She watched the snow-white eyebrows rise in surprise, but he didn't speak. He waited for her to continue.

"It's strange, but basically we think we may be the reincarnation of Rafe and Maria Cumberland. She was one of the women who worked in the brothel. They had a son named Timmy who supposedly died under rather strange circumstances."

"That's quite a story, Ms. McCoy. Are you expecting me to believe it?"

Her eyes sought his. There was challenge there. "Yes, I do, Mr. Gibson. It's the truth, or as much truth as I know."

"And you came here to see if I was that long lost son? That maybe I hadn't died?" He paused to give her a long, silent stare. "Do you want to know the truth, or are you looking to ease a guilty conscience?"

His words struck her nerves like a cat o'nine tails. She saw Timmy's face from the photo in her mind, and the pain of his voice reached out to her again.

"Yes. No. I don't honestly know."

A smile suddenly broke on his face, and some of his warmth eased the hurt in her heart.

"I'm not condemning you, Ms. McCoy. It's a bit much to digest all at once." He watched her for a long stress-filled moment. "I think I believe you. You seem sane enough."

"Thank you." She didn't know why it meant so much to her for this man to believe her, but it did.

"Don't thank me yet."

"I promised your daughter I wouldn't keep you too long. I appreciate your time, though."

"Ah, Lorenia means well, but she smothers me sometimes. You've brightened an old man's day with your presence. You're a pretty young lady."

"Th...thank you." The compliment felt good. "I'll bet you were quite a dandy when you were young."

"Don't tell my daughter." He winked, and the smile remained on his lips. "Ms. McCoy?"

"Yes?"

"In the bureau over there—open the top drawer." He raised a long, thin hand and pointed to the tallboy in the corner.

Faith walked to the dresser. Pulling the drawer open, she gazed at a myriad of items.

"See that blue envelope down on the left side? Bring it here."

He indicated she should open it. Pulling the old photograph into the light, she gasped. Stinging tears flooded her eyes. Rafe, Maria and Timmy stood together in front of an old-fashioned Christmas Tree. Like most old-time photographs, they stood stiff and unsmiling.

"I think you have more right to it than I. I know they weren't my family."

"I...don't...understand." Faith struggled with her composure.

"My mother was Delta Delange. Her legal name was Annie Gibson." He raised a restraining hand as she started to speak. "I was a year old when she died."

"But your daughter just told me she died an old woman."

"The woman who pretended to be my mother died an old woman. She wasn't my mother. She gave my grandparents money to help with my care. She sent gifts when I was married and when my daughter was born. I believed her to be my mother, but her real name...was Maria Cumberland."

Faith slumped in the chair. She had hoped that today she would learn a great deal. This wasn't quite what she'd had in mind.

"I'm confused. Why did she pretend to be your mother?"

The old man smiled. "Just before she died, I went to see her." His eyes took on a distant cast. "She told me the truth that day, about her own Timmy dying so tragically. I believe she was trying to make up for things she couldn't change."

Tree branches rubbed against the wall outside, startling Faith. Tim Gibson's voice sounded weary all of a sudden.

"She gave me the house, asking me to never again allow it to become such a place. We'd both been hurt so deeply by that house and all it represented. She made one stipulation. The observation room must be sealed and never seen again."

"Did she tell you why?" Faith's voice was barely a whisper.

"Yes. Are you sure you're up to this? You look worse than I do, and I've got a good eighty years on you." His concern for her brought a smile to her lips. "That's better. Come here for a moment." He extended his hand, clasping hers in his and settling them both beside him in the bed.

"Her husband died there. She hadn't been in that room since his death, though many of her treasured belongings were there. Each time she tried, her heart broke all over again. She was with him when he died." His fingers tightened around hers. "It was so hard for her to talk about it even after all that time."

"Then she didn't have anything to do with his death?"

"I don't think so. What gave you that idea?"

"Something someone said." A portion of the burden lifted from Faith's heart, but the weight still seemed great.

"You resemble her very much. I can see her eyes in yours." His voice caught, and he patted her hand. "Forgive me. Forgive yourself. Forget it all," he whispered. "Lord knows I've spent almost a century trying."

"What do you have to forgive yourself for?" she whispered.

"There are many errors in a man's life. Some I had no control over. Like what my mother was. I wish I'd pushed harder to know the woman who tried to make up for what my own mother couldn't give me. Her last days were lonely. We could have been good for each other."

"Probably." Further words failed her.

"On that last visit, she asked me to take her for a drive."

Faith didn't want to ask to where, but she did anyway. It took him a long time to answer.

"To a hidden grove. Hand me that atlas on the third shelf over there." Once the heavy book was nestled on his narrow lap, he flipped pages until he found what he wanted. "Look here. See that mark by the town of Altman?"

Faith nodded.

"That's where their farm used to be. Pretty little place, covered with aspen. That day they were as golden as I'd ever seen them."

"Why did you go there?" Faith could barely get the words out. Suddenly, an image came into her mind, and she knew. She had to hear his words, but she already knew. Her two men were there.

"There are graves back in the trees. She wanted to see them

one last time. She knelt down and sobbed as if they'd just been buried. I've never heard such heartache."

Faith felt the soul deep pain. Knew exactly what he was talking about. "You are a special man, Timothy Gibson."

His eyes closed, and Faith bent to kiss the paper-thin skin of his cheek. A melancholy smile tugged at the edges of his lips as a tear slipped between his closed eyelids.

"It's good to see you again—Maria," he whispered. "Good-bye, Faith." He didn't open his eyes. "Put some flowers on those three graves for me, would you?"

Ten

Rain hit the windshield just as Faith pulled onto the highway and headed home. The slapping of the wipers was loud in the silent car. The antique photograph sat on the seat next to her as she maneuvered her car north through Denver, the silent, lifeless eyes staring up at her. She hadn't put the photo back in the blue envelope, unwilling to hide the images again. They had been put away in a drawer for so long. At the second stop light she jumped when a car horn sounded, and she looked up. The light had turned green and traffic whizzed past. She turned the picture over.

Even the back of the tattered gray board, which the photo was mounted on, couldn't block out the images. Maria's hand on Rafe's shoulder, possessive and comforting. The way Rafe's head tilted toward hers, as if keeping her within his peripheral vision. The strong hand curled around Timmy's tiny waist as he leaned against his father's knee. A warm inviting portrait of the Christmas holiday. Despite the staid pose, she saw the love in their eyes.

Suddenly, the vision from the other night jumped into her mind. At the next light, she grabbed the picture and turned it over, searching its black and white surface. She didn't care if every car in town honked.

There, under the tree sat the toy bear Timmy had excitedly brought into her fantasy bedroom. The bear the wind had stolen away. Where had the bear gone? She didn't remember it being in the trunk. A lump wedged in her throat.

Memories of Faith's own childhood crowded in, of her childish tears at the loss of a beloved bear. Just one more pain she shared with the little boy.

Shadows engulfed the city. The evening had control when Faith turned onto her street. Exhaustion—both physical and emotional—threatened to overwhelm her. She looked forward to a soak in a nice warm tub.

The headlight beams sought out a path through the quiet residential neighborhood and found the familiar street. A battered blue jeep sat on one side of her driveway. Surprised, Faith stepped hard on the brake.

She sat in her car, debating about turning around and going to the convenience store a couple blocks away to call the police.

She slipped the car into reverse when a figure separated itself from the shadows on the front porch.

Swallowing a cry, she watched the figure take shape. A thick head of hair glinted in the dim starlight. Broad shoulders filled a worn leather jacket. He stepped into the eerie glow of the streetlight with a vaguely familiar swagger.

Cord.

A sigh of relief escaped her lips and then transformed into a frightened cry of uncertainty. Clarissa's words from yesterday rang through the empty night. *Rafe murdered Delta DeLange.*

What could she do? If she turned around and called the police what would she tell them? There was a murderer at her house? She could hear some sergeant asking her, "Who did they kill? When?" And she'd reply, "About a hundred years ago. A psychic told me?" Oh, that would be good. She had to face him, but she needed a couple minutes to prepare.

Cord isn't Rafe, she reminded herself and forced her thoughts and her heartbeat to calm. She punched the button on the garage door opener and drove inside. Quickly, she punched the button again and the door slid closed. She knew Cord stood on her front step, but she needed time to think. Time to hide the picture. To put all the information she'd learned in the past twenty-four hours into perspective.

Then maybe she could face the man whose existence was changing from a recurring dream into a never-ending nightmare.

***

The sun had slipped behind the mountains, leaving a blanket of shadow across the town. As the sun dipped, so had the temperature. Cord had almost given up, planning to go some place for a cup of coffee and to warm up.

When he'd seen headlights coming down the road toward the house, he knew it was Faith. No other cars had passed this way since he'd arrived.

For several long moments after she'd entered her garage, he stood on the front step, looking around, waiting. The tiny, baby-blue house fit her. A small verandah wrapped around part of the front and one side of the house. An old-fashioned porch swing hung on the far end. He pictured her there on a warm day, sipping iced tea and gazing out at the mountains. The view was lovely from the hill on which the house sat.

A cut glass window and a lacy curtain were all that prevented him from seeing inside. There'd been no indication earlier that she was home. Now a faint light shone through the lace. Raking his fingers through his hair, Cord pushed the little lighted button beside the door. Chimes echoed through the house in a soft, lonely sound.

The rain had stopped, and a gentle breeze slipped through the air, causing the swing to creak as if in invitation. If he had to, he'd use it. He had time to wait for her. After last night he had no choice.

He paced, burning off the nervous energy that had kept him company for what seemed like an eternity. The debate he'd held with himself all the way here repeated itself in his mind. In the end he'd given in, knowing he had to try to figure things out. He'd never been one to ignore a problem, and he wasn't about to start now.

He was patient for the first few minutes, then he bypassed the doorbell and rapped on the doorframe. What was taking her so long, he wondered? He knew his being here was a surprise, but she wasn't hiding from him—from their disagreement yesterday—was she? The old glass rattled, announcing his presence all over again.

A meow sounded on the other side of the door. It didn't stop until Faith turned on the porch light and opened the door. A streak of white that Cord assumed to be a cat sped past his legs and disappeared around the corner of the house.

"I hope he'll come back." Cord smiled at her, unable to control the warm desire spreading through him. The hall light haloed around her hair and caressed the smoothness of her brow, her cheeks, her lips... He caught himself before he leaned forward.

There was no smile on her face for him. She stood slightly behind the door, as if it were a shield. "When he gets hungry, he'll come begging for his dinner." Belatedly, he realized she was talking about the cat.

"Hello, Faith." He shoved his hands into the pockets of his jacket.

"Hello, Cord. How did you find me?" Faith's fingers squeezed the doorknob, as her heart pounded hard against her ribs. Why was he here?

"Opal has your address, remember? May I come in?" He didn't wait until she agreed but brushed past her.

Cord's height and bulk filled the small foyer. The hall light glowed in his dark hair. He turned away, looking at her house.

"Nice."

She'd always been proud of her little home. Items from her various travels, and from her parents' home, filled the nooks and crannies. Some thought it hodgepodge. She liked it. A shiver of pleasure shot through her at his approval. She quickly squelched it.

A cool breeze slipped through the open door, reminding her it was still open. She quickly shut it. The house grew immediately warmer, but she felt trapped and closed in with him so near.

"I'll have to speak to Opal about keeping my address confidential," Faith mumbled as she walked past Cord and into the front room. With a flip of a wall switch, soft recessed light bathed the room. Out of habit, she also flipped the companion switch that turned on the gas logs.

The bouncing flames in the stone fireplace sent shimmering light about the room, and Faith regretted the impulse. She wasn't willing to admit the error and turn it off. The constant warmth of the flickering gas flame usually gave her comfort, but not tonight. Cord's presence was too unsettling.

Clarissa's words suddenly leaped into her mind, and Faith rubbed her hands nervously up and down her arms.

This isn't Rafe.

This is Cord.

Maybe if she repeated it over and over enough times, she might actually believe it.

"Why are you here?" she whispered. Her eyes didn't meet his, but her gaze traveled over the rest of him.

"I..." He suddenly grinned at her. "I was wondering if you'd had dinner."

"You drove all the way from Cripple Creek to see if I'd had dinner?" She crossed her arms in front of her, finally meeting his gaze.

"Well, no." He shifted on the balls of his feet. "Have you had any more dreams?"

"Sort of." She recalled the vision and the toy bear. "You still haven't answered my question. You could have called to find out if I had more dreams. Opal has my number, too."

"I tried calling, but all I got was your machine. Besides, Johnny takes over whenever I need a break...and I need a break."

He walked across the room, coming uncomfortably close to her. Lifting one booted foot, he set it on the raised hearth and stared into the flames.

Dancing light caressed the even planes of his face, and Faith's heart softened. Her eyes followed the light's path. She remembered how his skin felt against her fingers. His lips would be warm and firm against hers...

"C...can I get you something to drink?" Faith moved away before her traitorous fingers reached out and touched him. "I've got some wine in the fridge. Or iced tea?"

"No vodka?" His voice teased, but his eyes didn't smile. "Tea will do."

Cord turned away from the fire and watched Faith walk into the kitchen. With the flames at his back, he looked around, more than a little curious about the woman who lived here.

The couch and matching loveseat looked old-fashioned, yet new. A bright floral print added light to the room. An antique rocker sat near him with a matching table and dainty lamp beside it. But what drew his attention most was the wall of photographs. There must have been a couple dozen in various coordinated frames.

Were they her work? A large print of a man and woman standing beside a tent dominated the grouping. The man, older and balding, smiled formally. The woman had Faith's features, though her gray hair was cropped short and serviceable. Her parents. How long ago had this picture been taken?

Groups of family and friends stared back at him. Home and family reached out, pressing unfamiliarly close. He'd never known what it was like to have a family like that. He doubted he ever would. Faith was the first woman to ever make him even think about the long haul.

He turned his attention back to the pictures. Other than the single photo of Timmy Cumberland, Cord had never known a photo to move him so deeply. These did the same thing, and he tore his gaze away.

Antiques. Knickknacks. Family. They were everywhere, reaching out to him, clearly announcing they were very different than his life in a casino.

Faith returned just then, a large glass in each hand. "Did you take these?" he asked even though he already knew the answer.

"Many of them, yes."

He nodded, returning his gaze to the photos. "For a book?" He knew better but hoped to put some distance between himself and the appealing homeyness they exuded.

She set his tea on the table before answering. "No, personal."

He returned to the couch. Sitting, he let his head drop back and his eyes close for a moment.

The silence stretched between them, heavy and thick. Faith didn't speak, and he didn't ask anything more. Instead, she stirred the ice in her drink, breaking the silence with the clink.

"You look tired," she commented as she sat down in the antique rocker near the hearth. The old chair was safe and strong, comforting to her frayed nerves.

"I am. I didn't sleep much last night. I kept thinking about you." His gaze was intent as he leaned forward. He sipped the drink, his blue eyes looking at her over the rim of the glass.

"Oh. The dreams." She stared down at her own drink, swirling the liquid around in the glass. He was silent for several moments, and she finally looked up at him.

"Yeah, that too, but no. About how good it felt to touch you," he whispered.

The fire in his eyes had nothing to do with the gas logs a few feet away, though Faith tried to convince herself it did. She took a deep gulp of her drink. Its mellow dampness soothed the dryness in her throat and the tightness in her chest.

"I...we can't." She couldn't sit any longer. She stood and paced. Her shoes brushed against the thick carpet, the whooshing sound the only noise in the room.

"Stop." He stood and reached for her. Unmindful of the tea splashing across them both, he pulled her into his arms. He took her glass out of her hand and set it on a nearby table. The front of her shirt was damp and clung to her skin.

"You're driving me crazy." He pulled her close, his hands moving up and down her back, and his face buried in the softness of her neck.

"Cord, please." Her plea was halfhearted. It felt so good, so right to be with him like this.

"There's no storm this time, have you noticed? We're safe here."

"There's so much you...we don't know." Faith wanted to share what she'd learned with him, but the thought of telling him tore her apart. How could she discuss the violence of their shared past? What would he say? How would he react? A shaft of fear tripped through her, and once again she repeated Clarissa's warnings in her mind. She had to stop this. She struggled in his embrace and against herself.

His voice was strained when he spoke again. "I really don't give a damn about anything right now but you and me. Here. Now. Like this." Cord didn't give her a chance to argue, didn't give her any more time to think. He simply took her lips in a demanding, soul-searing kiss.

His lips were hard and warm against hers, seeking what she was sure she couldn't give him—her heart. But as the moments passed, the magic of his kiss seeped past her hastily erected barriers. She relaxed against him.

Hesitantly, her arms crept around his neck, and the curls at the nape of his neck teased her fingertips. This man wouldn't hurt her.

His vitality and warmth were stronger than any evil that might have once been a part of him. At the reassurance, her mind grew blank, seeing nothing but the gossamer warmth of her desire.

The cushions of the couch pressed against her back, and the warm weight of his body stretched across hers. The heavy, solidness of his thigh between hers was intoxicating.

Levering up on one elbow, Cord gazed down at her, a teasing smile hovered on the edges of his lips. "Isn't this better?"

The movement of his lips mesmerized Faith as they formed the words. She nodded in agreement, coherent speech long gone.

"Sorry about spilling your tea." He didn't sound at all remorseful. He reached out and traced a damp circle near the top button of her blouse. With gentle care, he pushed the white pearl through its hole and pulled the fabric apart, exposing her neck and collarbone to his searching lips. As his mouth warmed a trail down her skin, his fingers moved to the next button, opening the fabric over the swell of her breast. The fabric parted and his mouth followed, pulling the dainty lace of her bra away with his teeth.

Heat exploded over her skin. Faith moaned from the fire traveling through her. As his lips closed around her nipple, she cried out. Gently, she urged for more with her fingers at the back of his head. His laughter wasn't a taunt, but an expression of his enjoyment.

With growing urgency, Faith let her fingers travel over the T-shirt covering his chest. She tugged at the white cloth, successfully pulling it from the waistband of his jeans. With one swift movement he pulled it over his head, and a sudden rush of hot desire shot through her as his chest pressed against her naked breasts. Her gasp echoed through the room.

"You're not him," Faith whispered as she pulled his lips back to hers. "You're not," she repeated as he pulled away.

Lifting away from her, Cord looked down into her eyes. "Not who?"

"Rafe. You can't be him."

"Ah, damn." He sat up, raking the fingers that moments before had played magically against her skin through his thick mane of hair. "I've spent the last day and night trying to escape those images. Will there ever be a time these dreams won't be a part of us?"

"I don't know. Maybe they *are* us." Faith pulled her blouse back together and sat up. Torment blazed in his eyes. She wanted to take back the words. Her arms ached to hold him again. Her heart ached to return to that magic place where they didn't think, just felt.

"I'm sorry," she whispered.

"It's not your fault." He stood and paced, stopping only for a moment to pull his shirt back on. "I'll be glad when this is all over."

"When what's over?" Faith stood, gathering up the glasses and walking into the kitchen with them.

"The dreams." He followed her, standing in the doorway as she put the glasses in the dishwasher.

"What makes you think it will end?" She couldn't face him, couldn't let him see how much she wanted the dreams to go away, too. But that was like wishing history to change. She couldn't do that. No one could.

"It has to. Don't you see?" He reached out, pulling her around to face him. "We've had these dreams for years, but never met. Now that we've met, all kinds of strange things are happening. Something has to give sooner or later."

"Yeah, like our sanity."

"No. I'm not ready to give up. You want to know the real reason I came here? I wanted you so badly I couldn't stand it." He smiled as the blush crept over her cheeks. "And I wanted to talk to you about what we're going to do."

"Do?" Uncertainty shot through her. He needed to know about Rafe, and yet what would he think? How would he feel? What would he do?

"Clarissa," she said aloud.

"Who?"

"A friend of mine. She's a psychic."

"A what?"

His smirk of disbelief was comical, and Faith laughed. "I've known her a long time. We met at the library yesterday. She knows about everything."

"Meaning you told her about it? I realize she's a friend, but are you sure she's not a nut case?" He looked as skeptical as she had been yesterday.

She frowned at him. Clarissa was not a nut case, though Faith knew many people would share his opinions.

"I've never told her about the dreams because that's all I thought they were. She knew about Timmy." The color drained from Cord's face. "You should meet her. I'm calling her." She walked to the phone and dialed the familiar number of the coffee shop. The answering machine picked up. Knowing she must be busy with customers, Faith left a brief message.

"Well?" Cord leaned against the counter, his long legs stretched out in front of him. He crossed his arms over his chest. "If she's a psychic, wouldn't she know you were calling?"

Faith glared at him for his sarcasm.

"Now what?" He looked away.

"Is that invitation for dinner still open?" She tried to smile, but couldn't. She knew it was dangerous to stay here alone with him, but he didn't seem in any great hurry to leave.

The doorbell rang, and Faith breathed a sigh of relief. Leaving Cord in the kitchen, she went to answer it.

Clarissa shoved two brimming grocery bags in her arms as Singe raced in through the opened door. The cat's yowl of anger told her he'd been in another scrape with the neighbor's cat. She'd have to tend to him later.

"There're two more bags in the car. You take these and I'll get the others." Clarissa rushed back to her car, leaving Faith to stare after her.

"Yes, ma'am," Faith mocked and took the bags into the kitchen as instructed.

"What's that?" Cord took one bag from her and peered inside. The white cartons and unlabeled wrappers didn't tell them what was inside. The scent of ginger announced the presence of Chinese food. Jalapenos hinted at Mexican. The front door banged shut, and both Cord and Faith turned to see Clarissa enter the room. Faith saw Cord's eyebrow shoot up in silent question.

"Cord Burke this is Clarissa Elgin." She wanted to tease him about his earlier sarcasm but held back.

"Nice to finally meet you." Clarissa extended her hand while juggling the paper bags. Rather than shake her hand, Cord took the bags and smiled in return. The crease between his eyebrows remained, though.

"I just left you a message," Faith said, a twinge of relief leaping through her.

"Oh good. Well, not so good. I'm not there. Anyway, what was it about?"

"The dreams." Faith was surprised to see Clarissa stop and stand still. For a long moment silence claimed the room.

"I'll make you a deal." Clarissa turned to face them. "A psychic without sustenance is worthless. That's why I brought all this food. After dinner, we'll talk, okay?" There was a plea in her voice.

Faith and Cord exchanged uneasy glances before turning to help Clarissa unpack the bags.

"What is all this?" Cord lifted a large white box.

"Well, I couldn't make up my mind what I wanted, and I didn't know what you two liked, so that's Mexican—enchiladas, tostados extraordinaire. This one." She held up another white box. "Is Chinese." She hugged it to her with a decadent smile. "Mine. Faith, that's ribs. I think I managed to get something for everyone."

Clarissa was frequently a chatterbox, but this was definitely nervous energy. Faith watched her, seeking but finding no clues as to why.

"How did you know we were here?" Faith asked Clarissa, looking at Cord with an I-told-you-so smile.

Clarissa looked up sheepishly. "I...uh drove by earlier and uh...you should close your curtains." With her boxes of food piled in her arms, Clarissa bolted from the room. Faith's cheeks warmed with her blush.

"I guess we can eat by the fire." Faith didn't look at Cord. She grabbed the bottle of wine, paper plates and food and followed Clarissa into the living room. Cord chuckled but quickly swallowed the sound when Faith turned to glare at him.

Spread out on the hearth and coffee table, there was enough food for a dozen people. They managed to make a healthy dent. Friendship permeated the room, and Faith savored it. She and

Clarissa hadn't been able to spend much time together lately, and Faith missed her friend.

Cord entertained them both with tales of his various travels. He'd lived more places than her parents had visited. As he talked, she watched him over the rim of her glass. Was Cripple Creek just another place he intended to pass through or was he planning to stay this time?

Before she could ask him, Clarissa reached over and replenished her wineglass. "I think I'm up to this."

Faith looked closely at her friend. "I would like to know what's got you so on edge."

"Yeah, me too," Cord echoed.

"Oh, why do you want the difficult stuff first?" Clarissa moaned. Closing her eyes, she took a deep breath before opening them again. When she did, she didn't look at either Faith or Cord. She stared into the depths of her wine.

"I had a dream last night. At least it felt like a dream. It wasn't one of my usual visions." She fidgeted with her wineglass. "It's as if the image were being forced, like a television signal just barely at the edges of the reception area."

"A dream?" Cord's voice was husky. "What about?"

"Well, it wasn't a what. It was a who." She didn't elaborate.

After several long, silent minutes, Faith leaned forward, unable to stand the suspense any longer. "Clarissa. Who?"

Clarissa gulped her wine. "I saw Timmy last night." Finally, she looked up. The room was silent. Faith wished she'd put on some music—anything to fill the awkward silence.

"He was in the dark somewhere in the mountains, looking for you. He clung to an old-fashioned Teddy bear."

"Where was he?" Cord sat on the couch and leaned forward, resting his elbows on his knees, as if he needed the support. His eyes were distant and cool.

"I...I don't know." Clarissa lifted her hands. "All I saw were trees, him and the bear."

"Wh...what did the bear look like?" Faith trembled. Her images and feelings about Timmy were the most painful part of all this. She was afraid of what Clarissa saw.

"Ragged and dark brown. It wasn't called a teddy bear then, was it?"

"No, not till a few years later," Faith answered absently.

"He was so sad." Clarissa's voice broke then. "There were tears in his eyes. Talk about my maternal instinct kicking into overdrive. I wanted to hug him forever."

Faith's heart cracked. Tears filled her eyes. She stood, meeting Cord's startled gaze, and then rushed from the room, away from the pain and questions there. She retrieved the picture Tim Gibson had given her from the drawer where she'd hidden it. The tiny stuffed bear rested innocently beneath the Christmas tree. So joyful. So innocent. So painful.

"Oh, Timmy, where were you?" she asked the empty air. No words came to her ears, and she knew there would be none. She slowly returned to the living room with the picture.

Cord looked up, concern filling his face as she sat down next to him.

"I...I went to see someone today," she said. "I wasn't going to tell you until I had things figured out, but, well, he gave me this." She handed him the picture and moved to the hearth.

"Who gave you this?" Cord held the picture gingerly as if it might vanish.

"Tim Gibson."

He stood, anger filling his face and walked toward her. "You weren't going to tell me? What the hell did he say to you? Is that why you were so damned suspicious earlier?"

Faith could only return his stare. He had a right to be angry, had the right to not trust her. She hadn't trusted him.

"May I?" Clarissa stepped between them and took the picture from Cord's hand. Her interruption broke the tension between them. Cord returned to the couch.

"The bear." Clarissa cried aloud, holding the picture close to examine it. "That's the one."

Faith's mind tumbled back to the vision. "The other night, I saw a scene. I don't know what it was." Her gaze sought Cord's, needing his support. "It was Christmas morning. Timmy came into our room, the one with the quilt and the brass bed. He had that bear. He said Santa had given it to him." Her voice broke as she remembered his childish joy. "The only thing was, suddenly the wind came in and snatched the bear away. He was heartbroken."

Clarissa was silent for several moments as she stared at the photograph. She shook her head. "I'm not getting anything new." She laid the picture down, a frown creasing her brow.

"It's spooky, isn't it? To see your face on a picture you don't remember posing for." Cord stared down at the photograph.

"Yes." Faith went to stand beside him. "I didn't mean to

deceive you. I....” What was she trying to tell him? That she’d never had to deal with problems, that her father had always seemed to do that for her, that she’d only recently taken control of her own life. “It’d be easier to just walk away.”

Cord reached out and ran his fingers along the edge of her chin. “You can’t this time.”

“I know. The dreams aren’t going away. They seem to be getting worse.” His hand felt so good, so right, so strong.

“They’ll continue to do so, won’t they Cord?” Clarissa pinned him with a stare.

She knew. How the hell...? Cord stared in shock at the woman he’d at first thought a flake. She knew about his dream. The dream that had brought him awake with cries of anguish. Cries that were his own screams echoing through the years and through his room.

“Yes. They’ll get worse. Much worse.” He looked down at Faith, knowing she too would soon be crying out in the night, screaming with the pain of the past.

Eleven

Cord sat before the never dying gas firelight. Flames lit the room enough for him to see shapes and shadows combine.

He stared at the wall of pictures he'd examined earlier. Dozens of faces stared at him, all smiling and happy. A little girl in a pinafore in one photo caught his eye, and he knew from the tilt of her little smile and the bright copper curls that he was staring at a much younger Faith.

His heart twisted. The wanton woman in his dream and the woman who'd once been that innocent child were worlds apart. The dream woman was like half the women he met in the bar and casino trade. They didn't necessarily have to be hookers for him to know they had only one purpose in mind. Taking care of themselves and no one else.

Faith, on the other hand, confused him. Her fear when he'd first arrived had pulsed in the air. After Clarissa arrived and they'd talked, she'd relaxed. He wasn't sure who was more surprised when she'd offered him the couch for the night. He'd had several glasses of wine, but he'd been nowhere near drunk. He'd gladly taken her up on the offer, though it felt strange to have someone take care of him, to fuss over him. He couldn't remember the last person who'd done that.

He turned back to the fire. No, Faith was nothing like the women he was used to. She wore her heart in her eyes and cried tears for total strangers.

Disturbed by his own thoughts, Cord paced, avoiding the staring eyes that seemed to watch him from the wall of pictures. He thought of the single photo he had of his own parents. Old. Tattered. Lying in the bottom of his dresser drawer.

He didn't fit into Faith's world. Never would. But a part of him wished he could. What would it be like to have a family and a home? He'd built the closest thing he knew to a home with his casino. Johnny was as close to family as Cord got. He knew he should return to it, but not yet. For just a little while he wanted to believe he could have Faith's world.

Besides, it fit into his plans. The images that had invaded his mind last night returned, images that he knew she'd soon experience.

He wanted to stop them. He'd expected to arrive here today and find her in emotional pieces. When she went about business as usual, he'd known she hadn't shared his dream last night. Odds were, she wasn't far behind.

He headed to the kitchen and put on a pot of coffee. He needed something to do, something to occupy his mind.

As the coffee dripped, he turned his gaze to the small, orderly kitchen. A pile of bills and letters scattered near the phone provided the only disorganization.

The corner of a handwritten note caught his eye. He knew he was snooping, but he wanted—needed—to learn more about Faith. The letterhead spoke volumes. Reverend and Mrs. McCoy. He slid the paper from the stack, glancing down at the scrawled signature. *Love, Mom.*

He cringed. A preacher's daughter. Figures. He couldn't remember ever setting foot in a church. What a contrast to his life, as well as the Cumberland's. Suddenly, her hesitancy to gamble that first night made sense. No wonder she resisted the very thought of being Maria.

The bright red lettering of *Past Due* across several papers caught his attention. A mortgage. Utilities.

She needed the money from this book. That was what drove her, kept her working. What did she have planned after that? Something told him she'd pay the mortgage, find Mr. Right and create the proverbial 2.5 kids.

A rolled tube of paper sat wedged against the blender. He recognized blueprints and unrolled them. A handwritten note stuck to one corner. "Check out these plans. Just perfect for you." The strip mall sketched on the page looked new and modern. A big red "x" on one section drew his attention. The same handwriting had scrawled "portrait studio."

There weren't any strip malls in Cripple Creek. How much further from his world could she get? A cold knot of loneliness settled in his chest.

Uncomfortable, Cord filled a large mug with coffee and returned to the living room. As the hands slowly maneuvered around the face of the clock, he sat. Waiting. Watching the flames, and dreading the pain to come. His normal life was miles from hers, but for now he'd be here for her. He hoped and prayed, for the first time in his life, for strength.

***

On the other side of the locked door, Faith listened to Cord moving about the house. Her mind filled with images of him spreading out the bed linen she'd given him for the short, narrow couch. Of him pulling his shirt over his head. His tight jeans sliding down his thighs...

Stop that. She moved away from the door and turned toward the bed. She would *not* think about him.

She jerked back the covers. Turning off the lights, she snuggled under the down comforter. The bed felt cold and empty. She tried to ignore the urges telling her she should be sharing it with him.

Sleep. She'd go to sleep and soon morning would be here, then he'd head back to Cripple Creek.

Why did she find little comfort in that knowledge?

Despite her hectic thoughts, exhaustion tugged at her. Sleep battled with images struggling to form, as if having difficulty separating themselves from the darkness. Even when the images did emerge into the light, the gloom clung to the edges of her dream.

Rain fell in sheets. The town's dirt roads turned into a quagmire, tugging at her shoes and the heavy, wet hem of her skirts. Giving up, she pulled the thick fabric above her knees. To hell with propriety.

His voice floated on the wind. "Mama?"

She followed its lead. She had to get to him. Had to protect her baby.

The buildings fell behind as she struggled through the clinging mud. "I'm coming, sweetie," she cried, unsure if her voice carried through the wind and rain.

From out of nowhere, Rafe appeared in the clearing ahead. As she drew closer, the lantern's golden light illuminated his features. She stopped, searching his face for an answer. His red-rimmed eyes met hers and then skittered away, looking at some spot behind her. She saw dampness on his cheeks—the rain?

"Where's Timmy?" She ran the last few yards. "I heard him calling."

Rafe wasn't alone. Several other men stood nearby, still and silent in the dark.

His big hands reached out to hold her as she moved to pass him. She shrugged off his touch. Other arms tried to reach her. She had the strength of ten men. She pulled from the grasp of the strong, burly miners.

A tiny form lay on a pallet, beckoning to her, pulling her gaze. The men's arms fell away. They couldn't stop her. Nothing could keep her away. Like a wheat field under a summer wind, the group parted.

"No." Her voice tore away on the night. Her heart stopped beating. Timmy lay covered in a man's coat, a coat she vaguely recognized. She stumbled and crawled the last few feet through the mud. "Sweetie, Mama's here. I'm sorry it took me so long to find you." She reached out for him. His skin was cold and pale. "We've got to get you warm. It's so chilly."

She heard no response. No welcoming snuggle from his tiny arms. The footsteps nearby were loud and grating to her ears.

Rafe knelt beside her, and she looked up at him, realizing tears did indeed slide down his face.

"He's gone, honey. Timmy's dead."

"No. You're lying." She pulled her son's tiny body close to her chest, rocking back and forth as if she were in the wooden rocker in the nursery instead of here in the freezing mud.

"Maria, please." A sob broke Rafe's normally strong voice.

"Rock a by baby," she sang in a soft, tear-filled voice. "On the tree top..."

Rafe sank into the mud, his head bowed and his face buried in his work-roughened hands. Sobs shook his big body. Time barely moved.

From out of nowhere, arms reached out and took Timmy from her. The cold and damp had weakened her grasp, but still she fought. "No, don't take my baby. Stop them, Rafe. They're taking Timmy. Stop!"

The voice echoed across time and into the room where Faith struggled in her sleep. She awoke in the darkness, the feel of the damp pillow against her cheek, and the pain of Timmy's death an unbearable agony. Jumping from the bed, she fumbled with the lock and then tore open the bedroom door.

The gas logs in the living room glowed and hissed. Their unchanging flame became an odd comfort, a testament she was in modern times, not that long ago day a century past. The faint aroma of coffee teased her, reminding her she was awake.

"Now you know why I stayed," Cord said, his voice barely above a whisper. He looked up at her from the wingback chair, a mug of coffee between his big hands. She saw the pain reflected in his eyes.

The firelight danced, sending shadows to and fro in the room. She couldn't seem to move. He sat there, so close, so real. What would he think if he knew she ached to fling herself into his arms? The broad, bare expanse of his chest invited her to seek comfort...and something else. The something else made her hold back.

He set the cup aside. "Come here." He extended a hand and after a moment's hesitation, she ran to him, seeking his comforting embrace.

She knelt before him, and he pulled her tight. His warm skin was reassuringly real and alive. "It was awful, Cord. It hurt so much."

"I know. I went through this last night. Dear God." He buried his face in her hair, anguish strong in his voice. "We found Timmy in the mine shaft and carried him to the surface. Watching you—her—sing to him, in that sad, pitiful voice nearly did me in."

Both Cord Burke and Rafe Cumberland had been taught men don't cry. Yet, no man, no matter what his strength, could have fought off the horror of that night.

"I'm not Maria." Faith lifted her head, desperation in her voice. His face and pain-filled eyes were so close. "She hurt too much. I'm Faith."

"Faith," he whispered her name, kissing first one eye, then the other. With his thumbs, he wiped away the damp trail on her cheeks. "Faith," he repeated.

Her hand came up to cover his, pressing his palm against her cheek. For a moment she closed her eyes, savoring the warmth and stability of his touch. Reality.

She let her eyes drift open. "I need you, Cord. Now. Tonight."

"I don't think that's a good idea," he whispered but didn't move his hand away.

She wanted him and didn't stop to wonder why. Thoughts of the past and their pain faded. Moving closer, Faith pressed her lips to his, seeking comfort and passion and finding both in his arms. His fingers moved to cup her chin, holding her lips to the kiss he professed not to want.

The magic of the night in his office swept in. Quickly, she pushed the frightening images of the storm-shattered window from her mind and thought only of the warmth seeping through every inch of her chilled body.

His fingers moved from her chin, along the curve of her neck and down the sides of her body. She felt him shudder and his growing arousal pressed against her belly. His hands reached her hips, and he lifted her to his lap where the heat of him nestled intimately against her.

A sigh and then a gasp escaped her. His kiss swallowed the sound. The hem of her nightgown tempted him, and he played with it before sliding his hand beneath.

"So soft. So sweet," he breathed into her mouth.

She had responded to his caresses in the past, but this was different. She burned hotter.

With his fingers, Cord drew tiny circles on her inner thigh. Slowly they slipped between her legs, touching her tenderness, teasing and tempting through the thin barrier of her panties. She whimpered when his fingers moved away—and upwards.

A shiver shook her as he grazed the top of her panties and the sensitive skin of her abdomen. When he found the soft underside of her breast and gently stroked, she nearly shattered.

With shallow breaths, she fought to slow her pounding heart. No one had ever made her feel like this before. So alive. So real.

He played her body like an instrument—an instrument of pleasure—caressing her in all the places aching for his touch. After what seemed an eternity, he found the curve of her breast again and brushed her nipple. She cried out. The pleasure, while expected, bloomed stronger than she'd thought possible. He rubbed and stroked her, building heat along her nerve endings.

She wanted to pleasure him and ached to feel his body beneath her fingers. She slid her hand across the broad expanse of his chest, enjoying the tickle of the rough hair covering his bare skin. Her hand brushed a hardened, male nipple, and she heard a low groan in his throat. She couldn't stop the smile forming in their kiss.

His stomach muscles were taut and hard beneath her touch, his skin warm and smooth. She moved her hand over him, touching each inch, unsure if she'd ever get enough of him.

When her fingers touched the top button of his jeans, his hand shot out, catching hers and stopping her progress. "Not yet, love. We've only just begun." He guided her hand back up to his chest.

To distract her, he tugged the hem of her nightshirt upwards and over her head. She moved to lean against him, but he held her away for a moment, gazing at her in the dancing firelight. "You're so beautiful."

He dipped his head, taking one distended nipple into his mouth, rubbing it with the damp, insistent tip of his tongue until she moaned aloud with pleasure. He moved to the other breast, repeating his actions until she whimpered in delight.

Hot sparks flashed behind her closed eyelids. She leaned into him, burying her fingers in his hair and holding his head to her breast. She longed to touch him, but she found herself incapable of doing anything except feeling and accepting the magnificence he offered. She gave herself up to him.

"I want you," she whispered through her parched throat. "Cord!" She called his name as he shifted her to the floor in front of the chair and nearer the fire.

He knelt over her, watching as the firelight played across her skin. With one hand, he slipped off the tiny barrier of her panties and traced a tormenting pattern upward across her bare skin. With the other, he took her hand and returned it to the button of his jeans where he'd stopped her earlier. "Now."

She pushed the metal button through the frayed buttonhole. His zipper slid down, the sound loud and provocative. She smiled as he impatiently took over and quickly shed his clothes. Her eyes drank in his every action, looking at and memorizing each inch of skin revealed.

Her breath caught in her throat as he knelt beside her again, naked, aroused and exactly as she wanted him to be.

"Mmmm," she sighed as he leaned over and captured her lips with his, filling her mouth with his tongue, in a provocative imitation of his intent to fill her in other ways.

He moved closer, the length of his body matching her curves. He thrust inside her, pausing when he realized this was her first time. She blushed, and he smiled and carefully pushed forward. After she'd adjusted to him, they moved together, rocking in a motion as old as time. The heat, intensity and depth of his touch astounded her.

Her fierce reaction came as a surprise. She held him, wanting him to stay within her for eternity. Fulfillment lay ahead, and she waited with increasing anticipation.

She hung upon the edge of a precipice, clinging to him and returning kiss for kiss, thrust for thrust, and cry for heated cry. The joy came, filling the world with a radiance she'd never seen before and her body with the sparkle of release.

In response to her climax, Cord let go and gave in. His head was thrown back, and the firelight danced on his sweat-glazed skin. In awe of his abandon, she pulled him closer and he folded her into his arms. He held her tight as the last of their passion spent itself in the quiet, shadowed night.

When her breathing had slowed, Faith stirred in his arms. She nuzzled his chest, and her arms tightened around him. "Cord?" she whispered, lifting up on one elbow and gazing down into his eyes.

"Yes?"

Her hair fell in a curtain between her face and the firelight, distorting his expression with shadow. "Thank you."

He chuckled. "Any time." His arms encircled her, pulling her into the crook of his arm between the angle of his shoulder and chin. "What's going through that pretty head of yours?"

"Not much. I'm tired. Would the bed be more comfortable?"

"Than what? The couch or the floor?"

"Either. Come on." She moved away from him and stood.

The glow of the fire created shadows on his body and she realized how deeply she wanted him again. Instead, she turned toward the bedroom, and he followed. She absently flipped off the gas fire, plunging the room into darkness. Only the dim moon through the skylight provided illumination for the hallway. At the door of her dark bedroom she stopped.

"It's okay. If the dream returns, I'm here," Cord promised.

His hand settled in the small of her back, guiding her to the bed. After they crawled into it, he pulled her close and tucked the blankets snug around them.

"There. Get some sleep." He pushed her head back into the comfortable niche of his shoulder, placing a soft kiss on her forehead.

"Cord?"

"Mm hmm?"

What did she want to say? The words that nearly fell unheeded off her tongue were those of love, words that came too easy to mind. Words she dared not speak because she wasn't sure they were hers.

"Nothing." Instead of speaking her thoughts, she let her hand slip beneath the blankets. Suddenly, she was no longer sleepy. The warmth of his skin against her fingers sent them both deep into the vortex of desire.

The night slipped away, filled with soft, passionate sounds.

She felt a belonging she'd never known before, and she wanted it to last forever. When the first fingers of morning filtered into the room, she watched him as his eyelids slipped closed. The pink and gold of the sunrise tinted the room, and she snuggled close, holding tight for just a little longer.

Faith managed to doze in the circle of Cord's arms. The dreams remained at bay, but with the growing of the day, her mind filled with the dream's remnants.

Carefully, slowly she slipped out from the warmth of the covers, smiling when Cord moaned and pulled her pillow into the empty spot she left. A smile lifted the corner of his lips, but he didn't awaken.

She showered and dressed and settled onto the window seat with a cup of coffee. The morning rituals helped her get back on an even keel, get back to feeling like herself. She sipped the warm brew and watched Cord sleep.

Lord, he was handsome. His dark tousled hair fell over his forehead begging for her to smooth it back with her fingers. His bare shoulders looked big and dark against the white linens. Warmth washed over her when she remembered how tightly she'd clung to those strong shoulders last night.

Breathing in slowly, she fought to calm her racing heart, but it was an impossible task when she couldn't tear her gaze away.

Cord Burke was different. From the minute she'd met him he'd taken charge, taking care of her and others around him. He took care of Johnny when he drank too much. He'd picked her up when she fainted and whisked her off to the doctor to tend her wounds. He drove here when he knew the dream was ahead.

Her heart hurt as she recalled Timmy's death, but not as much as it would have if Cord hadn't been here. She shuddered, knowing that if he hadn't been, she'd have gone insane.

He was someone she could count on. *Cord.*

Rafe. The names whispered through her mind, and she shivered. She could still see his face as it had been last night in the dream. Distraught with grief, he'd let his tears flow, uncaring that the world saw his pain, uncaring that she saw it. He'd been a strong man, too.

Faith closed her eyes and let the two images form. She knew now that she'd always been attracted to the dream man. She also knew she was dangerously close to falling in love with his real life counterpart.

***

Vaguely, slowly, Cord's mind started to function. The scent of lavender tickled his nose, and for a moment confusion took over. He rubbed his face against the sweet scented sheets, and recognition filtered into his mind. A smile tugged at his lips.

Faith.

Reaching out, he found the spot where she'd slept. Empty. A flash of loss invaded his heart before he squashed it. Opening one eye, he surveyed what he could see of the room. Opening the other eye, he lifted his head, taking the time to look around.

Everywhere white lace greeted him. Even the blanket that pooled around his hips as he sat up contained more lace than blanket. Elegant dove gray covered the walls in a peaceful tone. He liked the room. It fit Faith.

Light filtered in through a large window. Turning, he looked at the bay window and saw her.

She blended in with the décor of the room, wearing a white lace shirt and form-fitting white jeans. The stark color of her hair caught his eye, like a single copper stroke across a canvas.

Her knees were drawn up, nearly to her chest. A mug sat perched between her hands on top of her knees. Steam wafted up past her face where it dissipated in the morning air.

She stared out the window, her eyes distant and sad. What was she thinking about? The dream? He pushed his own memories away. Not now. Maybe never.

He leaned back against the white, carved headboard. He didn't want to disturb her thoughts—and yet he wanted to know them all.

"Morning." Her voice came out in a husky whisper. She didn't look at him, just continued to stare out the window. She lifted her cup and slowly sipped its contents.

"Morning." He waited, holding his breath in anticipation of her next words. Would she ask him to leave? Tell him last night was a mistake? He pushed his luck. "Regrets?"

Finally, she turned her head to look at him. A smile played on her lips. "No. No regrets." Her smile didn't reach her eyes.

"Then why the pensive mood?" He pushed harder, letting go of the breath trapped inside.

For several long minutes she returned his stare and then faced the window. "I've been trying to figure out how to tell you everything. There's a lot." She traced the lip of the mug with her finger, round and round.

Relief washed through him. She wasn't regretting last night. "Does this have to do with your visit to Gibson yesterday?"

She nodded, her hair glistening in the sun. "Some. There's quite a bit I've learned through Clarissa, too." Her eyes turned to his, no longer hiding her pain. "I don't want to tell you."

"Why? It couldn't be any worse than what I've already seen. I can ask Clarissa."

Maybe he should. Maybe it would be better if Clarissa told him. No, she had to tell him. They had to start dealing with it themselves. Besides it sounded as if Clarissa only knew part of the information.

"Mr. Gibson inherited the house when Maria died," she said.

"Did he meet her?" he prompted when she didn't continue.

Faith nodded. "She knew she was dying and asked him to come see her." She shrugged and took a deep swallow of her coffee. "That's when she asked that the observation room be forever closed."

"Why?"

Her voice shook. "Rafe died there." She swallowed hard.

Cord's mind fell back to the day he'd gone into the room to see the trunk. The blinding pain. "H...how did he die?"

"Dr. Jamison told me Rafe was shot. Maria was there. She never went back into that room again." Faith slipped off the window seat and set the coffee cup on the dresser. She paced at the foot of the bed.

"Don't give up on me now." Cord sat forward. "Who shot him?"

She shrugged. "No one seems to know for sure how he was shot. Oh, Cord. I don't know what to think. Yesterday, I was so frightened of you." She stopped and clasped her hands in front of her.

"Why?"

"A...at the archives yesterday..." She hesitated. "We found that same article in the old newspaper. Another article took up half the next page. There was a picture of the girl I saw in the mirror at the casino." Her shoulders rose as she took a deep gulp of air. He remained silent. His arms ached to hold her, but he feared he'd spook her.

"She was murdered. Her name was Delta DeLange. Clarissa says she's been haunting us as revenge." Faith paused, fidgeting with the lace curtains. The silence stretched until he almost couldn't bear it. "Clarissa said you murdered Delta."

Talk about a sucker punch. Cord stared at her. "*I* murdered her?" Anger exploded inside him, surprising him and burning its way through his gut. "You mean *Rafe* murdered her."

They'd both struggled to keep the dreams and reality separate. After last night, after the determined way she made sure he knew she was Faith, he'd thought they'd gotten their identities straight, but obviously not. Betrayal and jealousy shot through him, and he couldn't sit there any longer.

He threw off the covers, uncaring of her modesty. Images filled his mind. Not images from a past life—but from this life—his childhood. Of his mother and another man. Of his father's heartache drowning in a bottle.

"So, who the hell did you think you were making love to last night?"

Twelve

Faith stared at the closed bathroom door. The sound of the shower was the only thing that broke the silence. That and the beat of her heart, hard against her ribs. In that instant, the instant where anger filled Cord's eyes, she'd known fear. The same fear that had overwhelmed her yesterday when she'd found him in her yard. The same shiver of fear that confirmed his accusation.

Guilt washed over her. Was he right? Was she confusing him with Rafe? Only a few minutes ago she'd been thinking of how much alike the two men were. A hard lump grew in her throat and she tried to swallow it. The ache remained.

She couldn't honestly tell if the desire she felt was real or remnants of the dreams. She stood and paced, reluctant to see who came out of the bathroom. Cord the lover? Cord the protector? Cord the gambler? Or Rafe the murderer? She was even more afraid that she wouldn't know the difference.

Stop it, she mentally yelled at her overactive imagination. Purposefully, she called to mind images of Cord's kindness last night. He'd held her together when the dream had been so real. Heck, he'd done more than that. Her cheeks flamed as she recalled all the wonderful things he'd done to her.

She stared at the door again, suddenly realizing that on the other side, beneath the familiar spray of her shower, he was naked. Her mouth went dry.

She swallowed and took several deep breaths. What was wrong with her? Was she more Maria then she wanted to be? Even as she wanted to yell at him and hurt him as he'd hurt her, she ached to feel his arms again. She'd never lusted after a man like this before.

Who was she kidding? She'd seldom had the opportunity to lust before. Her sheltered childhood had extended well into her college years. After that she'd buried herself in her career.

Sure, she'd had a couple of relationships that bordered on serious, but even as she remembered them, she discarded the comparison. They were nothing like this. Nothing that threatened to sweep her away in its wake.

And there would be a wake. Cord was a man, but while he'd held her and loved her last night, there had been no promises.

He wasn't the settling down kind. He lived in the back of his casino—at work. Building a home and job for himself were entirely different than looking at life as something to share with someone.

His stories last night at dinner told of a life spent moving from place to place, from town to town, looking for the next job. The fact that he'd taken off to come here was a perfect example of the practice. Even his commitments were only part time. There would be no promises of tomorrow from Cord. Disappointment shot through her, to be swiftly replaced by anger.

How dare he.

Was he just like her father and all the other men she'd encountered? They wanted to make all the decisions about how things should be. About when she could and could not have a relationship.

Could he so easily turn off his feelings? Was she really just a fling to him? No, she couldn't accept that. The tenderness in his touch and in his eyes had been more than fleeting, hadn't it? No one could pretend those types of feelings...could they?

She buried her face in her hands, finding fewer answers behind her closed eyelids. She looked back at the door again. She had to know. Had to have some sense of who he really was before she moved on. Before she decided what to do next.

She walked to the door, pausing with her hand on the doorknob for only a moment. Steam wafted out the open door, and she prepared herself to face the lion in its den.

***

Cord's anger washed down the drain with the warm water beating down on his back in sharp, welcome bursts. However, the unsettling frustration remained. He braced his arms against the tile and let her words and the shower wash over him.

Fool. He called himself that and a few other choice words, too. Faith wasn't like other women. He'd known that last night when he'd stared at her pictures, had been convinced of it when he'd held her in his arms, and seen it in the hurt on her face when he'd yelled at her.

Both he and Faith were having trouble keeping each other straight from the dream. He'd slipped up several times before and so had she. Why had it bothered him so much this time?

Because he'd believed she was different than the other women who'd been in his life. Still believed it on some level, like the fool he was. She'd gotten under his skin and he'd let himself care.

Had last night really been just a continuation of their dreams? Was Faith only reaching out for Rafe? That suspicion ate a hole through him. He'd had plenty of one-night stands. Hell, that was all he'd ever wanted, wasn't it? So why did the thought of waking up in that lace bedroom every morning hold so much appeal?

Images of last night came to mind. Okay, there were certain things he wanted to know more about...and most of them had to do with her body.

He recalled her face outlined in firelight, a face that begged for tomorrows and forevers. Things he swore he didn't want, didn't need. Things he'd never before wished he could have.

He brushed those thoughts away impatiently. Tomorrows always brought broken promises, and forevers weren't real.

Cord grabbed the bar of soap and rubbed it viciously over his chest. *Rafe.* The name whispered through his mind. Rafe Cumberland, a murderer? No, it wasn't possible.

And why not? he chided himself. Hell, he was as bad as Faith, acting as if he knew the man. Neither of them did. Just because he and Rafe shared a face didn't make them in any way the same.

Damn it. This whole situation was ridiculous. A hundred-year-old murder? Ghosts?

He slammed the water off, no less frustrated than when he'd stepped into the shower. For a minute he stood, listening to the water falling down the drain, then shoved the shower curtain aside.

A blue towel smacked him in the chest.

"Men are such idiots." Faith's gaze challenged him to contradict her.

He didn't. She sat perched on the only seat in the bathroom, indignant and adorable. He felt his resolve slip and shored it up with his reservations about her and the situation. "Women make us that way." Briskly, Cord dried off and wrapped the towel around his hips before stepping out of the shower.

"So, this is my fault?" Faith stood, hands on hips, blocking his exit.

He glared at her. "I'm not sure anyone's at fault." The bathroom's acoustics made his voice vibrate around them. "But it sure as hell isn't mine. I've lived in Cripple Creek for two years and never had to deal with any of this until you showed up."

"By *this* do you mean us, or the ghost?"

"Both. Excuse me." He pushed by her, ignoring the heat that shot through him when his bare skin touched hers. She jumped back, letting him pass, but followed him into the living room.

His clothes spilled across the carpeting in front of the fireplace where he'd thrown them last night. Hot memories flooded back. His body responded, and he cursed. He wanted her, but she wanted someone who existed only in her dreams. He had enough trouble keeping track of himself without competition.

Cord grabbed his jeans and dropped the towel. He heard her breathe in sharply and watched her eyes widen as her gaze raked over his body. Her cheeks flamed, but she didn't turn away. A wicked part of him enjoyed her discomfort, and he took his sweet time pulling on the faded jeans.

He ached to touch her, to pull her close and then down onto the rug where he'd erase any thoughts of anyone else. But then he'd be back to those forevers and tomorrows again.

For an instant, time stopped as their eyes met. Something flickered in hers. Uncertainty? Fear? Cord grabbed the rest of his clothes and stuffed them into his bag. He pulled out a clean shirt.

"I know exactly who I was with last night."

Her words stopped him cold. He paused a long minute then turned to face her. "Are you sure?" He didn't believe her and that bothered him. He could tell his doubt reached her, too, and he saw the hurt in her eyes.

"I don't lie, Cord."

He knew that, but a part of him couldn't ignore the lessons he'd learned too hard in life. Women didn't stick around and honesty was an illusion. She'd thought of him as another man. It didn't matter that it was Rafe. Someone he may have been. What mattered was that it wasn't him she'd been thinking of—the man he'd struggled so hard in life to become. Someone he was proud to be.

Anger and pain at her distance and betrayal tore through him. He grabbed his duffel and stalked toward the door.

Faith followed several feet behind, unsure what to say to stop him. "Cord, please, talk to me." She stepped in to his path.

"About what?" He closed his eyes as if trying to calm the anger in his voice or shut her out, she wasn't sure. "You've got what you wanted. The casino pictures. Excuse me, I need to get back to my work."

He wasn't the only one with work to do. Something tore inside, something she ignored and buried in anger. He was leaving, and he hadn't made any plans to come back.

"It's time to move on, Faith." Cord threw the duffel over his shoulder.

"There are too many questions. I need to know what...what happened."

"You and me both, babe. Look, last night was great. Maybe even necessary for us both, but I'm not the settling down kind. One night doesn't make a relationship."

"I didn't ask for one." She glared at him, hiding the growing love she'd discovered earlier.

"Didn't you?" He lifted his arm, taking in the whole room with one sweeping gesture. He reached out and snagged the picture of her in the pinafore off the wall. "This is you. Your world. It's permanent. Quaint little house. Your family all neatly lined up there on the wall, watching and taking care of you."

She grabbed the frame from his hand. "You're not making any sense."

"Yes, I am." He glared at her for a long minute, then stepped past her and through the door. The screen smacked against the wall, loud and harsh in the morning air. "I never had a family like that. My father was a drunk, and my mother never had time for anyone but herself. I don't know how to fit into your world. I doubt they would accept me."

He stalked to the car and jerked the car door open, throwing the bag into the passenger seat.

She watched him, feeling lost, adrift, cast aside and angry. "So, you won't even try?" He was putting up walls between them. She saw it in his eyes and felt it in her heart.

"I know who you are," she said. She reached out and touched his arm, needing to feel he was still here. He jerked away and climbed into the car. He'd barely slammed the door when he shoved the car into gear and backed away.

Frustrated, she flung the picture frame she still held toward him. It hit the bumper and bounced to the cement. The tinkle of breaking glass seemed loud until he gunned the engine.

"Rafe," a soft voice called through the trees.

"No!" Faith screamed as he glared through the mud-splattered windshield at her. She realized he'd heard the voice, too. "Wait." She hurried after him, but tires squealed as he roared away.

Delta was here. Had he thought Faith had called out to him? No. "Damn you, Delta." Anger clouded her senses. "Why are you doing this?"

Nothing but that damned laughter answered her...that and the squeal of Cord's tires as he disappeared around the corner.

***

Cord's mind remained blissfully, angrily blank for about half a mile. His knuckles white on the steering wheel, he squealed tires around nearly every corner he took. The sooner he got out of this damned town the better.

Rafe. The name echoed through Cord's brain like a mantra. She hadn't even bothered to hide her mistake. Despite her claim that she knew who he was, he didn't believe her.

Rafe the murderer. He tried to shut it out, but found it permanently recorded there. With each mile it repeated itself. He wasn't sure where it came from, and he didn't really want to know. Someplace dark was all he knew.

He had no experience to draw on to deal with...this... this... Hell, he didn't even know what to call it. Faith was a preacher's daughter. She had her background to draw on, an upbringing that surely held long-entrenched beliefs in an afterlife, in her family.

Her family. He wanted to growl.

He shivered instead.

As he drove through Denver, he thought about stopping to see his mother. He almost laughed out loud. Yeah, right. From the frying pan into the fire.

She'd never had time for him when he was a kid. That hadn't changed any now that he was an adult. That was part of why he'd chosen to live with his dad after the divorce. At least the old man needed him.

Cord seldom believed in anyone, or anything—sometimes not even himself. Buying the casino had been the first thing he'd let himself believe in, had been the first time he'd hoped for something better. Last night with Faith had been the second. He slammed his fist against the steering wheel in frustration.

He'd faced knives, gun barrels and men's fists in his years of chasing his father from bar to bar. Later, working in those same bars, he'd faced worse. He'd survived in only one way—by trusting no one. He'd just been reminded of those lessons once again.

Taking life day-to-day was all he believed in. Things like his work. His ambitions. His saloon.

The world Faith lived in, the family, the forevers were as foreign to him as the dream of the Cumberland family. Family and fantasy were too close in his dictionary.

She wanted him to be Rafe? He was *not* Rafe Cumberland. Rafe had murdered Delta Delange. Why should he, Cord Burke, feel responsible a hundred years later? The urge to right old wrongs sounded too pat, too clichéd, even to him. Rafe could rot in hell for all he cared.

Cool, mountain air filtered into the open window, and the harsh edge of his anger dimmed but didn't fade as he shed the city. The turmoil quieted, and all he heard was the sound of his tires on the pavement and the loud thud of his pulse in his ears.

He'd come so close—too close—to trusting Faith. To giving her a piece of himself.

Luckily, he'd come to his senses. Now he just had to stay that way.

As he drove the winding two-lane road up the mountain, he concentrated on clearing his mind, on looking ahead not back. The one thing he couldn't seem to do was dull the ache deep in his chest that seemed to intensify with each beat of his heart.

Thirteen

Faith's anger boiled and nearly bubbled over. She stared down at the broken picture frame. The shattered glass spider-webbed across the face.

"Damn you, Delta," she yelled to the bright blue sky. "If you weren't already dead, I'd kill you." When there was no answer, she wondered if she'd even heard the voice. Was she going crazy?

She bent down and picked up the frame, then stalked inside. She tossed it into the trash with a loud thud. Her childhood face stared up at her from the trash. She had the negative, but she didn't have time right now to process another print. The photo was one of her father's favorites, and he'd notice it missing the next time he came over. She still hadn't called him, and she certainly wasn't up to doing it now.

He taught repentance, but he also taught responsibility for one's actions. She'd always agreed with the last half, if not the means by which he taught it.

She tried not to think about what he'd say about the last few days.

Singe walked by, rubbing her ankles with a warm, fluffy tail. She picked him up and stroked his fur. "Maybe he did us both a favor," she whispered. The cat gave her a blank stare and swished his tail as if in agreement. "Besides, he and Dad would never have gotten along." The cat merely blinked and purred. She hugged him tighter, blinking away the emotional tears.

Suddenly, the house felt very empty and quiet.

And lonely.

Enough of this. She had work to do. Grabbing a slice of cold pizza and a diet soda from the fridge, she headed to her darkroom. As she worked, she found solace in the process. The angry words still hung in the air, but they'd lost their power to hurt. No more laughter or whispers interrupted her. Maybe she had imagined hearing it after all.

The overhead light was bright, but in a few minutes, she turned it off in favor of a red lamp, which protected her film. She set out the chemicals and opened a film case. She must have over a hundred shots. It'd be a long day, possibly stretching into the night. It didn't matter. She doubted she'd get much sleep anyway. Especially not in the bed she'd shared so satisfyingly with Cord last night.

No more of those thoughts.

She'd numbered each roll as she removed them from their cases, and she followed the same sequence in developing them. It helped keep her focused on the project. It also showed her how close she was to her goal. Excitement stirred inside her.

Other photographers initially used contact sheets. Faith often did, but this time she wanted to see the full-size effect of her work. The first set of pictures came out clear and dried on the line as she opened the next roll.

The second roll started with the first interior shots of the brothel, those of the parlor and front room. She planned to use them to illustrate day-to-day life.

Faith reached into the tray with her clamp, moving the first print around a bit, dampening each inch of the paper. Even after years of doing this work, the process by which the photograph appeared on the paper amazed her. The grainy figures grew into recognizable shapes. The carved chair. The Victrola.

Suddenly, the shapes shifted. They continued to grow beyond what she remembered seeing through the viewfinder. Faith stared at the picture. Several young girls stood in the room, each touching and apparently talking to a gentleman.

One young girl caught her eye. The girl's gaze met hers, as if she had been staring into the lens of the camera. She recognized her as the face in the newspaper and the mirror.

Delta.

Faith dropped the clamp. The loud clatter it made startled her. Taking several calming breaths, she reached for the clamp again. She lifted the picture and stared at it, wondering if the chemicals were getting to her.

The image remained.

Faith tried to hang the print on the line with the others and only succeeded in dropping it. Finally, three tries later she succeeded, then she ran to the kitchen phone. Her fingers shook, and she dialed Clarissa's number twice before getting it right. The answering machine picked up, and she slammed the receiver down.

Now what? She leaned against the wall, her eyes closed. On a hunch, Faith reached for the phone again and called the coffee shop. Clarissa answered.

"Thank goodness." Relief flooded through her. Faith smiled, though her voice shook. "It's me. Can you come over?"

"Why? Another dream?"

"No. I need your help." Faith glanced at the darkroom door. "I'm developing the film. There are images appearing on the prints that weren't there originally."

"Really?" Silence filled the phone line for several long seconds.

Faith's uncertainty grew and she took a deep breath. "Clarissa, I'm scared. Cord left this morning. We...we had a fight."

Clarissa was silent for a moment, as if pondering Faith's words. She hoped Clarissa wouldn't ask what they'd fought about. She didn't know how to explain what she didn't really understand herself.

"I can get out of here in about five minutes. I'll be there as soon as I can."

"Thank you."

After she'd hung up, Faith went back to the dark room. What if she kept going? Curiosity urged her on.

The next few photos were normal, no surprises. The last photo on the roll was of the upstairs hallway. Faith remembered snapping a shot of the wall hanging covering the observation window.

The picture developed, the hallway formed, then the observation window—without its concealing covering. Two dark figures materialized inside the observation room. Once again it was Delta. She stared directly at the camera lens.

This time Rafe Cumberland stood beside her. He held Delta tight in his embrace as he ardently kissed the side of her neck. His were eyes closed as they made love...just the way Cord had with her last night.

Anger boiled in Faith's blood. Green, jealous anger. She sent the photo flying across the room. *How dare he!*

As quickly as the anger formed, it faded. She picked up the photo. The doorbell rang—Clarissa. Relieved, Faith covered the chemicals then hurried to the door, blinking several times in the bright daylight. Clarissa stood on the front step, her arms loaded with books.

"What are those?" Faith took part of the stack, and together they walked into the living room. The books thudded to the floor where Clarissa dropped them.

"Research. I've never had anything to do with images appearing on film, although I've heard a great deal about it. I brought these few books from my collection to see if we can learn something. If we need more, we can go to the library. Where are the pictures?"

"I've only finished the first two rolls. They're in the dark room."

"Let me see."

Faith dreaded seeing the pictures again, but she led the way down the hall. Opening the door, she found the darkroom still shrouded in shadows. She flipped on the overhead light, confident she had taken the precautions to protect her chemicals from the light.

The photographs hung on the line. Now that they were dry, she took them down. She reached for the two with the extra images. She gasped. They were exactly as she had seen them through the viewfinder. The images had vanished.

Frantically, she pulled the pictures down from the line. "They're gone," she whispered over and over again as she tore at the photographs.

"Hey, hey. Slow down." Clarissa gently touched Faith's arm. She took the photographs from Faith's fingers. They were bent and cracked from the grip she had on them.

"I'm not crazy. There were people in those pictures. In this." Her finger angrily stabbed at the photograph on top of the battered pile. "Cord was kissing that woman in the paper." She glared at the picture. "Delta."

"Remember, Cord is *not* Rafe." Clarissa looked at the pictures on the table.

"I know. I know," Faith whispered, rubbing her forehead in frustration. "What's going on?"

"You're absolutely sure you saw the images?" Clarissa pinned her with a demanding stare.

"I am not imagining things. I know what I saw. I looked right into her eyes."

Clarissa moved around the table, spreading out the pictures to see them more clearly. Several times she held one in her hands and closed her eyes. Occasionally, she shook her head and put that picture in a separate pile. When she finished there were two piles of pictures. One held the majority of the pictures. The other had three photographs in it. "I feel something in these." She handed them to Faith.

They were the photographs Faith had seen the images on earlier, plus one that was foggier than the others. She remembered Cord had been with her, breaking her concentration.

"That's them." Faith sank down onto a stool and wished everything away. When she opened her eyes, the photographs and Clarissa were still very much there.

"Let's redevelop them," Clarissa suggested.

Faith hesitated. "What have we got to lose?" She stood and turned off the overhead light. The red glow created an eerie feeling. The room, small anyway, had become cramped with Clarissa joining her. She had difficulty setting up her chemicals. Her fingers shook, and like an opening night performer, she trembled. What would—or wouldn't—develop on the pictures?

"Relax, Faith. It's okay."

Under Clarissa's watchful eye, Faith repeated the familiar process. Images formed on the paper that had seconds earlier been blank. Clarissa leaned over the trays, watching the progression of the print with fascination.

"There." Faith's cry interrupted the silence, and Clarissa leaned closer to see. The image of a woman formed on the picture of the parlor. She smiled into the camera lens.

"It's her." Both women stared at the print.

Then suddenly, as if the chemicals went bad, the development of the picture stopped. In the next second, the picture completely faded away, leaving the page blank and white.

Faith looked up at Clarissa. "It was there, wasn't it?"

"Yes. I saw it. Delta sent a message, but I'm not sure why. And I'm not sure why she wants only you to see it." Clarissa moved from the table to a stool in the corner. "This is very puzzling."

Faith flipped the light switch, unmindful of the chemicals. The close, quiet darkness of the room she had always loved suddenly wore on her nerves. Both of the other pictures had developed completely blank, and Faith knew she had followed the routine as usual. She'd been doing this work so long, she could do it in her sleep.

"So." Faith sagged against the wall. "Now what?"

"I'm not exactly sure. I think it's time to do a little research."

Together, they left the dark room. Time stretched out as they sat on the living room floor, poring over Clarissa's books. While they learned many important facts, there were no answers to their particular questions.

"I give up." Faith shoved the book across the floor and

rubbed her tired eyes.

"I've got an idea."

"What?"

"Why don't you develop the prints—alone. I'll wait out here, if anything shows, I'll come in."

"What will that prove?"

"Nothing. But we'll finish getting the message. I doubt you've seen all the pieces she wants you to see. How many more rolls do you have?"

"At least four."

"Well, get started. Once we've got the whole message, we can start analyzing."

Faith gulped back her fear. It was difficult enough facing the prospect of seeing those images with Clarissa's company. Alone, it was daunting. Still, she knew she had no choice.

"Okay." She stood, running her suddenly damp hands down the sides of her jeans. Her heart pounded as she gazed down the hall at the closed darkroom door. "Might as well get to it."

Once again, she prepared the chemicals, opened film cases and set to work. Several times she caught herself looking over her shoulder.

With each developing image, she expected to see new, unknown images, but there was nothing. The photographs were exactly the work she'd been hoping to achieve, and she couldn't resist smiling. The love for her work soothed her fears. The publisher would be pleased when she delivered them.

The final canister was open and in the trays. Cold air swept past her. The dark room occupied a back corner of the house, making it normally cooler than the rest of the house, but this was different. Something out of the cold north settled over the room. It took most of her strength to look into the developing tray.

As before, an image she hadn't photographed appeared on the film. Delta DeLange lay across the brass bed that had been in Faith's dreams of late. She stared with the sightless eyes of the dead. The picture continued to develop, and Faith saw the dark stain on Delta's chest.

In the foreground a figure formed, and Faith gasped. It was Cord...no, she corrected herself...it was Rafe. He held a pistol in his hand.

The look in his eyes frightened Faith. No remorse, no regret. He'd intended to kill her. The smile turning up the corner of his mouth boasted pride, as if he'd set out to accomplish some great task.

Dear God, he'd killed her in cold blood.

Terror, strong and unbending, filled Faith and the room around her. There was no escape.

Three photographs remained in the trays, waiting to be immersed in the final chemicals that would bring them to life. Or, in this case, to death.

"Faith?" Clarissa's voice came through the door, and Faith's heart slowed slightly.

"Y...yes. Wait a minute." Hastily, she covered the undeveloped pictures and pulled the door open. She yanked Clarissa's arm and slammed the door behind her. "Quick, look at the images before they fade."

She pulled Clarissa to the print trays. The figures were clear, though they quickly withered.

"Oh, merciful heaven." Clarissa watched until they were completely gone, leaving a blank white page.

Clarissa paled and her eyes widened with shock. Faith watched the golden curls on her head tremble in the dim light.

"There are three more pictures to develop," Faith whispered, afraid of startling either of them.

"I'll be right outside the door. Can you do them all at once?"

"Yeah. I'll do just like before. When I call, get in here quick, before they're gone."

It took several minutes for the next two pictures to develop, as if something slowed the process. Still there were no new images, but the last photograph sent terror shooting through Faith.

Delta stood before the camera. Laughter danced in her eyes. The laughter from earlier echoed in Faith's memory. Delta held a gun in her hand, a gun pointed directly at the camera.

The image wavered and Delta faded away. The image behind her tore a scream from Faith's throat. Cord lay on the floor of the old-fashioned bedroom. Not Rafe. Cord.

He wore the same clothes he'd been wearing the first day they'd met in the casino. Jeans. Flannel shirt with the sleeves rolled up to just below his elbow. No mustache decorated his upper lip. His eyes stared wide and lifeless. A dark stain covered the front of his shirt.

Suddenly, bright golden flames appeared in the picture, eating away at the image. "No." Faith screamed. "No."

The sound of the door crashing open vaguely registered as Clarissa ran in.

"How can I beat a ghost? How?" Faith's voice broke with fright. Her eyes met Clarissa's as the last of the images faded to black. Faith saw her own terror reflected in Clarissa's face.

Clarissa guided Faith to the living room—a solid, normal room. Then she went back and closed the darkroom door. Neither of them needed to return there any time soon. They'd gotten the message.

"She's going to kill him." Faith wanted to run to the phone and call to see if he was okay. One glance at the clock told her he probably hadn't yet reached Cripple Creek. If she left a message with Johnny would Cord even return her call? His anger came back to her, deep and strong and painful. Frustrated, she resisted the urge to kick something.

Clarissa rushed across the room and picked up a book. Thumbing through the pages, she stopped about half way through it. "Here it is. There has been some research, primarily by Dr. Waylon Marshall at a university in California, that suggests spirits use film images to send messages. Some say good-bye to loved ones; others seem intent on revenge. They tease their victims through horrific images."

"Tease? Oh, that's the word. But what message is she sending?" Faith buried her face in her hands, the image of Cord's lifeless body indelibly burned into her mind's eye.

"It means she's got a plan. To tease you. To make threats. The question is, will she follow through? Can she?"

Faith had no doubts about Delta's intent. "So, we just sit back and let her kill Cord?" Anger brought Faith to her feet and she paced. "It's not like I can have her arrested. Or shoot her with a gun. Even vampires have wooden stakes and werewolves silver bullets. Can't you unbolt Frankenstein's head?" she babbled. "But how do you stop a ghost?"

"Hold on. We don't know if she has the power to do it."

"We don't know that she doesn't."

There were no more answers—none that Faith wanted to hear anyway. Pain penetrated her shock. "I can't let him die."

"He's got to get out of Cripple Creek. He'll be safe here, I believe." Clarissa stared into space, her brow creased in a frown.

"I...I'm not so sure about that."

"Why?" Clarissa's gaze focused on Faith.

"I think I heard her laughter this morning. That's part of

why he left."

Clarissa crossed her arms in an unmistakable sign she intended to get the whole story.

"He thought I wanted him to be Rafe. She called Rafe's name, and he thought I said it."

"Great." Clarissa threw up her hands. "What about the dreams?"

"I had another one last night." The terror of the dream returned along with the memories of how Cord had taken the pain away. "About Timmy's death."

"I don't think those are coming from Delta," Clarissa said and at Faith's look of surprise, she explained. "For one, they aren't things Delta would know about. I think they're memory whispers. Leftovers from the past."

Memories of the past. They were back to the same old problem. Were they Rafe and Maria reincarnated? How they'd dealt with the recent dreams infused her cheeks with warmth. Did Cord think she was Maria? Last night had gone a long way in helping him think that.

The rat. She wanted to kick something again and gave the trashcan a shove. Broken glass tinkled, breaking the silence. So many pictures destroyed today...

Destroyed. "Oh, God."

"What?" Clarissa looked up.

"My pictures. They're ruined. I can't print those in the book."

"Maybe she just ruined the prints."

Faith doubted it, and from the tone of Clarissa's voice, so did she. Faith rushed back to her darkroom. The developed film that she intended to cut into strips later hung beside the prints. She pulled them into the light, looking for something, anything.

Every frame was blank. Nothing remained of all that work.

Her eyes burned, and she rubbed them to stall the tears. What more could go wrong?

Fourteen

After Clarissa left, the panic set in. The events of the past few days tumbled about in Faith's brain. The destroyed pictures. Delta's unearthly threats. The argument with Cord...making love with him. With that thought, she dropped to the couch and buried her face in her hands. Heat warmed her cheeks and other parts of her body.

If she returned to Cripple Creek would he think she was following him? Would she be able to stand her ground and resist him if he touched her? She groaned, the sound muffled by her hands.

Going back was no longer optional. It was mandatory. Her deadline loomed like a black cloud on the horizon—a black cloud lined not with silver but red past due notices.

What was worse was not knowing who she feared facing most—a ghost or Cord.

"I refuse to be intimidated," she whispered to Singe who barely moved a whisker in response. "Oh, what good are you?" She hugged the animal to her chest. "I should at least warn him, right?" Again the cat simply stared. Even if Cord was still angry, he deserved to be warned. But that was all. She dialed the casino. This was simply a business call.

"You've reached the Double Barrel Saloon," Cord's prerecorded voice slid across her nerves, tingling with the memory of his touch. She closed her eyes and listened, disappointed when the beep came and she had to leave a message.

What should she say? A simple, "Call me" was all she left. As the evening wore on, she stared at the silent phone. She left a second message, but another hour dragged by. She fidgeted and paced, barely taking notice of Singe until his tail smacked her leg.

With the setting of the sun, the shadows and darkness that lurked around her house intensified and grew. Had they always been like that? She flipped on light switches, and while the fireplace banished the encroaching darkness, nothing really helped.

In her mind's eyes she saw the photo images again, too vivid to ever forget. She shivered, despite the warmth of the room. Where was Cord? Was he already hurt...or dead? She forced her mind away from that possibility. Why hadn't he called?

She hated to admit that she already knew why. He was still angry. He didn't buy any of this stuff, and if he did, he didn't want any part of it. He probably thought she was desperate, calling him like this.

That same uncharacteristic indignant anger threatened to return, but she refused to let it. Outside the wind picked up, smacking the branches of the lilac bush against the siding. Faith jumped nearly a foot. "This is nuts." She bent down and picked up the cat. Several minutes later, she had packed a small bag and stuffed the cat into his carrier.

"It's been awhile since we saw Mom and Dad," she explained to the cat who stared at her through the wire door. "Let's go visit."

She climbed into the car and quickly backed out of the garage. For the first time since she'd bought the tiny house, it didn't feel comfortable. Her vision blurred for just a second as she stared at her home. Home. Was it really a home, or just a place to hang her hat? Again, she couldn't answer her own question.

Instead, she drove into the night to her parents' townhouse. At least there the shadows faded.

***

Battling traffic the next day, she finally reached the mountains by mid-afternoon. Fall foliage brought tourists and gamblers from all over the state—and the country—this time of year. Faith tapped her fingers on the steering wheel as she followed a line of cars up the two-lane road. At this rate, she'd never get to Cripple Creek before dark.

She'd left her parents' as early as she could without concerning them, which meant sharing breakfast, a meal that lasted longer than her usual cup of coffee and toast on the run. She'd toyed with the idea of asking her father's advice about the Maria-Rafe situation but quickly discarded it. How could she explain to him about Maria? Or her relationship with Cord? No, her father wasn't someone she could turn to now. That knowledge bothered her. She wanted to be independent, but somehow knowing her parents weren't even an option disturbed her.

The taillights of the car in front of her glowed red and she hit the brakes—again. Cursing the traffic and her own impatience she forced her mind to concentrate on the road.

The winding highway climbed toward Pikes Peak. Where an old mine shaft cut into the hillside, she slowed and pulled over at a wide spot in the road. She stepped out of her car. Maybe if she waited, the rush would disappear.

She looked across the incredible valley. A few wispy bits of cloud settled on the horizon of a gold and green carpet. She snapped off a few shots as the mournful sound of a train's whistle echoed across the valley. Heaviness settled in her chest, and with it, an emotion she recognized as homesickness.

Homesickness for what? For her house? She didn't think so. For a time and people long gone? Maybe. Her throat ached. She climbed into the car and pulled back onto the two-lane highway.

The road wound tighter and higher. Sharp turns revealed steep drop offs. Not paying attention up here could be deadly. How she'd managed to stay safely on the road in that horrid rain the night she'd run from here, she didn't know. Even in daylight the road was treacherous.

Just before she reached the first tunnel she saw the spot where she'd stopped that night. She turned off the road. Her palms sweated against the steering wheel. That tree. She'd seen the vision of Timmy there. She stared at it. Nothing appeared now.

Something did catch her eye, though. A dirt path to the right of the tree. Curiosity raised its ever-present head. An eighteen-wheeler passed just then, creeping by. She had plenty of time if the line of cars behind the truck was any indication.

She swung her camera over her shoulder, locked the car and pocketed her keys. The clear blue sky indicated a good day for a hike. She glanced down at her sweatshirt, jeans and tennis shoes. She was even dressed for it.

Pushing past the broad boughs of the tree, she stepped through its shadow and into the bright sun. A wildflower-covered meadow swept away from her. Late summer grasses grew thick and green, and aspen trees bloomed golden. She took a few pictures, enjoying the contrast of the gold against the deep sky.

The path cut across the edge of the field, disappearing in places as a light breeze bent the tall grasses. Excitement bubbled in her blood. Instinct told her something good would be at the end of the trail. Her mind conjured up images of a mineshaft. Maybe the skeletal remnants of the workings were buried in the field grasses. Great lighting today. Ideas perked as she walked.

At the top of the rise, she stopped and surveyed the valley below. Beautiful. Click. Click. The path divided where the ground leveled out. One trail widened while the other narrowed to little more than patches of dirt between tufts of grass. The fainter one intrigued her, seeming forlorn in the open field. It meandered toward the aspen grove to the left.

Some shots of the sky from beneath the golden leaves would be beautiful. She hurried her step until she hit rough ground. Caution would be a good thing here. She didn't relish the idea of hurting herself and being stuck out here until someone found her—which by the looks of this path could be years.

A few late summer flowers bloomed at the base of the trees where they were sheltered from the cooler breezes that announced the coming of fall. Their vibrant reds and golds filled the viewfinder. The trees closed around her with a welcome embrace.

Finishing a roll of film, she took a break to change it. The calm, quiet air relaxed her for the first time in what seemed ages, and she breathed in the sweet-scented air.

In the distance, weathered, gray wood caught her eye. A structure of some sort lay ahead. She hurried toward it. The trees parted, and she found herself looking at a house, or what was left of one.

It was small, but not uncomfortably so. One story, it sat nestled up against a hill, as if to protect it from the cold winds. A verandah ran along the front. She envisioned a pair of rockers there. The windows were long gone, though the tattered remnant of a curtain hung in one of the side openings. No breeze stirred the fabric.

She stepped closer, her heart in her throat. She'd expected an abandoned claim, or even a played out mine with its shaft house and rigging reaching toward the sky. This hard-bitten mining district didn't even hint at a quaint family atmosphere. She loved surprises and smiled at this one.

Sticks crackled beneath her feet. Hesitantly, she climbed up onto the verandah. The wood, while faded and gray, held beneath her weight. She moved carefully, just in case.

The small parlor and kitchen stood empty. The only other room, the bedroom, was large compared to the rest of the house.

Not one stick of furniture remained. No pictures hung on

the walls. The only object left was the wood-burning stove. Even the cook stove was gone.

The building remained, but the people left nothing of themselves behind. Saddened by what she did—and didn't—find, Faith didn't like being here.

The back door stood open, and she walked through to a tiny porch. She reached for the railing, which wiggled. She pulled her hand back. Gingerly, she stepped to the ground.

A distant rumble sounded. Looking up, she noted that while the skies were clear, faint wisps of clouds slid by. She shrugged off the apprehension creeping up her spine and headed back around the house.

The thought suddenly struck her that she hadn't taken any pictures. She shivered. She didn't want to take any pictures, not of this empty, lonely place. She rounded the corner and headed toward her car. The thunder indicated a storm despite the lack of clouds overhead.

Her toe hit a stone. She stumbled and fell into a soft bed of leaves at the base of an aspen stand. She laughed at her own clumsiness and rolled to see what had tripped her. The corner of a gray stone peeked out from the leaves.

It was unnaturally smooth. She reached out and brushed the leaves away.

A tombstone.

Rafe Cumberland. The name reverberated inside her head. Was that sound a scream? Tim Gibson had said there were graves somewhere in the hills. She dug around in the mildewed leaves, sending dirt and leaves flying around her. She found a second gray stone. "Timmy Cumberland. Sleep with the angels." This time she said the words aloud. She knew she did, they echoed back at her.

"No." She hadn't planned to do this. What had brought her here? She looked around. "Delta. Is that you?" Anger built inside her. "Stop this. What do you want from me?"

No answer came back to her. She faced the stones, so lost here in the woods. Wasn't there anyone to watch over them? The forlorn air of the house answered her.

Her heart hurt as she turned to leave, but she couldn't leave. Kneeling again, she brushed the leaves and debris away. She wanted—no needed—to clean the lonely graves. A drop fell onto her hand. She looked up at the sky. Only the wispy clouds were visible. She was crying, not the sky.

"Oh, Timmy. Rafe."

She cried Maria's tears. She cried her own tears. She shed every mother's tears. She let all the emotions of loss she'd kept bottled up inside wash over her as she shoved leaves and dirt away.

Suddenly, her knuckles scraped something else hard, and she rocked back on her heels. No. She didn't want to brush any more leaves away. She wanted to turn and run.

Another drop of wetness hit her hand. This time it wasn't a tear. The clouds had arrived. The leaves bounced with the force of the drops.

Nature revealed what Faith had been too afraid to see. *Maria Cumberland.*

Faith ran. She knew she'd gone the wrong direction as soon as the forest closed in around her. The trees were too thick, but which way was the trail to her car? She kept going, hoping she'd find the meadow. Her thoughts still spinning.

Her own grave. Images filled her mind. Tim Gibson's words, or her own memories, she wasn't sure, but she remembered kneeling beside the two graves. She remembered the fervent prayers, the begging, and the pleading. She remembered warm hands helping her to her feet and comforting her. She'd made Tim Gibson promise right then and there to bring her here with them when her time came.

He'd kept his promise.

She stumbled. Her hip hit the ground hard. Her shoulders followed. The fabric of her jacket tore. Slick, wet dirt offered no purchase. Each bump bruised and jarred her bones.

The camera strap snapped. Its familiar weight fell from her neck. The heartbreaking sound of cracking metal and plastic vaguely registered as she slid farther down the steep slope.

***

Cord pushed the play button on the machine again. Damn her. Couldn't she just let him go? The sound of her voice filled his office. Soft and warm, she asked him to call her.

And he had called. Twice. She hadn't answered. He dialed the number again, slamming the receiver into the cradle when her machine picked up—again. Where the hell was she?

Every muscle in Cord's body ached. He'd driven himself and Johnny harder than he'd ever thought possible. Pausing for a moment, Cord leaned back in his chair, staring unseeingly at the view. Johnny was out back unloading the shipment that had just arrived. Gamblers filled the main hall, and there wasn't a seat to be had at the bar. Business was good. He should be thrilled.

Maybe she was out taking pictures. He envisioned her bending low, trying to get the right angle, the right light...he loved the way her jeans clung in all the right places when she did that.

He could almost see her there in the woods. Suddenly Cord realized he *was* seeing her. The newly replaced window reflected an image. He stared. What the—?

Frozen inside the glass, Faith screamed. He couldn't hear her, but he saw her face. His heart heard her pain. She ran through branches and thick mounds of fallen leaves. Where was she going? Who was chasing her?

Clenching his fists, he watched helplessly as she tumbled. He saw her fall farther down the side of the mountain. A nasty precipice appeared.

"Faith!" he cried. The image vanished, and he found himself staring at his own white-faced reflection as it mingled with the view on the other side. Where the hell was she?

***

"Help!" Faith tumbled farther down the slope. The hard trunk of a ponderosa pine stopped her fall. She laid there, her breath coming in quick panting breaths. The cold rain splashed onto her face. Every inch of her ached.

Her feet dangled over an edge. She didn't want to look. She didn't want to know.

"Hey. You okay?" Footfalls heralded the arrival of an old man, his hair whitened with age and the ebony of his skin creased with time. He knelt beside her and she immediately recognized him as the maintenance man from the museum, Ned. Where had he come from?

"Mercy, girl. You tryin' to kill yerself?"

"No. No. I tripped." Faith shivered from the cold and his macabre words. She gingerly sat up, testing every joint. She'd be sore, but no permanent damage.

"Goodness, you gave me a scare. These sudden storms can catch ya by surprise. Ground gets pretty slick." The old timer moved back. His poncho shed the rain, creating a puddle at his feet.

Faith's heart pounded against her ribs. "I was trying to get back to my car."

"The main road's clear over that a-way." He pointed behind his back.

"I figured that." She hated admitting she'd gone the wrong direction. She didn't want to explain what had scared her enough to confuse her. He'd think she was nuts.

"Here, let me help you." The old man reached down and with surprisingly strong arms, lifted her to her feet. Once she was standing steady, he took a step back. "We've got to stop meeting like this," he teased.

She hadn't been sure if he'd recognized her. She blushed. "Thank you." She attempted to brush the mud off her jeans. It was hopeless. Her icy cold clothes were plastered to her skin. Now that she stood, her hair hung in her face. She pushed it back, feeling twigs and leaves caught in the mass. *Yuck.*

She avoided looking at the ravine they stood so dangerously close to. Instead she peered at the man. She had to tilt her head back to look into his face.

"I can show ya a short cut back to the main road."

"I'd really appreciate that." She hoped it didn't involve going past that old house, or past the graves. She shivered. At least she'd have company and that comforted her. There was something warm about him, something reassuring in his voice.

"This way."

Ned moved surprisingly quick. He wasn't soaked to the skin or wearing tennis shoes, she noted. He wore the slicker and heavy hiking boots. The steep incline she'd fallen down shifted to the left, and he followed a ridge that looked like natural stairs. When they reached a landing, he stopped. She nearly ran into him.

"Isn't it beautiful?" he whispered. Faith followed his gaze and gasped.

The entire valley lay at their feet. The summer greens and autumn golds blended into a breathtaking palate. Late afternoon sunlight shafted through the breaking clouds at the edge of the storm. On instinct, Faith reached for her camera. Pain shot through her heart.

The old man continued the climb. "Wait. I lost my camera."

"You ain't gonna find it now."

"I have to!" She heard the panic in her voice and turned to go back and look. The old man sighed and followed her down the hill.

Despite the rain still pouring over them, they searched the

field. Up and down the hill. She shivered violently, and her teeth chattered long before she was willing to admit the camera was gone.

"I'll see if I can find it later after this clears up," Ned said.

He came up beside her, and she jumped, startled. She rubbed her hands up and down her arms in a pathetic attempt to get warm. "I don't want to bother you, but it's really important to me."

"You need to get warm and dry." He put a big, warm hand on her arm and she didn't argue. Disappointment washed over her. They didn't speak again, and in a few minutes they stepped out of an aspen stand where her feet met the paved highway. Her little car sat only a few yards away. Relief washed over her.

Spinning around, she started to thank him. He was gone. "Ned, where did you go?" She looked around the road and trees. "Thank you," she yelled, hoping he heard her. Only silence answered.

Water dripped off her hair and clothes. She sneezed. "Damn. Now I'll probably catch cold." She struggled to pull her keys from her sodden jeans pocket. It took several minutes before her cold fingers cooperated enough to turn the ignition.

Her hands shook, but she convinced herself it was the cold. She slammed the door of her mind on the things she'd seen out there in the woods.

***

Cripple Creek never looked so welcoming, and the hotel was an oasis. After checking in, she hurried to her room and quickly stripped. She couldn't get into the hot bath fast enough.

She slid into the bubbles, soaking up the heat and the scent. Would she ever stop hurting? Several abrasions stung, and she made a mental note to get some ointment at the drugstore. This town was hazardous to her health. She laughed. Big shock there. It would be so easy to get hysterical at this point.

Suddenly, someone pounded on the door of her room. She closed her eyes. Now what? She didn't want to know, didn't want to see or hear or talk to anyone.

"I'm busy right now," she yelled, hoping they'd get the hint.

They didn't. The door nearly flew off its hinges. She ducked beneath the bubbles, but that did little to calm the racing of her heart.

Cord stood in the open bathroom doorway, all broad

shouldered and gorgeous...and totally angry. The little muscle in his cheek practically jumped to life. She could only stare.

"What the hell are you doing back here?" he growled, the sound echoing around the room.

She didn't have the nerve to tell him she was taking a bath. That little bit of sass would probably have him going for her throat. She swallowed. Even the thought of his touch set her blood on fire.

What could she say to him? Where did she begin? She leaned her head back on the edge of the tub and closed her eyes. Laughter bubbled up from her throat. Laughter that would have sounded cool and uncaring if her eyes hadn't betrayed her by filling with tears.

"Damn it," he growled, more softly this time. "Now what?"

He stepped closer, his manly scent warring—and winning—with the soft bubble bath. The pictures she'd developed in her dark room leapt into her mind. He wasn't dead. He was alive and well and here with her.

He was safe. A tear slipped from beneath her closed lids and slid across her cheek.

For now.

Fifteen

"You fell, didn't you? Halfway down a mountain." Cord's words were quiet but hard. He had to force them from his chest.

Faith opened her eyes and stared. "Yes. How...how did you know?" Her teeth chattered.

"I saw it." The images flashed through his mind. Images of her legs dangling over a precipice. Similar images of Timmy's tangled body at the bottom of a mineshaft.

"How?"

"In that damned window in my office. Like a movie or something." Next week he fully intended to buy drapes—heavy drapes—for the cursed thing. "Hell, I'm going nuts."

Here he stood, a woman in front of him wearing nothing but soap bubbles, and he wasn't even thinking about her body. Okay, now he was. Cord turned and stomped out of the room. He slammed the bathroom door between them.

"Cord, wait!" she called.

"I will. Out here."

Her suitcase sat on the luggage stand. She hadn't even opened it. The room looked clean, old-fashioned, and serviceable. His gaze roamed to the large, iron double bed in the corner.

The scent of soap bubbles teased him and his anger grew.

What was she doing here? His livelihood depended on keeping his world on an even keel. He focused on that while he waited for her.

The bathroom door opened, and Faith stepped out wearing a thick, fluffy white robe. He immediately thought of waking up in her white lace bedroom. Heat engulfed his body, and he fought against reaching out to her. He swallowed his desire. She'd washed the grime from her face and hair, and the mass of curls hung long and damp down her back. She looked so damned beautiful, her skin still dewy...

"What are you doing in Cripple Creek?" He stepped back. Sadness and fear, and something else he couldn't quite read, settled into her eyes. She looked away, hiding from him.

"I had to come back. I have to re-shoot everything." A frown creased her brow.

"Why?"

She shook her head and looked up at him. "Delta destroyed

everything." She clasped her hands together, from nerves or the cold he wasn't sure.

"What are you talking about?" he prompted when she didn't elaborate. He'd probably be kicking himself for this later. Did he really want to know?

"I started developing the pictures after you left. Oh, Cord, it was awful."

The pain in her voice tore at him, but he stood his ground. He reminded himself of their last meeting, when she'd called him Rafe. "Go on."

If she noticed his distance, she didn't show it. "There were images I didn't take on the film. Four total. The first was of Delta looking right at the camera. It was spooky. When I tried to show Clarissa the pictures, the images faded away. Clarissa said Delta only wants me to get the message."

"And what's the message?" He took a deep breath and held it. Faith looked up at him, her chin lifting. He resisted the urge to smile at her attempt at defiance.

"The second photo was of Rafe kissing Delta. The third was of Delta. She was dead and...Rafe held the gun."

"She's showing you the history we already know. What's the point?" He turned away, staring outside. The sky remained remarkably blue and clear. He relaxed, a little. "We know Rafe killed her." He'd almost grown comfortable with that knowledge. Almost.

"There was one more."

He heard her move and wasn't surprised to feel her fingers lightly touching his arm. He closed his eyes, letting himself enjoy it for just a moment. He opened them again and turned to glare at her. She didn't move away.

"It was of you. Not Rafe." Her voice caught in her throat, and she cleared it twice before speaking again. "You were wearing the clothes you wore that day when we were at the museum." Tears sparkled in her eyes, and she hastily blinked them away.

"You were the one shot this time. Oh, Cord, you were staring into the camera, but there was no life in your eyes." Her voice broke on the last words. "We can't let her win."

He'd spent several long minutes afraid he'd actually seen her die. Now she claimed to have stared into his lifeless eyes. His fear returned. This time he gave into his need to touch her, needing to feel something real. He pulled her into his arms, roughly finding her lips with his.

She tasted sweet and so very much alive. Even with her here in his arms, the fear clung tight.

She resisted his kiss for a moment, pushing against his chest. Then her touch shifted, and she melted into him.

Where she'd shivered before, she was now heat. He knew he had to stop this. All those promises and tomorrows he'd fought so hard against loomed around him, and for the first time he wondered if he'd even get a chance at them. She leaned into him, alive and vibrant. The robe parted, and he knew he was lost.

He lifted his head, gazing down at her, taking in every detail of her face.

"What?" Faith whispered, looking hard into his face. Dark emotions clouded his eyes. His lips thinned as he stared at her.

"When I saw you in the window...falling down that hill... Now this business with Delta." He swallowed hard, and she watched the muscles of his throat work. "I...just...damn, I'm not good with words." His brow puckered with a deeper frown.

Faith reached up and pressed her palm to his cheek. His day's growth of beard rubbed against her skin. She smiled, enjoying the feel of it, of him. For several long, silent seconds she met his gaze, nearly falling into his beautiful eyes.

"Then show me." She leaned up on her tiptoes and pressed her lips to his. "Show me," she whispered.

Cord's lips held an urgency she'd never felt before. His arms tightened, and she slipped hers around his neck.

All the fear she'd lived through with Delta and then the fall bubbled to the surface. She tightened her arms, pulling him closer, but not close enough. Never close enough.

"Damn, I want you," Cord growled across her lips, lifting his head just enough to move them across her cheek. As he kissed a trail down her neck, she trembled so hard that she was sure she'd fall. Only his strong arms held her up.

His hands moved. Up and then back down over her ribs. His long fingers curled around her waist. At the edge of the robe, he reached in. The rough calluses of his fingertips scraped across her belly. She moaned, letting her head fall back.

"That's it, honey." His voice caressed her. His lips captured hers before she had time to react to his words. For someone who had trouble speaking his feelings, he sure managed to get his message across.

Faith felt her entire body smile. Her lips were too busy tasting his. She leaned against him, letting him feel how he affected her. She relished his reaction, the way his body hardened in response.

Time shattered and melted away. Nothing existed outside of him, outside of this embrace. Her breath came hard, and with each intake of air, her breasts rubbed against him. It almost hurt to touch him like this, through layers of clothing.

"I need you." Faith reached for the buttons on his shirt, pulling and tugging until they came open. The warmth of his skin against her hands soothed her. So solid and strong.

As if reading her mind, Cord leaned closer, whispering in her ear. "I need to touch you. Feel you around me." He didn't wait for an answer, but pulled the robe all the way open and off her shoulders. She shivered, not from cold, but with anticipation of his touch.

Skin to skin, the passion erupted. He lifted her and carried her to the bed, where he ripped back the covers. Gone was the patience, the little steps to discovery of the other night.

His eyes roamed a path over her skin. She felt his gaze and her body's reaction. "Cord," she breathed his name, letting it fill the room.

In an instant, he lay beside her, his clothes tossed carelessly to the floor. Her fingers moved over him, wanting—needing—to memorize every hard, muscular curve and plane.

"Please, Cord. Now." She gulped out the words. "I need you inside me."

"Hush," he whispered. He kissed her then, gentling her, slowing the pace. "Savor it," he instructed.

Surely, he'd gone mad. He'd driven her to the edge, only to pull up short. Oh, but the things he was doing to her now. The heated trail his tongue forged along her skin, down her neck and over the hill of her breast. He hesitated at the peak, tasting her until she cried out in frustration. He laughed, then continued lower.

Slowly, oh so slowly, he nibbled his way down her abdomen, reaching the curve of her hip after what seemed an eternity. The heat only intensified as he moved lower, tasting places he'd only touched before.

He kissed every inch of her he could find. The tender skin of her inner thighs. The warm, wet opening that ached to be filled with him. His tongue did magical things, creating an ache she thought might never ease.

"Cord," she cried his name as she shattered. Called out to him, begging him to join her. He did. Pushing her farther over the edge as he drove inside her.

"Ah, babe," he whispered as he held her. "Faith." He prayed her name and threw back his head, letting go.

She marveled at his intensity, at the depth of which she felt him in her body and in her soul.

Time stopped and then slowly returned to life. As they lay there, listening to each other's even breathing, darkness cocooned them. Night took hold of the city, driving away everything but the feel of his arms around her. Faith smiled, enjoying him. The warmth that seeped from his skin to hers. The way his breath moved like a subtle caress over her skin. She could stay like this forever.

The world intruded slowly. A door slammed down the hallway. A car horn echoed from the street below. The windowpane rattled...

No! Faith turned her head to look out the window. Clouds scudded across the sky, blotting out the stars, hiding the moon and its friendly light. No, please...Her arms tightened around Cord, and he stirred at the sudden pressure.

"What?" he mumbled, snuggling against her, his whiskers rough against her skin.

"Cord, a storm." Her voice cracked at the same instant a flash of lightning lit the room. Thunder rumbled so loud and close on its tail they barely blinked between.

A roar ripped through the room. The windowpane shattered. Faith screamed. Down the street something exploded.

Cord threw back the covers and ran to the window. She ran after him. A golden glow painted the planes of his face orange.

Flames shot from the roof of The Double Barrel. He stared in disbelief. Then he turned to her, and his eyes filled with pain.

"Damn it." He grabbed his clothes from the end of the bed. He pulled up the zipper of his jeans as the next flash came, outlining the beautiful lines of his body with it's white light. "This is impossible. Why don't I get a break?"

Not waiting for her reply, he grabbed the rest of his things, turned and strode from the room. The door smacked the wall before bouncing closed. Faith doubled over as the pain hit her full in the heart. She'd seen the accusation and the distance in his eyes. And the blame. He'd blame her for this just as he'd always blamed her for everything...

Painful images of his anger, of him storming away, assaulted her, images she knew weren't from this life. Tears burned her eyes and all the sweet love seeped out of the room.

***

Flames licked the sky, sending sparks up into the night. A fire engine's wail broke through the crackling roar as it rumbled down the street. Cord ran along the sidewalk, barefoot, bare-chested, and bare-souled.

How could he have been so stupid? The vision of Faith all enticing and beautiful in that white robe tore through him. He forced down the pain in his chest. The pity party came later. Now he had to save his life. He met the fire crew as they piled out of the truck.

He knew every one of these men. They came in to gamble, did the necessary inspections, and were his friends. Now all emotion had been erased from their faces. They had a job to do. They barked orders, shoving him aside as they worked.

Hoses were hooked to the hydrant, and a great wall of water poured into the shattered front window.

"Where's Johnny?" Cord pulled on his shirt and shoes, and then he wove through the growing crowd. "Doug?" he called to one of his bartenders.

"Boss. I...I don't know what happened."

"Is everyone out?" Cord looked through the crowd, counting heads. Everyone he knew to be on duty tonight was accounted for except Johnny. "Where's Johnny?"

"He was back in the office—" one of the waitresses called.

Cord headed to the other side of the building. Darkness shrouded everything, but he found his way to the window. Damn, he'd just replaced these.

Johnny was in the office, stuffing papers into boxes. *Idiot.* Cord slammed his fist against the glass, and Johnny looked up. He waved and grabbed the box. He headed toward the door. Cord banged on the window again and shook his head. If Johnny opened that door he'd be stepping into an inferno.

Johnny touched the door and seemed to feel the heat. He backed up and headed to the window.

"Get the hell out there," Cord yelled as he shoved the window open. He half dragged Johnny through it. "What are you doing?"

"Trying to save the paperwork."

Cord wanted to ring his neck. "It'll keep. Come on."

They rounded the building. The crowd had grown, and the fire crew was having as much trouble controlling the crowd as the flames.

"You take that side, I'll head to the other. I don't want anyone hurt, do you hear me?" Cord met Johnny's stare.

Between the two of them, they got the crowd back enough for the fire crew to do their job. Smoke billowed into the night, blackening everything in its path. Cord coughed, wondering if he'd ever feel clean again.

Time crept by, tearing at Cord's soul. He tried not to stare, to feel the loss. When darkness fell, he fought the pain. The hiss of the flames faded. The fire crew stepped back, white-toothed grins breaking through the soot on their faces. Cord couldn't muster even a faint smile as he stared at the blackened shell of his life.

He blinked repeatedly to remove the soot from his eyes as he stared at the building. He had no idea what they'd see in the light of day. His stomach clinched at the thought. Would everything be gone?

The crowd thinned and finally moved away. Johnny sent the staff home. Cord didn't say a word. He couldn't move, couldn't stop staring.

"Hey," Johnny walked up to him. "Cord?"

"Yeah."

"I sent the crew home. Told them we'd have a meeting tomorrow. Everyone's okay."

Relieved, Cord let himself relax a little. "Thanks."

The night grew quiet except for the sounds of the fire crew packing up and beginning their investigation. The distant noise from the other casinos mocked the silence of the Double Barrel.

Finally, Cord turned away, unable to watch any longer. A lone figure stood across the street. Her hair hung in mussed ringlets around her face. Even in the dim light she looked as if she'd just crawled from his bed, which she had.

He stood there for a long minute, watching her, seeing her as she had been in his arms just a short while ago. And then in the image in the window, falling down the mountainside.

Someone was trying to tell him something, and he was finally getting the message.

He strode across the street, unable to control the pain, the fear and anger that ate at him. "Get out. Get the hell out of my life and this town."

"Cord—"

"Get out," he repeated, nearly pleading as well as ordering her. "Nothing like this happened before you came here." He knew he was hurting her, knew it from the tears that glistened in her eyes. If he had to hurt her to save her, he would. He also knew that if she looked close enough that same agony would reflect back at her. "I don't need you here anymore." Even as he said it, he knew he lied. He'd give everything he had for her—even his own life.

But he couldn't risk hers.

"Just go home." Home where she was safe from the harm that seemed to await them here.

Faith stood there in the cold night, her arms wrapped around her middle. He walked away, his back ramrod straight.

She'd seen that look in his eyes before. That same look of desperation and pain. In the dream after he'd carried Timmy's body up from the mineshaft and knelt beside her in the mud.

And on that first night under the lamppost.

Now she could put a name to that look. Loss. Loss of everything. Something she suddenly realized he knew entirely too well, because he'd lost everything tonight. His casino, his life, his dream, but she'd lost something, too.

She'd lost her heart to a man who didn't want it.

Sixteen

Cord roamed the streets in a pattern that seemed distantly familiar, as if he'd done this before. He listened for the quiet of the night that hid behind the noise of the other casinos. The fire crew would be working for several hours on their investigation. Even then, would his room in back be habitable? Was there anything left of it?

Desperation settled into his chest, a desperation like he'd never known before. He'd fought so hard for his casino, and it was gone in just a few minutes.

The thought of taking a drink crossed his mind. Had this been how his father had felt all those years? All those lonely years? Cord shivered. He didn't drink, though he knew how it felt to be drunk. Even now he could remember the bliss of oblivion, the escape that came from the bottom of a bottle. He'd been underage when he took his first drink. His old man had passed out on the couch, a half-empty bottle tipped over on the floor. Cord remembered picking it up. It tasted nasty, but he'd kept drinking. There had to be a reason why his father kept drinking. All too quickly he found it. He conjured up those memories now. He recalled how it felt to escape, and yet never quite being able to. Reality lurked on the edges, never going away, just keeping its distance.

Cord stopped walking. Surprised, he looked up. How had he gotten here? The museum looked almost forlorn in the darkness.

He sat down on the old lawn chair that Opal had left on the front step. He didn't have any place else to stay. The haunting image of Faith's eyes as she'd stared at him after the fire came back. She had a hotel room...with a comfortable bed...

No, that was not an option, though his body ached for the soft distraction of her bed, of her arms...of her body.

"Hell." He propped his feet up on the rail. Not too bad. He doubted he'd sleep much tonight, or that Opal would mind.

"That doesn't look very comfortable." Opal's voice startled him. He laughed as he put his feet down on the floor.

"It'll do."

"Don't be ridiculous." She climbed the steps and inserted the key in the door. With a flick of a switch, she turned on the foyer light. He noticed that her eyelids drooped and her shoulders sagged, as if the long day and night weighed on her as well.

"Quite the excitement tonight. I'm so sorry about the fire." She led the way inside.

"Yeah. Me, too. Thanks," Cord sighed, shrugging his tired shoulders. "It'll be a lot of work to get things back into shape."

"Where are you staying?"

"I've got a room in back of the casino. I'll stay there after the investigation is done."

"I'm sure it's a mess." Opal put her purse in the closet. She turned and stared up at him. "You surely can't get it ready tonight. There's a spare room in the back here, if you'd like to use it."

"That's generous of you, but..."

"I won't have any arguments, my boy. I know there's not a hotel room to be had in town. I close up by eight each night." She headed down the narrow hallway and he followed.

Opal led him to a small room underneath the back staircase. "This room was used by the man who worked as the bouncer in the old days. It was used for storage for a while. We've never had the money for its restoration."

The sparse room held an iron bedstead with serviceable bedding. "Thank you, Opal. I'll probably only be here tonight."

"Oh, whatever you need. It'll be nice to have some company around here."

"You live here?" He had thought she lived someplace else.

"Oh, yes. Have for years. The maid's rooms were converted into a lovely little apartment when the previous owner was too ill to use the rest of the house."

The previous owner...too ill. His mind recalled the information Faith had received from Tim Gibson. That previous owner would have been Maria. His heart sank at the thought of her growing old here, alone. Guilt over Rafe's actions nagged at him.

"Can I get you some supper?" Opal's eyes lit up.

"No. I'm not very hungry." He saw the crestfallen expression cross her face. "Thanks for the offer."

"You're welcome. Well, I'll be turning in for the night. I'm afraid I get up at the crack of dawn. Comes from spending so much of my life on a farm. Goodnight, Cord." Opal smiled and turned away.

"Opal?"

"Yes?"

"Did you ever meet her, the former owner?" Cord found the words emerging from his lips before he could stop them.

"No, I'm afraid not. My husband and I moved here a couple years after Mr. Gibson took over the house."

"Oh, I see." Why was the disappointment so strong? Did he really want to know how lonely Maria's life had been?

She'd survived, and he knew how she'd made her living. He'd always thought he'd feel disgust or at best indifference to a woman who lived that way. Instead he found a measure of respect. Survival for a woman in that era, so shattered by her life's events, was an accomplishment.

Opal's retreating footsteps brought him out of his thoughts. "Thanks, Opal."

A faint blush tinged her wrinkled cheeks. Cord realized Opal had probably been quite beautiful as a young woman.

"It's nice to have someone to care for again. Since my husband died, it's been rather lonely. You're welcome to help yourself to the shower. It's right through there." She pointed to a door a few feet away. Still smiling, Opal turned and headed down the hall toward her apartment.

Cord listened until her footsteps disappeared behind the doors of her rooms. Then he turned into the bathroom, thoroughly enjoying the shower. He didn't have much choice of clothes, but at least he was clean.

A small lamp sat on a table beside the bed in the room. Moonlight filtered through the thin white curtains. The full, white orb lit the room nearly as well as if the lamp remained on.

Despite his best efforts, his thoughts turned to Faith. His anger and disappointment kept most of her images and his desire for her at bay. With nothing to distract him now, she came back with a vengeance.

The memory of her eyes filled with pain and fear floated in his memory. He had to chase her away. It was the only solution. He hadn't given her a chance to speak, and he doubted the chance would arise again.

How could he have given in to his lust so easily? His body answered by reacting to the image of her against him. He felt the heat and hardness, and he groaned and rolled over. He banished her from his thoughts...but not his dreams.

***

Rafe was drunk. He'd stumbled around the building

searching for Maria for nearly half an hour. It seemed an eternity. With the heavy rain, it was a slow night and few people were about. The bouncer was getting used to throwing him out these days, but tonight Rafe lifted the gun. Even big Cyrus backed off. The house quickly emptied of the few guests and most of the girls.

Whiskey and remorse sent him over the edge. Wandering through the upstairs hallway, calling her name, he went from room to room. Each time he opened a door, he found only emptiness. Finally, he came to the observation room and went in.

He wanted his wife. He wanted his son. She was dead now, that girl who had killed Timmy. God, how could she have done it? As Delta had looked in fear at the gun, he still hadn't understood why she'd done it. She blubbered about how Timmy was hers, how she'd get him back. Rafe wasn't sure about anything Delta said. It didn't make sense. None of it did, and did it really matter? She was dead now. He tried to tell his soul not to hold so much glee.

His anger escalated as she described how she took Timmy to the old mine to hide him. He smelled burned powder and watched her stumble and fall back across the bed. Bright crimson blood spread quickly over the front of her dress. Her eyes stared in silent shock.

He didn't stop to think.

He ran.

Ran until he could run no more. Nearly five miles outside the city limits, he stumbled. Landing on his knees, he rolled to stare at the slowly emerging stars. Stars that blurred through the dampness in his eyes.

It took two days of alcohol to numb the horror. All he wanted was his Maria back. To hold her. To love her again.

But he couldn't find her. If she was here, she was hiding from him. Her steamer trunk sat in this room. He lifted the lid, wanting some part of her to take with him. Dear God, she'd shut their entire life up in this little box. He frantically took out familiar items, until he was throwing them around the room. Finally, his fingers encountered the softness of the toy bear. The plush animal had been Timmy's. Stroking the fur, tears burned Rafe's eyes.

"Papa?"

Rafe turned, shocked by the familiar little voice. He was

losing his mind. He blinked several times when he saw the beloved figure of his son, wearing the same nightshirt he'd died in. The one Maria had made him for Christmas.

"T...Timmy?" He clutched the bear tight in his strong fingers.

"It's all right, Papa. I know you hurt." His hand reached out and touched Rafe's arm, though Rafe couldn't feel the contact.

"I miss you and your Ma so much," Rafe whispered, setting the bear on the couch and reaching to pick up the bottle. He took a deep swig of the whiskey that had been his constant companion for two days.

"I see Mama cry lots of times. I think she misses us, too. Papa?"

"Yes?"

"What happened to that lady?"

Revulsion shot through him, and he took another deep drink. So, even his son now knew the truth. "She died."

"Oh." Timmy pondered his father for a minute. "Like me?"

"No. Oh, no. Not like you did." A sob shook Rafe's big body.

"Mama always said to wait and see. Things will get better."

"Mama doesn't say that anymore." Maria didn't say anything to him anymore.

"Does my bear make you feel better? He used to help me lots when you and Mama would go away from me."

"I...don't think so." Rafe picked up the bear and looked lovingly at it before extending it out to Timmy. "I wanted this to be buried with you, but your Ma wanted to keep it with her."

Timmy reached out and a sudden, blinding flash of light filled the room. When Rafe saw Timmy again, he hugged the bear. A joyous smile lit his tiny face.

"Thanks, Papa." His childish giggle filled the air. "I'll wait for you and Mama, okay?" Timmy waved at his father and Rafe smiled, waving back as the little boy faded away.

"Okay." Rafe stared, sure he was insane and just as sure that Timmy would wait forever. They wouldn't end up in the same place. Failures didn't make it where Timmy had gone. Suddenly, Rafe heard voices in the hallway. Through the fog

of his mind he recognized the soft tone of Maria's voice. She was scared and angry. She'd soon reach her boiling point. He chuckled to himself. Whoever was on the receiving end of her temper would be sorry.

"He's not here," she cried. Ah, she must still care. A comfort.

The door of the observation room slammed open. The crack of the wood against the wall startled Rafe for only an instant. "Evenin', sheriff," he drawled. Rafe smiled, tilting the bottle up to his lips again.

The gun Rafe had carried for two days was nestled in his hand. Timmy was waiting. He had to get going. He looked at the cold darkness of the gun. Raising the gun, he saw its power as the sheriff and his deputies scooted back behind the wall. Only Maria remained. The woman he'd loved so desperately, who was now a stranger.

"Please, Rafe. Put the gun down," she pleaded. Tears streamed down her cheeks.

"I can't, honey. It's the only way out." He stood, his legs unsteady as he walked toward her. Only a few inches separated them when he stopped. "I told you I'd take care of everything, but you didn't believe me. I love you, Maria. Really love you." He kissed her then, sweet and slow.

He took a step back and faced the sheriff. "What's done is done." The muzzle felt cold against his brow. "Good-bye, sweetheart." Her scream preceded the roar, and then the pain sliced through his mind. As quickly as it began, the pain halted, giving way to blessed cool darkness.

***

Cord sat up in bed. His heart pounded against the wall of his chest. No, it couldn't be true. He shoved his hand through his already tangled hair and then down over his sweat slick face. Dear God, don't let Faith share this dream. Even though he was angry with her, he couldn't wish this on her.

He had to see that room again. There were more answers there; he was sure of it. He pulled on his clothes then walked to the door. He opened it slowly, so as not to startle Opal. She wasn't used to someone roaming around here at night.

He followed the moonlight's path through the rooms and up the stairs. He flicked on the hall light to dispel the shadows.

It illuminated the room clearly. He walked to the spot where he'd stood with Maria in the dream. That same sharp pain stabbed at his head as when he'd first come in here.

Cord struggled against the discomfort. He moved to the couch and pushed against it. It moved several inches, and he found what he was looking for. Wiping the years of dust away, he saw the dim outline of a dark stain. Rafe Cumberland's blood.

Cord swallowed the lump in his throat and backed out into the hall. Sweat drenched him. He hurried back downstairs to his room. The sooner he got out of this place, the sooner he'd feel sane again. He left Opal a note and headed back to his casino. He'd check out the progress of the fire investigation and put the dream out of his mind.

The streets were empty. None of Cripple Creek's casinos were open after two a.m. and a glance at his watch told Cord their doors had been closed for well over two hours.

Heartsick all over again, he walked toward the Double Barrel. The beautiful building sat silent and black against the moonlit sky. The burned out section of the roof provided a ghastly reminder of how easily everything could be taken away.

His headache lingered, and he rubbed his temples. He didn't need this. He *really* didn't need this. He had enough to contend with in his life without taking on troubles left over from some other life, a life he was only partially convinced was his.

So, what was he going to do?

Fight. The word leaped into his mind as if lurking in some corner, just waiting for a chance at the limelight. Even as he thought it, he knew he could—and would—do whatever it took.

Cord had relived Rafe's desire to have his wife and son, but Rafe had given up. Cord wasn't a quitter. Never had been. Never would be. He didn't have a wife and son to ache for, but he had his own life. The Double Barrel was the first thing he'd done in his life that was his. His staff and friends were closer than his own family had ever been to him.

Cord understood odds, knew about winning and losing. He willingly took risks, aware of the payoffs. There was no changing now.

For several moments he stared at his casino. Instead of seeing the skeletal remains of his dreams, he saw the foundations and structure of new ambitions. This was his chance to build it over. To build it better. To raise it to a higher level.

A calm that he hadn't known in a long, long time settled over his heart. He would succeed...or die trying.

Seventeen

Despite the lateness of the morning, the restaurant overflowed with diners. As Faith scooted through the crowd, she heard snippets of conversations. Last night's fire was the main topic of conversation. There was speculation everywhere. How had it started? How long would the casino be closed? Would it ever reopen?

Faith had her theories about who had started that fire, but she kept them to herself. They'd all think she was crazy if she started telling ghost stories.

Way in the back, just outside the kitchen, Faith found an empty table. Everyone else wanted conversation. She didn't, not about the fire, or about anything else. The banging of the kitchen door, and the pots and pans beyond didn't matter that much to her. All she wanted was food.

A young girl rushed up to the table, a notepad in hand. "Can I get you anything to drink?" She smiled, but her exhaustion showed in her eyes.

"Busy day?"

"It's been nuts all morning. Everyone's still hyped up about the fire. Add that to the fact that everyone seems to be winning and spending their money."

"On food?"

"On anything." The girl looked harried, but also as if she appreciated the couple of minutes to stand in one place and rest.

"Bring me a cup of tea and a ham and cheese omelet," Faith said. The girl nodded, scribbling on her pad as she turned away.

"Ah, wonderful choice. My mother used to say anyone who orders a good breakfast is a smart one." The man's voice easily carried over the din of the room.

Faith looked up. Ned smiled at her from a nearby booth. She smiled back.

"Hello. I didn't get the chance to thank you for rescuing me."

"I heard ya." He nodded and took a sip of his coffee. She watched him close his eyes and savor the taste of it, as if it were brandy or some other special drink.

He suddenly opened his eyes and, for a long minute, stared at her. "Such sweetness," he said.

"Y...yes." The depth of emotion in his eyes left her to wonder if he referred to the coffee or something else. Just as the thought crossed her mind, he smiled and reached to the seat beside him.

"I was plannin' to drop this off at your hotel." He set her camera on the table.

"You found it!"

"I tried to clean it off. It wasn't easy. A lot of that hill went with you when you fell."

"I...yes." She reached for it, tentatively touching the case. Relief washed through her, and she blinked away the dampness. Like an old friend it settled into her palm. Out of habit, she checked it over. It looked fine. Maybe she'd imagined hearing it break. She'd have it checked out, anyway.

She smiled, emotions clogging her throat. "Thank you." Looking down, she noticed the film had been used. She hadn't taken any shots on this roll. She shivered, remembering the pictures she'd almost taken of the house. "Did you take any pictures with it?" Part of her wanted to hear him say yes. Another part hoped he said no. Why would he have any reason to use her film?

"Nope. I wouldn't know how to work one of them new fangeled things."

She believed him, but the twinkle in his eye made her wonder.

Just then the waitress set a plate of steaming biscuits and gravy in front of the man. His grin could have lit the whole room. Just like with the coffee, he took a bite and closed his eyes to savor it. Faith couldn't remember anyone enjoying a meal as much. She hoped her own was as good.

"You think I'm nuts, don't ya?" He suddenly pinned her with another of his intense stares.

"Well, not nuts, exactly." She tried to cover her discomfort with a friendly smile. "You seem very intense in your enjoyment of things."

"It ain't often I get a real home-cooked meal like Laverne makes here. I appreciate things right here in front of me." He stirred the gravy and enjoyed another bite.

Why did she get the feeling he was speaking about something else? She didn't have time to ponder it any longer as her own meal arrived. She had to admit it was good, but obviously nothing compared to his.

They each ate in silence for a while. Faith sat listening to all the conversations around her—conversations that made her think of Cord, of his pain and anger. One blessing in disguise became apparent about Cord not being open this weekend. If she believed what she was hearing, the other casinos were giving away record-breaking jackpots.

The old man stood slowly, as if even that were something to be experienced. He smiled as he dropped coins on the table. He seemed to have a pocket full.

"I see you're a winner, too," Faith commented.

"What?" He looked at her, then as if understanding dawned, he laughed. "Yes, but not just in a casino. You might say I've hit the big jackpot."

He had a way of talking in riddles. She was almost afraid to ask. He saved her the trouble.

"There's no greater treasure than love, my dear. Nothing better, but I can see you know that already."

"What do you mean?" She looked down, wondering what he saw on her face. She blushed, though she didn't know why. He couldn't know about her and Cord's lovemaking last night.

The old man shuffled across the short space between them. He reached out, placing his old, gnarled fingers over hers. "Treasures come in different packages. Some big. Some small. None more important than from other people." He reached into his pocket and pulled out an old-fashioned cloth bag. Small and white, she recalled her grandfather using something similar when he bought tobacco to roll his cigarettes.

"Here's a little treasure for you." He turned her hand over, placing the bag in her palm. Gently, he pushed her fingers around it. "Hold on tight, don't let it go."

Faith looked down at the bag. Gently, in order not to harm it, she pulled the drawstrings open. Tilting the bag, she let the contents fall into the palm of her other hand.

A simple golden band fell out. She caught it, afraid it would bounce onto the floor and be lost among all the busy feet. "It's beautiful, but I can't..."

"It ain't mine," he explained. "Opal told me you were at the brothel askin' about Rafe Cumberland."

"Yes...I have."

"My Daddy worked in that house until Ms. Maria closed it. He was the bouncer and took care of...business for her."

"Business? Like what?" Faith didn't think she wanted to know the answer.

"Like getting rid of problems. He helped take care of Mr. Cumberland after the accident." The old man looked around and leaned in closer. "When she closed the house she had no money to pay him, so she gave him this. Told him to sell it for whatever he could get."

"Why didn't he?"

"He knew she'd want it back someday." With a wink and a smile the old man turned and shuffled through the crowd.

Faith stared at the ring, then looked up and found he'd vanished again. She stood, trying to see over the crowd, but he was nowhere in sight. She sat back down, unsure what to do next. She couldn't keep this. Why had he given it to her?

The metal felt warm and smooth in her hand. Faith slid her finger in and out of it. Even her thumb fit inside with extra room to spare.

It sparkled in the light as if it had been kept well polished. The nicks and scratches indicated someone had worked hard while wearing it. It wasn't totally round either. She held it up to the light, noticing the oblong shape of it.

Something was engraved inside. Faith tilted it, hoping to read it more clearly. The words were nearly worn off. She couldn't make them out in this light.

Hastily, she headed for the cashier. She paid her bill and stepped out into the sunshine. It winked off the metal, but she could see the curls of the fancy lettering inside.

She'd know that name anywhere.

Rafe.

Tears formed in her eyes and she closed them, holding the pain inside. *This can't be happening.* Inwardly she laughed at herself. After everything else, it was a little late now to think that.

Faith opened her eyes again, looking down the street at Cord's casino. The burned out shell held a macabre beauty to her photographer's eye—its blackened frame against the bright blue sky. His home. His dream.

She looked down at the ring in the palm of her hand. Rafe had lost his home, his dreams, his life...everything.

I can't let him lose it again.

Where had that thought come from? Shoving the ring back into the bag, she stuffed it into her pocket. There were answers somewhere. She didn't know exactly where to look, but she knew she had to try.

Faith headed toward the brothel. Delta had some explaining to do.

At the museum, Opal sat in the kitchen having an early lunch. She waved Faith in with a smile. Upstairs the observation room remained unlocked, though no efforts had been made to clean it or make it a part of the tour. Even though the mystery of what was here had been solved, there was still the promise Tim Gibson had given Maria to keep the room closed. A promise he would keep. Faith admired him for that.

Bringing her mind back from its wandering path, Faith pushed the door open. The room felt different. Empty and dusty.

Sudden flashes of memory came and went in her mind. She tried to bring them into focus, but they refused to adjust. As quickly as they appeared, something snatched them away.

Sadness settled over her. Heavy sadness that threatened to fall from her eyes in great big tears. Staring at the painted-over window, Faith remembered her dreams of Rafe standing on the other side of the window watching her. He'd been so full of life. So full of desire. So driven by pain.

Turning away from the memories, Faith knelt beside the trunk and lifted the lid. Opal had put the blue dress back inside. Faint water stains marred the delicate fabric. The reality of what she'd done hit her. Feeling guilty, she wondered what Opal thought and how she could repay her for the damage. Making a mental note to talk with Opal, Faith glanced at the trunk's contents again and saw the red box. She looked through the jewelry.

The brooch must still be with Delta. All Faith found here were more questions.

Shaking her head, Faith dug deeper into the trunk, but she found nothing that gave her more answers. "Damn." She closed the lid and sat on the trunk. The mirror in the corner reflected her as she sat there. No other images filtered in. It all looked the same.

It didn't feel the same.

Delta was gone.

How did she know that? And yet, she did. Delta wasn't anywhere in the house. Leaving the observation room, Faith walked down the hall to the room where the familiar quilt lay across the brass bed. The pictures she'd seen before flashed through her mind in a horrific kaleidoscope, but there were no new images.

She wandered in and out of each room. Nothing.

Delta had definitely left this place.

So where had she gone? The casino? The hotel? Someplace else?

After talking to Opal and making arrangements to reshoot her pictures, Faith left. She needed to get the camera checked before she started work. As she walked down the street, modern day gamblers meandered up and down the sidewalks, enjoying the warm sunshine and the fresh mountain air. Even the small shops were filled.

The blackened exterior of the Double Barrel hovered at the end of the street. Was that where Delta had gone? Had she started the fire? Or had it been something simple like lightning or some electrical problem? Faith shook her head, knowing she wouldn't find any answers just standing here.

She headed back toward the hotel, having to cross the street to avoid the crowds. On the next corner the front page of the local paper hung in a storefront window. She looked up and read the old fashioned lettering on the glass. The Crusher, Cripple Creek's oldest newspaper, lived inside. The blazing headline of "Fire" caught her eye, as did the photo of the Double Barrel as it glowed orange against the dark night sky.

The camera suddenly weighed heavy in her hand, and she remembered that some of her film had been used. That newspaper photo...Did it mean they had a darkroom? Was there even anything on the film in her camera? Curiosity pushed her through the door.

***

Cord stared at the casino from all the way down the street. The beautiful, historic building—what was left of it—stood silent and dark in the afternoon sun. Grief and loss stabbed at his heart. All his plans and dreams gone up in smoke. Each day the casino was closed he lost revenue. While insurance covered the building it didn't pay his workers wages or his other bills.

At least the casino hadn't been condemned. He and Johnny would have a place to live while repairs were made, albeit a grimy one. His earlier attempts to find a hotel room had proven fruitless. A large convention filled every room in town. And there was no way he'd spend another night in the museum. He controlled a shudder.

"Tough break, bud." Johnny said behind him, and Cord turned to see his friend's welcome face.

"Yeah. What a mess." Together the two men walked down the street, side by side, partners against the disaster. Their boot heels rang in unison against the pavement.

A thick, metal chain held the front doors shut. The heat of the fire had melted the handle. Johnny pulled a key from his pocket, and after releasing the padlock, handed Cord the key.

Johnny's broad shoulder pushed against the water and heat warped door. After several futile attempts, Cord lent his shoulder to Johnny's efforts. The scrape of the door across the once polished flooring grated on Cord's nerves. They managed to open the damaged door wide enough to pass through.

Cord tried to prepare himself for the devastation, but there was no preparation for this. He sucked in his breath as frustration enshrouded him.

Stale smoke and the scent of wet wood permeated the air. Damaged slot machines filled the room. The once shiny metal frames were warped and blackened. One machine's metal arm bent awkwardly toward the ground, melted by the heat. The money sat safely in the bank, thanks to Johnny's efforts.

Cord's throat tightened as he walked around the room. The beautiful hand-carved bar, Cord's pride and joy, now formed a black, charred lump in the center of the room.

He stopped dead in his tracks. A fresh rose lay on the once polished surface. The thorns had been removed. He reached out and touched it, afraid it was an apparition, and almost as afraid it was real. Black ashes clung to the velvet petals as he lifted the flower to sniff the sweet scent. He'd smelled it before. Upstairs in the brothel the day Faith had fainted. How had the rose gotten here? Cord hesitated, afraid he already knew the answer.

"Has anyone been in here since the fire?" He turned to Johnny. The other man didn't speak until he'd finished pushing two charred tables toward the back door, in preparation to throw them out, Cord realized.

"Not that I know of, I locked 'er up pretty tight."

Cord stood for several seconds, gazing around at the devastation. The fire investigator had concluded that faulty wiring in one of the slot banks had caused the fire. That same junction had been inspected less than a month ago.

Absently, he picked up the rose and rubbed it along his cheek. "I will win, Delta."

"You say somethin'?" Johnny asked.

"No." Cord crushed the delicate flower between his fingers and threw it out the open door. The afternoon breeze carried the petals down the curb, and murky water running in the gutter pulled them down into the sewer grate at the corner.

***

"I'd never survive without developing my own pictures," The Crusher's editor said. Faith smiled and thanked him for the use of the dark room.

The room was nothing more than a converted closet. She didn't like being alone, but there was barely room to turn, much less have company.

With a deep breath, she opened the camera and went to work.

She developed the photos as quickly as possible. She wasn't looking for quality at the moment, she just wanted to see them. The first prints formed in the trays, and she gasped.

The house in the woods took shape first. It looked new, freshly painted and clean. Figures wavered in the doorway. Closing her eyes, Faith braced herself. Slowly, she took a deep breath before opening her eyes.

Warmth filled her chest, warmth that she now recognized and understood as love. She smiled.

Rafe carried a young Maria over the threshold. His strong arms held her close. He stood at the door, their lips pressed together in a sweet, heart-melting kiss.

The next developed quickly. A tiny swaddled bundle rested in Maria's arms. She gazed down at her son with obvious love.

Faith especially liked the one of Rafe bouncing a three-year-old Timmy on his knee. Laughter shone in their eyes, and for a minute Faith thought she heard it. The thick darkness of Rafe's hair was mussed and hung in his eyes. His shirtsleeves rolled up, he looked every inch the gentleman farmer.

Other images formed. The family sat at the dinner table. Rafe twirled Maria around the room to the Victrola on the table. Timmy chased a tabby cat across the parlor floor.

Tears gathered in Faith's eyes. She did hear the laughter. Felt the warmth from the old wood stove. Knew the love Maria had for these two men. Her men.

She brushed the dampness off her cheeks. "Please," Faith whispered. "Don't let these fade." She hung the pictures to dry. She reviewed them again and again, thrilled and frightened by what she saw.

When they'd dried, she carefully stacked the pictures then slipped them into a large manila envelope. She resisted the urge to hug them. Such sweet precious images.

For a minute, fear struck at her. Why had Delta sent these images? To taunt her? To show her what she'd lost? If that was her plan, it did little to ease or increase the pain already settled in Faith's heart. The dreams had dug them deep. Gathering the photos, she left the darkroom.

In the newspaper office daylight poured in the windows, and she blinked several times. The editor sat at his computer, engrossed in an article. She thanked him then made her way out to the street. Hustle and bustle surrounded her. The word "home" whispered on the sweet mountain breeze.

Faith headed toward the casino. Hugging the picture envelope close, she smiled. She and Cord had a past. A wonderful past cut short by terrible circumstances. Cord would probably throw her out again, but she had to share these with him. Show him that Maria and Rafe and Timmy were real people.

In the shadow of the tall building she looked up at the workmen on ladders over her head. They scraped at the blackened paint in preparation for the future.

Standing there, holding the pictures, she realized she'd do anything to help Cord make his dreams real again. In the large window she smiled encouragingly at her own reflection. Cord appeared on the other side of the glass. He glared and turned away. Her heart skipped a beat.

Anything.

Eighteen

"Now what?" Cord stood hands on hips glaring down at her. For some odd reason his anger couldn't dampen her mood. Maybe it was the realization that she loved him. Maybe it was the pictures.

She smiled at him, ignoring the frown he threw her way. "Come see these." She walked to his desk, now neatly cleared of papers. She saw the sooty documents had been packed into boxes. She opened the envelope and pulled out the photos. Laughing at herself, she turned them over. Her smile faded. They were blank on both sides. Empty glossy paper stared up at her. Not a hint of the shadows remained.

"Damn her." Faith threw the stack of used-to-be photos on the desktop.

"What?" Cord picked up the blank pages. "What are these?"

Faith closed her eyes. In her mind she saw the images. The sweetness of Timmy's smile. The passion of Rafe's kisses. "I didn't imagine them," she whispered, swallowing the sudden tightness in her throat. "They were us...I mean, Maria and Rafe and Timmy. Happy. At a house I saw yesterday in the woods, before I fell."

Opening her eyes, she banished the thoughts and the pain. She picked up the papers, rifling through them, hoping to find something—anything—left. It hurt to lose the images. Hurt deeply. As if she'd lost a memory.

"Nice try."

Faith fought to control her anger. At Delta as well as Cord's stubbornness. She had needed to show him these pictures were real. Why that mattered so much to her, she didn't know, but it did. She could redevelop them, but would they develop at all? A dull ache formed in her chest at the thought of him never seeing the images. She looked up at Cord and realized it hurt nearly as much as the possibility of never seeing the smile in his eyes again.

Standing, she moved to the window. The afternoon sun beat down warm on her shoulders. Amazingly, the beautiful window had been spared in the fire. She looked up at it, remembering how it had shattered so easily before. He'd loved her that night. At least something had survived the fire. "I supposed this will vanish, too."

She reached into her pocket and pulled out the bag the old man had given her. She tossed it to Cord. He almost caught it. Instead, it flew past his fingers and landed on the pile of pictures.

Like a blossoming flower, the images spread over the photo paper. Timmy, Rafe, Maria, the house, they all returned to full vibrant color.

"What the..." Cord stepped back, startled. He stared mutely at the pictures.

"Oh, my God." Faith rushed to the desk. She picked up the bag that held Rafe's ring. The images faded instantly. She opened the bag, looking at the ring again. The inscription remained.

"The old man who helped me when I fell on the mountain was in the diner this morning. He gave me my camera and this." Faith lifted the ring, presenting it to Cord.

He reached out and took it, fingering the worn metal with his thumb. She watched the muscles of his throat work as he swallowed and closed his eyes. "Who did you say gave this to you?"

"He said his father worked for Maria. She gave him that when she didn't have the money to pay him."

Cord stood so close she felt his breath against her skin. His anger was gone now, but what was he thinking? He opened his eyes then, pinning her with a stare filled with wonder and pain.

She took the ring again and laid it on the pictures. Amazed, she watched the colors blossom once more. They seemed even clearer, brighter now.

He picked up the pictures, careful not to dislodge the ring, and looked closely at them, not saying a word. "They seemed happy," Cord whispered. He looked up and their eyes met. Emotions flickered across his face, and Faith struggled to read them. They vanished quickly, a distant stare taking their place.

"Maria." The name whispered through her mind and the room. She looked around. No one but the two of them were here. Had Cord said it? Or someone else?

Doubt fluttered around her, tapping gently on her heart. She refused to let it in, but she knew it was out there...waiting. She moved closer to him, looking over his shoulder at the pictures.

"Look, here's one of you and Timmy playing in the front room." She smiled, the warmth chasing away her doubts.

"You still think that's us, don't you?"

She hesitated, daring finally to look up at him. What did she have to lose? "Yes."

"Well, it isn't." He tossed the ring and the pictures onto the desk, the metal clinking as it landed. It bounced and slipped off the desk and rolled underneath. He didn't try to retrieve it. "These fit right in with *your* dreams."

"What do you mean?"

"I told you before, and I'm telling you again. I'm *not* Rafe."

"I'm not so sure."

"I am. You want the perfect little family." He grabbed a fading picture, nearly crushing it in his grasp. "This is the man you want?"

"I don't know if that's true." And at the moment she didn't. The emotions staring back at her were frightening and confusing.

"Rafe Cumberland was a fool. He lost his cool when his family needed him most. He took another life, and then he killed himself when he couldn't face the consequences."

Cord turned his back on her, staring out the window, the picture still mangled in his fingers. The silence reeked of anger and pain.

"How...how do you know...?"

"Another dream," he whispered. "Pray you don't relive it. Just leave Faith. What you're looking for isn't here."

She stood there for several long, excruciating moments. "You're right," she said. "You aren't what I'm looking for. Maybe Rafe was...maybe he wasn't, but at least I know he tried." She turned away from him and stomped out the door. The fact that she didn't slam it told him she was way beyond mere anger.

Cord closed his eyes and let his head drop back. Over the past few hours he'd had a lot of time to think. Even when he was giving orders to the cleanup crews, nagging thoughts of Faith hung out in the back of his mind. They'd sneak up on him and surprise him when he least expected it.

He'd hear her laughter and turn to find she wasn't there. He could close his eyes now and conjure up the taste and feel of her. For an instant he'd felt a flicker of hope—a hope that had lived in her eyes as she showed him the pictures. A hope that died when he realized she wanted some imaginary coward.

He'd never forget the stark pain he'd seen in her eyes last night when he'd yelled at her. That pain had quickly returned just now.

Why couldn't she just leave well enough alone? Did she ever give up? She'd left here and kept searching for answers. She'd come back, even when she knew danger waited. Even after he'd pushed her away, she'd come back...not like anyone else he'd ever known.

Realization dawned slowly. She wouldn't give up on him, either. Her idea of normal meant permanent. He admired her tenacity, even loved her for it. Loved? He couldn't love her. He didn't know how to love like she obviously needed to be loved, did he?

A rough wind howled outside, and tiny pebbles pinged against the window. How long had he been standing here? The image of her when she left a few moments ago filled his mind.

Her hair hung in soft ringlets around her face while her eyes sparkled with unshed tears. Even angry, she looked lovely.

He didn't know how, but he had fallen in love. A smile spread across his face. When had it happened? How had it happened? He hadn't let his feelings surface like this since his teens. His parent's bitter divorce had taught him the pitfalls of caring. Faith had lit all his hiding places, freed his emotions.

Kneeling, Cord retrieved the ring and shoved it into his pocket as fat, wet raindrops fell, splattering loudly against the windowpanes. So, now what was he supposed to do?

He didn't have a clue. He'd think of something as soon as he found Faith. The thought of hauling her into his arms warmed him.

The sound of a hammer echoed through the open doorway and brought Cord out of his thoughts. He walked into the casino to find Johnny high on the ladder. The chain holding the overhead chandelier slowly slid through the pulley.

"Careful up there," Cord cautioned as he walked into the room.

"This needs to come down while they check the roof."

Cord nodded, wondering if they'd ever get the soot off the crystals and brass. He was amazed it was intact. Maybe clean it would show damage. He hoped not.

"I've got a box for it in the back room," Johnny explained.

The storm's intensity grew outside, and a bolt of lightning split the sky. Cord shivered, appreciating the relative warmth inside. Suddenly, the chandelier lit up. A loud pop filled the air, and Cord looked up just in time to see a jolt of electricity arc through Johnny. Johnny jerked and tumbled down the ladder, landing with a loud thud.

"Lay still," Cord said as he ran to his friend, who moaned as he lay at the foot of the ladder. "You could be seriously hurt."

"I'm okay." Johnny's voice sounded weak as he tried to sit up, rubbing his head.

"I thought the power was off. Damn, you scared the life out of me."

"And what do you think it did to me?" Johnny growled. Cord offered to help Johnny to his feet, but Johnny shrugged away his assisting hand.

"Let's get you to the doctor. I think I can handle it tomorrow. We've made a good start," Cord said.

"Oh, and I'm sure you'd like that, wouldn't you?" Johnny turned angry eyes on Cord. "Tomorrow all I'd hear about was the way I slouched off today. You'd lord it over me all day, bragging to that woman how lazy I am."

"What?" Cord stared at Johnny. He must have taken more of a jolt than it had seemed. Maybe he hit his head when he fell. "Let's head to the clinic." He reached for his jacket draped over a charred chair.

"I ain't goin' to no doctor. I'm fine," Johnny yelled, kicking the ladder in frustration. The ladder slammed down the wall, gouging tracks in the heat-damaged wallpaper and landing with a crash only inches from Cord's feet.

"What's wrong with you? Are you trying to kill me or yourself?" Cord turned on his friend, his own frustration and exhaustion taking over. "Now let's get out of here. Don't make me pull rank."

Cord started toward the door when he heard a shuffling sound. He turned as Johnny launched himself through the air.

In the years they'd worked together, they'd had their fair share of disagreements. Cord could hold his own with Johnny. He wasn't afraid of a few blows, but he feared the look in Johnny's eyes. He'd seen that look only once before in another man's eyes. In the alley behind a bar in San Diego. It was the look of a man intent on a fight to the death. How had it gotten into Johnny's eyes? "What's wrong with you?" Cord yelled.

Johnny's big frame knocked Cord to the ground. Cord's back slammed against the hard floor. The element of surprise gave Johnny a slight edge. Cord rolled toward a table. He shoved Johnny back into the oak pedestal. Rolling away from his friend, Cord stood. He had the advantage as Johnny struggled from under the table.

Cord stood ready, feet apart. Fists lifted in front of him. He tried to anticipate his friend's next move.

"That wasn't fair," Johnny whined, as he struggled to his knees and then his feet.

"Fair?" Cord stared at him incredulously.

Johnny shook his head, looking down at the ground. When he once again returned his gaze to Cord, that look was back. Cord tensed for the coming impact.

Johnny's fists flew toward Cord's jaw. Cord ducked aside, barely. He slammed his own fist into the other man's stomach. A loud whoosh of air escaped from Johnny, and he stumbled backwards. For several seconds Johnny wavered, recovering.

"Give up?" Cord questioned, unsure what would happen next. This wasn't normal. They never fought like this. Johnny knew when to quit.

"Hell, no," Johnny roared and once again launched himself at Cord. Both men fell backwards. The hard oak bar hit Cord just below his shoulder blades. The force threw his head against the brass rail.

Johnny's fists were quick. They connected with Cord's jaw, then just below his eye. Pain exploded in his entire face as his cheekbone popped. Johnny's fist hit his jaw one more time. Cord struggled free. His own punch met with Johnny's chin. Anger and pain gave Cord strength. Johnny stumbled backwards.

"I don't know what your beef is, Johnny." Cord struggled to catch his breath against the pain. "This is no way to settle it." Cord reached up to wipe his face. Bright red blood mixed with ash covered his hand. His head throbbed in time with his heart.

"You don't, huh?" Johnny laughed, but the sound wasn't his normal laughter. A higher pitch overshadowed the familiar baritone.

Cord stared at him. He tried to focus with both eyes, which was difficult with one nearly swollen shut.

"I've waited so very long for this day, Rafe."

Cord's head whipped up. Had he heard right? "What did you say?"

"You heard me." Johnny's fists flew toward Cord. Cord moved away and managed to put the charred blackjack table between them.

"Who the hell *are* you?" Fear shivered through Cord. He could battle Johnny, but he suddenly knew this wasn't Johnny. Only one person that he knew of could do this. Delta.

"Wouldn't you like to know." Johnny shoved the table

toward Cord. Cards stored in the drawer below skittered across the floor. Chips clicked as they hit the ruined wood.

Cord stood ready for the next assault, prepared to give back whatever he could. The fight had changed. Cord fought for his life now. Somehow he had to knock Johnny out.

A big, meaty fist slammed into Cord's chin, sending new blinding pain through his head. He punched Johnny in the stomach again. Both men stumbled. Johnny landed against the wall. Cord wasn't as lucky. His heel caught on a barstool, and he went sprawling. He heard the wood of the stool crack.

Before he could struggle to his feet, Johnny came toward him again.

Johnny reached out and snagged a leg from the broken stool. He hoisted it into the air.

Cord watched the wood rise above him. He expected Johnny to hit him in the head, and he lifted his arms protectively. Johnny surprised him and slammed it into his knee. Cord's cry of agony echoed through the room.

Tendons and muscle shifted with the impact. Red, blinding pain shot up his spine and into his brain. Blackness beckoned him, but he fought against it. Faith's face drifted before him. The thought of never seeing her again ate a hole in his gut. He had to see her and tell her he loved her.

Cord slumped back against the floor, clutching his knee and fighting the overpowering pain.

Johnny stood a few feet away. His chest heaved as he breathed. Cord watched him under lowered lashes, trying to anticipate the next attack. When none came, he watched Johnny, waiting for the next move.

Johnny walked over to the bar and grabbed an unopened bottle of whiskey. Twisting off the lid, he drank a deep swallow. After putting the liquor down, he wiped his sleeve across his mouth.

"I rather like this guy. He's nothing like me." Johnny looked into the soot-smeared mirror hanging over the bar and rubbed his jaw. "I'm not sure I could handle the shaving bit. What do you think, Rafe? How would Johnny look in a beard?"

"Like an ass." Cord struggled to sit up, putting pressure on his knee. The pain caused him to gasp and lean back against the wall. He wasn't far from the fire door, but it might as well be down the block.

Sweat drenched Cord's body, as much from the fight as

from the pain. He longed for a cool breeze, but they'd nailed boards over everything, shutting it up tight as a drum. The storm lost its impact. Even the pounding of the raindrops on the roof seemed softer than before.

He wiped a sleeve across his brow. He still wore his jacket. Leaning forward, he tried to struggle out of it.

"What do you think you're doing?" Johnny spat.

"Taking off this damned jacket, if you don't mind. It's hotter than hell in here." He scooted a few inches toward the door.

"You'd know about that wouldn't you?" And suddenly as if he'd made a joke, Johnny giggled insanely at his own reflection in the mirror.

Cord watched him, wondering what to expect next. There was no deciphering what went on in the other man's mind. The Johnny he knew was gone. Or at least buried deep in there somewhere. Was Johnny still alive? The thought that he might not be sent grief deep through him. Johnny wasn't perfect, but he was the best friend Cord had ever had. He wouldn't take his loss lightly.

"So, what exactly are you planning?" Cord heard the ragged pain in his own voice.

"Planning?" Johnny's eyes shifted, meeting Cord's. "I'm not sure yet. I was thinking about that. I could kill you now. I know Johnny has the strength to break your neck."

"Not without one hell of a fight, which you aren't even sure you'd win."

"Hmmm." Johnny lifted the bottle and took another swig. Cord hoped he'd keep drinking. Johnny drank with the best of them—and went under the table first. Johnny was often teased about what a "cheap date" he was. Did this person know that?

Person? Was this a person? Cord's head hurt just trying to figure it all out. He could wait as long as Johnny could drink.

Leaning his head back, Cord looked at the burned out room. It was a mess, just like everything else. Like a slide show images popped into his mind—images of Faith.

What a fool he'd been, hurting her and pushing her away. He saw her there in his mind, as he had hundreds of times today. The moonlight playing on her hair that first night. The irritation he'd seen on her face when he'd teased her that first visit to the museum. The soft smile that hovered on her sleepy lips after they'd made love. The hurt he'd dished out far too easily.

"Hey." Johnny moved away from the mirror and towered

over Cord. “What are you planning?” The words were more accusation than question.

“Nothing.”

“Don’t lie to me, Rafe.” Johnny grinned, a smile barely reaching his lips, let alone his eyes.

Cord turned his head away, an action he immediately regretted. Johnny’s booted foot shot out, slamming against Cord’s injured knee.

Cord fought the cloying blackness, barely recovering before another wave of pain swept over him, pulling him under. Suddenly, Johnny pulled something from behind his back. Not the whiskey bottle as Cord expected, but a gun. The last image he saw was the barrel aimed directly at his heart.

Nineteen

Men were so stupid sometimes. Faith stomped up the street, the sound of her feet against the pavement ringing around her. Some men more than others. Cord Burke in particular.

She'd passed three casinos and two gift shops before her pace slowed. Her heart pounded in her chest, and she took several breaths. She'd forgotten about the altitude. She grumbled, but her anger faded slowly.

At the hotel, she flopped back on the bed. Okay, now what? The ornate designs on the ceiling intrigued her for a minute. That done, she rolled over and stared out the window. A few wispy clouds floated by. Was that a giraffe?

Her chest ached and her eyes stung. She would not cry. She refused to let him drive her to that.

A tiny drop slipped out of the corner of her eye. Okay, she'd allow him one tear, but that was all. It fell to her hand, followed by another and another. She closed her eyes, but that didn't help either. He just appeared there behind her closed eyelids.

Handsome and tall. His eyes flashed and he smiled, a smile she knew started in the dreams and kept going.

She stood, rubbing her eyes and daring any more tears to fall. Cord had made himself very clear. He didn't want her. It might hurt, but she'd get over him. Her heart ached now, for him and for herself, but she'd survive. They both would.

Wind whipped, tapping against the window. She sat looking down at the street. Gamblers scurried inside for cover. Dark clouds hugged the mountaintops, mushrooming up toward the heavens. Lightning lit the sky then faded off with a whimper. The old trick of counting the seconds to tell how far away the storm was didn't work. Faith knew the storm was here, all around her, inside her.

From her window she could see the dark, charred outline of the Double Barrel's roof. Raindrops pelted the glass. She stepped back and let the curtain drop. Lightning spiked again, followed by a roar like she'd never heard before.

Faith's heart trembled, and she realized this was more than a simple, natural storm.

Delta was back.

She tore open the door of her room and rushed outside. Water fell down on her from the sky. Ponds formed in the streets and soaked her shoes. She ran on. Cord might not want her. He might send her away again. She couldn't—wouldn't—let him. Not yet.

Together they were stronger than Delta. Alone they were helpless. How she knew that, she didn't know. She just did.

She shoved her sopping wet hair from her eyes. Night fell quickly. Streetlights blinked on only to fade out with the lightning blasts. Inky blackness formed a wall before her.

Using her hands on the rough brick walls, she found her way. Two more doorways. The deformed handle of the Double Barrel told her she'd arrived.

She shook the door, but it didn't give. Even the rattle of wood against wood disappeared in the roar of the storm.

"Cord!" she screamed, the word ripping from her throat and flying away on the wind. She pounded on the door until her knuckles ached. No one answered.

Now what? The rain continued to fall, soaking her to the skin. She shivered. The back door. She followed the wall to the alley where she found the metal door by touch. It, too, was locked. No one answered her pounding this time either.

Where had he gone? A flash of light split the sky into black shards. Thunder rumbled in the ground beneath her feet. Faith covered her ears with her hands, shutting out the worst of the painful roar. As she did, the storm's tone softened.

A woman's laughter echoed through the air, low and distant. Faith knew that laughter, sensed the violence in it. She recalled the pictures she'd developed with Clarissa. Fear took hold of her and wouldn't let go.

"Cord," she screamed again, desperate for an answering cry in that deep voice she loved. But the incessant pounding of the falling rain provided the only reply.

She returned to the front of the building. Cord's jeep sat a short way down the block. He was nowhere to be seen. She headed towards it, hoping to find something, anything that would tell her where he'd gone. Suddenly, a shaft of golden light caught her eye.

It shone through the tall window of Cord's office. Shadows moved behind the glass. She ran to the window. The storm must have drowned out her pounding. Wiping the drops from the window, she cupped her hands around her face to peer through. A smile of relief tugged at her cold lips. He'd probably think she was a total idiot getting soaking wet for nothing.

She saw Johnny through the open door of the office. He knelt down, looking for something. Faith reached up to tap on the glass, but her hand stopped in midair as he stood. Her heart lurched.

Cord's tall frame lay stretched across the floor. She couldn't see his face as it was turned away. Was he...? No dark stain marred his chest like in the picture. She tried to calm her breathing. She tried the window. Locked. Frustrated, she watched Johnny switch off the light and walk away. She pounded on the glass. Still he didn't answer.

She dropped to her knees. Scrambling in the mud, she hunted for a rock, a board, anything hard to break the window. She found nothing. She stood again, and with her heel, she kicked the lower panes until they burst. She pulled off her shoe and beat at the broken shards until they fell away.

Ice-cold mud squished between her bare toes. She slipped her shoe back on, grimacing at the chill, and then climbed through the window. When her sleeve snagged on the frame, she tugged free. Inside, the building blocked and partially muffled the storm. The eerie stillness rang in her ears.

She was surprised when Johnny didn't come to check out the noise. Where was he anyway? Because of the fire, she knew the phones were out. He must be on his way to get help for Cord. She hurried through the darkened office only bumping a couple pieces of furniture on her way.

"Cord!" she cried when she reached his side, and she knelt beside him. Worry pounded in her heart. Gently, she turned his face toward her and gasped. A dark, angry bruise swelled and covered his left cheek. Blood stained the corner of his mouth.

"Cord?" She tried to rouse him, fighting the tears and pain in her heart. His head rolled from side to side, and he moaned softly. Pain cloaked his voice, but she thought he whispered her name.

"What?" She leaned closer, straining to hear the strangled words.

"Get out," he whispered.

"Forget it. You can be mad at me later. Johnny went to get help. What happened?" Fear cracked her words.

"Johnny?" Cord's eyelids fluttered open, then closed again. "Get out," he spoke carefully, deliberately. "Now. Get help."

"I can't leave you like this." She had to help him, but she didn't know what to do. Please, Johnny, hurry back, she prayed.

"Johnny should be right back," she reassured him.

Cord's hand shot out, surprisingly strong as it clamped across her lips. "No. Delta's got him."

"What?" She stared into his pain-filled eyes. The remaining color drained from his face as he looked past her.

"Ah...Maria." Johnny's voice boomed through the room in a strange, yet familiar voice. "What took you so long to get here?"

Cord struggled to sit up, managing only to lift up on one elbow. His chest rose and fell rapidly with the exertion. Faith turned to find Johnny leaning against the blackened bar. A wicked grin sliced across his face.

"Johnny what's going on? What happened?" she demanded with more bravado than she felt.

"Just a little unfinished business." Johnny leaned forward, pulling a gun from his belt. His wicked grin grew. "With more to come."

Faith had never stared down the barrel of a gun before. Sweat broke out all over her body, and she trembled.

"It's Delta," Cord explained. He slumped against a burned table, his breathing labored.

"What do you mean?" She rocked back on her heels, staring at Johnny and the gun.

"She's possessed him."

Fear that Delta had actually taken over Johnny's body speared through her. This whole thing was beyond reason, beyond accepting. "No, you're Johnny. Cord's friend."

Suddenly, Johnny threw his head back and laughed. The sound—a mixture of Johnny's familiar baritone and the haunting laughter she'd heard these past weeks—sent goose bumps along Faith's neck.

"What do you want?" Faith slowly rose to her feet. Maybe reasoning would work. Maybe she could get to the door and run. Would Johnny kill Cord if she did? Faith swallowed her fear. Panic wouldn't do either of them a bit of good.

"What's this all about?" She spoke softly, soothingly. She wished she'd read more of Clarissa's books. Maybe then she'd know how to drive Delta's ghost out of Johnny. "Why, Delta? What did we ever do to you?" If nothing else, she didn't want to die without knowing.

"So, sweet Maria." Johnny sneered, reaching for an open bottle and taking a deep swig. "Don't you know?"

"No, I don't. Tell me, Delta." Faith coaxed. "Tell me."

"Say please." Delta smirked.

Faith hesitated only an instant before whispering, "Please."

A smug look filled the face behind the gun. "You were always so good. You had it all. Now I'm going to take it all back." Delta reached up to the open V of Johnny's shirt collar and rubbed her bare neck. Anger sparkled in her eyes. Faith recalled Delta stroking the broach in the same manner. She tried not to enjoy the spiteful realization that it was gone.

As if reading her thoughts, Delta glared at her. Faith stumbled back from the intensity of the emotions emanating from Delta. Cord shifted beside her, and she glanced down. She forced all her love into her gaze, wishing she'd said the words before and hoping he could read it clearly in the dim light.

"Trust me," she mouthed and stepped away. "All this over a man? A worthless one at that?" Faith kept her feigned disgust low in her voice.

Delta rolled her eyes heavenward. "You think I'm buying that act?" She laughed and took another swig from the bottle. "Oh, honey. If it were only that simple I'd have beat you out long ago."

Faith controlled the urge to glare. "Then what is this about?"

"Don't you remember how I died?"

"I haven't forgotten. How could I? You keep reminding me."

"Yes." Delta leaned across the wooden bar with a feral smile. "I did do a lovely job with those photographs, didn't I? Did they scare you? Make you jealous?"

"They disgusted me."

"Oh, well, that will do." Delta walked around the bar, stopping beside Cord. He didn't move. His eyes were closed again. She reached out and ran a finger down Cord's bruised cheek. "We could have been good together, but you chose her." She raised the gun. "Open your damned eyes." She kicked him, but he didn't move. "Look at me while you die!" she yelled.

"No!" Faith screamed and ran toward Delta. She shoved hard against Johnny's solid body. The element of surprise gave her a moment's advantage, and Delta stumbled backward. Faith sprawled across Cord, shielding him.

Delta caught her balance but almost dropped the gun in the process. She gripped it even tighter. "Damn you. Maybe I should let him watch you die first."

Faith waited for the painful shot to pierce her body. When

none came, she breathed again. Frustration showed in Delta's face. She recalled Delta's words. *Look at me while you die.* There was something in those words, some meaning. Now she just had to figure them out in time. Faith prayed for Cord to stay unconscious, at least for now. She needed time to come up with a plan.

"Gun," Cord barely whispered the word. Faith fought showing her reaction. "Register."

Faith looked at Johnny. "He has it," she whispered back.

"No. Another."

She squinted and looked closer. Johnny had an antique gun. A dim ray of hope grew in her heart. She had to get the other gun.

Would it even work? Had the fire damaged it? She looked away from Cord, unable to concentrate when worry licked at her heart. She had to find a way around this...this...person.

Fragmented images flitted through Faith's mind. None gave her answers. None told her what to do. The withered image of an old man suddenly slipped into her thoughts.

"Timmy's still alive," Faith said, knowing Delta heard every word. It worked. Delta's gaze bore into her.

"No, he's not. I saw him buried." An evil glare formed in Delta's eyes.

"Not m...my Timmy." Grief over Timmy Cumberland's death pulled at Faith even now. "Yours."

The barrel of the gun wavered. Delta sucked in a deep breath, and her gaze faltered. "How? No. It's been too long."

"I saw him a few days ago. He told me about his life. I met your granddaughter. Her name is Lorena."

Again the gun wavered, but Delta didn't lower it. Faith halted her tale, half afraid Delta would squeeze the trigger accidentally. Slowly, as Delta digested the information, Faith inched toward the bar and the gun that could save them.

Delta spun around to face Faith. It was only a few feet, but it felt like a mile. Out of the corner of her eye, Faith saw Cord move, ever so slightly. His hand closed around a broken table leg.

"You're lying," Delta said.

"No, I'm not." Faith suddenly hurt for the other woman. She knew how it felt to lose a child, or at least Maria did. "Your parents raised him, didn't they?"

"Yes." A tear gleamed in Delta's eye. "They took him away.

They took my baby." A sob shattered through Delta, and she broke under its intensity. Her head bowed in sadness.

Cord moved. Delta spun around, deflecting the blow of the table leg in the same instant she kicked Cord's knee.

Faith took her chance. She ran to the bar. Running her hand along the side of the register she found the gun, wedged beneath the metal. She recoiled from its coldness, but knew she couldn't give in to her revulsion. Their lives depended on her.

Faith aimed the gun at Delta—in Johnny's body. "Put the gun down, Delta, or I'll shoot you right now." Her voice came out strong though her knees shook.

Delta faced her and laughed. She lowered her gun. "You think I care if you kill this stupid man?" Slowly, she sauntered toward the bar. "He means nothing to me. He's served his purpose."

Fear raced through Faith. How could she scare a ghost who had no fear of death? She'd never been a gambler, but she knew about calling Delta's bluff and kept the gun level with Johnny's chest.

"Go ahead," Delta taunted, leaning forward and flashing one of Johnny's familiar grins. "Shoot me. I'll just use another body...like maybe yours?" Pure madness glared out of Johnny's eyes.

Faith's hand trembled, but only for a moment. She felt invaded, violated by this person who knew her heart and mind all too clearly. She wished she knew more about Delta. She had to buy time, to find answers to this tangled web of their lives.

"Why? Can I at least know why?"

"Ah...you really don't know, do you? Didn't Rafe tell you?" Delta looked down at Cord and shook her head in mock disgust.

Faith dreaded hearing what Delta had to say next. "No. What should he have told me?" Did Cord know what Delta was talking about? If so, why had he kept that from her? If she asked him now, she'd alert Delta that he wasn't actually unconscious.

"She killed Timmy." Cord's whispered words filled the room. She sensed the pain in them, felt shock and hurt at hearing them. Eyes open now, he met her tearful gaze.

"You knew?" Faith's voice trembled, but the gun held steady.

He nodded. Struggling, Cord rolled and grimaced as he tried to move. Delta approached him. Faith moved quickly to stand between them.

"Stay away from him!" she screamed.

"He lied to you," Delta taunted.

For a long minute, Faith stood staring at Johnny's face. Tears streamed down her cheeks. "How could anyone do such a horrid thing to a child?" Her grip on the gun tightened as she fought her pain. Fought against the overpowering grief. Timmy was beyond saving now, she knew that, but Cord still had a chance. She'd grieve for the little boy later.

Delta stood glaring at her. "You should have taken better care of him."

Faith's stomach lurched with nausea and pain. To blame Maria for Timmy's death was cruel, and it hurt Faith clear to her soul.

"Rafe should have been a better husband." Delta's grin grew.

Like a warped puzzle, Delta's taunts began to make sense. No, it wasn't possible... "What if..." Faith turned the gun in her hand and aimed it at Cord. "You're right, Delta. He should have been a better husband. Should I kill him?"

Delta could barely contain her excitement. "Yes. He deserves to die, doesn't he?"

Suddenly, Faith didn't care what or who she'd been in the past. She *did* care about the man across the room and the memories they hadn't yet had the chance to make.

Like the images on the pictures, the dreams and memories would blossom to life when touched by love. She wanted to see those pictures. She had to win here.

"I...I don't know." Faith slowly lowered her arm.

"No!" Delta screamed. "You...you have to."

"Why?"

"He deserves to die for all he put you through."

Faith chose her next words carefully, playing along with Delta's warped scheme. She knew Delta didn't care about her or Cord. She had to find out what Delta really wanted. She forced her expression to remain calm.

"I see what you mean. He's lied to me. You told me that." Faith strolled over to stand nearer Delta. "You don't know Faith very well. I grew up in this life as the daughter of a minister." Faith hoped she looked more at ease and casual than she felt. "I'd gladly sacrifice this life's happiness to save his eternal soul," Faith said.

Delta rubbed her hands together in anticipation. The gun wavered but never left her hand.

"What happens when I kill him?" Faith forced the disgusting words past her lips.

"He's mine."

So that was what Delta wanted. Faith stared at Delta, pretending to ponder her words. "No, I don't think so." She didn't dwell on the ramifications of her actions. Maria had survived. She would, too. Her arm suddenly felt strong and steady. The roar of the gun echoed through the room and rang in her ears. She stumbled as if she'd been kicked.

Johnny flew backwards, his cry of pain breaking the night as the bullet slammed into his chest. Wide, incredulous eyes stared at Faith. Johnny crumpled to his knees.

"How dare you!" a strange voice that was a mixture of Johnny's and a soft feminine tone wailed. The antique gun lay at Johnny's feet. A metallic ping filled the silence. Rafe's wedding band spun and winked in the light.

Faith dove for the gun. When Johnny's big, beefy hand reached out for the ring, Cord lifted the table leg again and slammed it across Johnny's hand. His yelp of pain filled her ears.

After closing her fingers around the gun, Faith scooped up the ring and scooted back across the floor toward Cord.

"No!" Delta's spirit lost control over Johnny. A wisp of golden smoke rose above him. His body sagged, and he slumped to the floor. The golden light stayed above him, shimmering and turning. Faith's eyes never left the apparition. She recognized the image of the young girl she'd seen in the mirror, the woman in the newspaper photo. The woman who had killed Timmy and tried to kill Cord.

"You bitch!" Delta's voice echoed everywhere at once. Soul-deep anger filled the spirit's eyes, eyes growing darker as the seconds passed. "Prepare to die."

Delta's golden form moved and blinding pain shot through Faith's head. What was happening? She tried to think, but couldn't. Her thoughts scrambled. Darkness overtook her.

The gun and ring dropped to the floor with a clatter. Cord saw the fear and pain fade from Faith's eyes. Something else took its place—something cold, and he shivered.

"Oh, it feels so good to have a woman's curves again." In that instant, he knew Delta peered at him through Faith's beautiful eyes. She ran her hands up and down the sides of Faith's body, a soft moan in her throat.

"It feels so good to be alive. I can feel the blood rushing inside me again."

She picked up the gun and the barrel grazed the edge of Faith's breast. He swallowed hard, fearful for Faith.

Delta sauntered towards him, and he resisted the urge to move away. If he could get close enough perhaps he could get the gun from her and save them all.

"Not so eager, lover boy?" She ran her finger down his chest. He fought the urge to pull away.

"Go to hell, Delta." He purposefully used her name, wanting Faith to know, if she could, that he didn't mean her. That he knew the difference.

Each word, each touch, filtered through to Faith. Fog encased her, holding her captive, but she knew she had to fight, had to struggle, or Cord would soon die.

"Delta, release me!" she cried inside her own mind.

"Shut up, bitch." Delta spoke aloud.

"Faith," Cord called. She heard him. He sounded so far away. She knew he had to be close though. "Faith, come back to me."

"I'm trying," she said, knowing he couldn't hear her. She was trapped inside her own thoughts. No one could hear her except Delta.

Faith conjured the image of her father in the pulpit—his sermons and teachings ran through her mind. He could fire and brimstone with the best of them, surely some of it had rubbed off on her. She began to pray. To Maria. To Rafe. To Timmy. To anyone who might hear her, anyone who could help.

She tried to see Cord through the fog of her own eyes. She loved him. Not as Maria loving Rafe. No, this love was hers and hers alone. For the gentle way he'd touched her cuts. For the care and friendship he gave Johnny. For his attempts to protect her—even at the risk to himself. But mostly for the way he loved her with his body and his heart. He might not know it, but he did love her.

In that instant, Maria found Faith, binding her to Rafe through Cord. Thoughts and memories joined. Love and hate collided. Past and present fused. The depth and pain of Maria's grief swamped Faith and her knees buckled. The hard floor caught her as tears pooled in her eyes and spilled over.

Letting go, Delta left behind Maria's memories of the past and all its pain.

"Go ahead." Delta lifted up above Faith, her form dancing in the air. "Kill him, just like you killed me."

"She didn't kill you, Rafe did," Cord growled.

Delta laughed. "Tell him, Maria."

Cord turned to Faith and saw the anguish in her tear-drowned eyes.

"The day the sheriff came to the house...I knew he was there to arrest me." Faith closed her eyes, nearly crumpling with the pain.

"No."

She nodded, the memories clear and painful, too true to deny. "I killed Delta."

"No...I...Rafe shot her and then himself..."

Her tears fell harder as she shook her head. "To protect me. Oh, God." Faith doubled over, her arms hugging her waist as the pain in her grew. A pain Maria had lived with for too many long, lonely years. "You took the blame for me. I went to town to try to find Timmy. I got a job at the house."

"You worked in the brothel." They both knew that from the dreams.

"And I learned the truth. You saw me kill her. The agony I saw in your eyes..."

"You hate her now, don't you, Rafe?" Delta interrupted, barely containing her glee. "Enough to kill her." The antique gun skittered across the floor as if kicked. It clattered against the wood and spun before stopping just beyond his reach.

Silence like that of a tomb hung in the air. The storm had ceased and nothing stirred. The gun was useless against Delta so he left it where it lay. The pain in Faith's eyes tore at his heart. He ached to hold her, to make everything right again.

"No, I don't hate her." He lifted up and glared at Delta's apparition with what strength he had left. "I gave my life for her once. I'll do it again." And Cord knew he would.

Twenty

Waves of pain shot through Cord's entire body—physical pain warred with emotional pain within him. He had to get to Faith. His heart hurt too much watching her like this. She curled into herself on the floor, letting the misery swamp her.

Struggling, he dragged his battered body across the floor. Finally, he touched her shoulder, and she pulled away. Red-rimmed, tear-filled eyes turned on him. "No. Go away." Her anguish poured from her and through his soul.

"Don't let her win." He spoke softly and slowly. He had to make her understand.

"I killed her."

"And she killed Timmy." The horror that grew on her face told him that wasn't the right answer. "Maria killed her, not you. A hundred years ago. Before you were born."

His words finally seemed to soak in, and her eyes cleared. She sat up straighter, meeting his gaze.

"No!" Delta's voice echoed around them. Cord reached out and pulled Faith close. Delta's cry grew louder.

Somehow, the wind came into the room, ripping through in a black cloud filled with ash and soot. On its tail a flicker of flame snaked across the floor, kissing the back wall, which erupted in a ball of flame. The wind pulled at his arms, and he strained to keep his hold on her.

"Cord," Faith cried, her voice barely breaking through the roar.

Images slammed into Cord's mind, as vivid as if they were real. Another fire had torn them apart once before. That fire had leveled most of Cripple Creek. The fear that had gnawed at him then as he'd searched for her in the streets came alive inside him. He'd failed Maria then, but he wouldn't do it again. "Hold tight, honey." He gripped her tighter.

"I'm trying." The wind pulled harder, and the laughter grew.

He felt her slipping away. "No."

"I love you, Cord!" she screamed, her voice cutting through the storm like a knife. The wind fell. The flames died, and ashes fluttered around them like confetti.

"I love you, too, Faith." Before either of them could say anything more, he pulled her close, kissing her with every ounce of his strength, with every piece of his heart.

"You can't." A voice behind them whispered. Faith turned to look at Delta's fading image.

"Yes, we can and I do." Faith pulled from Cord's embrace and stood. "You know nothing of love." She stepped closer to the apparition. "Maybe if you did, Timmy Cumberland could have lived and Timmy Gibson could have had a mother's love."

"I wanted my baby. I...I loved him." Desperation rasped through Delta's voice. "He was mine, but they took him away. They kept calling him my mistake." Could a ghost cry? Or was the darkness around her so deep that there were no tears to cry?

Faith ignored the pain in her own heart. She couldn't risk Cord, Johnny or her life by letting the past hurt them anymore. She had to lay that past to rest.

"Why didn't you fight for him, then?"

"I did, but no one wanted to listen to a girl like me. Then you came to town that day. Only out-of-towners would have shopped those hours. Everyone else knew that was when we girls on the line did. But there you were, with my little boy clinging to your hand. He was so pretty."

A chill filled the room, and Faith shivered. She swallowed and waited for Delta to go on.

"You just had to flaunt him in front of me, didn't you?" Delta finally said. "He was mine. I hated you when he called you Mama. It felt so good to take him and hold him." Was that a sob in her voice?

Once she started talking, Delta couldn't seem to stop. Faith waited, listening, something she'd seen her father do hundreds of times with a troubled parishioner.

"Where did you take him?" Faith prompted.

"A line shack up in the hills. You'd have never found him there."

Delta was probably right. Faith tried, really tried, to understand this woman. She knew what it was like to have parents that didn't approve of your actions, but she'd never experienced that deep a level of distrust.

"He kept crying, and I started to wonder if my parents were right, that I couldn't care for a child." The self-doubt clung heavily in her voice. "I almost believed them, so I went to town to see if I could get help." She paused a long time, staring at Faith in a strange, unseeing way. "While I was gone, he got out of the cabin. I don't know how. I locked that door. I should have nailed it shut, but I didn't have a hammer."

Faith shivered at the thought of a child, of anyone, being nailed into a building.

"It was dark when he got out, but I finally found him. Backcountry is dangerous with all those played out shafts."

This time Faith knew ghosts had plenty of tears. Delta's glistened in the light. "I didn't mean to hurt him. He just wouldn't stop crying. And all he wanted was you."

Somehow, Faith knew that those words had been frozen deep inside Delta for a long time. Too long.

"Mother?"

Another voice—a familiar voice—broke the night. Faith's throat constricted with tears. Tim Gibson had use that voice. It must mean...Her hear ached for Lorena's loss.

"Timmy?" Delta answered.

"Yes, Mother, it's me. I've come to find you. It's time to go."

He sounded so patient and kind in comparison to Delta's sad insanity. "You came? Oh, I always knew you would come back to me."

In the distance thunder rumbled. Delta's voice faded into sobs and eventually those died, too. Lightning flashed through the room. Delta's glistening form evaporated into the darkness. For an instant the heavy scent of roses wafted through the room and then vanished as the storm rolled away.

"Is she gone?" Faith whispered in the unnatural quiet. Cord reached out and touched her arm. She knelt down and looked around the room. Johnny lay in the corner, silent. Delta was nowhere to be found.

"I don't know." Cord wasn't betting on anything right now. "Lord, I hope so."

Faith hurried over to Johnny. "He's still alive." The blood on his chest wasn't as bad as she'd thought before. His breathing was even and deep. Suddenly, his eyes fluttered open and Faith jumped back.

"Delta?" she asked hesitantly.

"Who?" Johnny tried to sit up, then collapsed as the pain seized him. "What the hell happened? The chandelier?"

Faith looked up. The crystal and brass light hung over their heads, covered in soot.

"Welcome back." Cord smiled at his friend, thankful to see the familiarity in his eyes. "We need to get the doc."

"I'm so sorry, Johnny." Tears filled Faith's eyes, and a thick lump caught in her throat.

"You didn't have any choice," Cord assured her. "Can you get to the clinic?"

"Yeah." Together they wrapped Johnny's wound the best they could. She hurried to the door, then turned around and gave Cord another short kiss.

"Do I get one, too?" Johnny whispered, and Faith's guilt lifted a little. She pecked his cheek before running out into the cold night.

***

Doc James couldn't remember a longer day. Or week. Between car accidents, unseasonable colds, and falls in the mud, he'd been busy patching up the residents and visitors of Cripple Creek since dawn. Now another deluge of rain kept him from making his way home.

The receptionist had left over an hour ago, when the rush had finally let up. He sat down in her vacant chair, staring out at the storm, hoping it would soon stop. He was heartily sick of these storms. His old joints ached more with each drop.

Next to his elbow the phone rang. He almost didn't answer it. He was tired and didn't want to do anything more than slip into a nice long nap. His instincts wouldn't let him ignore it, and he picked up the receiver.

"Clinic. Doc here."

"Doctor," a soft voice spoke through the phone.

He had to strain to hear the words barely whispered over the line. Several words were lost to him.

"...Double Barrel...help quick...gunshots...now." The line went dead in his hand. Gunshots? Reaching for the black bag he kept under the counter, he stood, cursing the aching in his knees slowing him up. Grabbing his coat off the rack, he slipped it on and stepped out into the rushing dampness.

He was halfway to the burned casino when a figure barreled into him. He nearly stumbled, but he caught the thin shoulders of the woman, and together they got their footing. It was the young woman he'd seen a while back when he'd stitched some cuts.

"Doctor," she yelled over the storm. "I was just on my way to get you."

"There's trouble at the Double Barrel. Sorry I can't help you right now."

"That's what I need you for." Relief washed through Faith.

She didn't take the time to figure out how he knew, she just thanked heaven he did. "Come on." Together they made their way through the soggy streets back to the casino.

"Check Johnny first," Cord instructed through his pain as the doctor followed Faith into the room. "I'm not losing blood." The old man moved to where Johnny lay.

Faith knelt beside Cord once again. He leaned against the wall beside Johnny, the effort of helping her and his friend evident in the tightness of his jaw and the pallor of his skin.

"You okay, honey?" Cord reached out to caress her face as she took his hand in hers.

Beads of sweat stood out on his forehead, and the bruises had already turned the majority of one side of his face a dull purple. His lip was split and dried blood clung to his chin. She reached out with the hem of her shirt and carefully wiped the stain away.

"I'll recover." As if the strength keeping her going vanished, a tear slipped over her cheek. "I was so scared."

"You were wonderful," Cord said.

She wanted to put her arms around him and blot out the horrible memories that would haunt them both for a long time.

"Well, now, boys, what have you been up to?" Doc's voice penetrated the intimate little circle Cord and Faith had created.

The doctor carefully cleaned Johnny's wound. Faith saw the pain in her friend's eyes and moved to sit closer to him. She knew the doctor was required to report all gunshot wounds to the sheriff. This wouldn't be easily dismissed. Cord could lose everything. She had to explain.

"Do you remember how we talked the night you stitched my cuts. About the Cumberland's?"

"Yes." The doctor pulled tools from his medical bag, glancing up at her for only an instant.

"Remember how you thought I resembled Maria?"

"Did I say that? I know I thought it."

"Did you ever think Cord might look like Rafe?"

The doctor paused then and gazed at Cord's battered face.

"When he's not so abused." She tried to smile, hoping to appeal to the old man's heart, not to his analytical mind.

"Just thought those were the imaginings of an old man," he mumbled more to himself than the others in the room.

"They aren't. I was Maria—in a former life. He was Rafe."

The doctor rubbed his chin, pondering her words. Faith held

her breath, hoping against all common sense that he believed her.

"And I suppose next you'll be tellin' me this is little Timmy?" Disbelief filled his voice.

"Hell, Doc," Johnny forced a laugh. "Even when I was a kid no one called me little."

The doctor continued his work, not saying anything more. Faith didn't know what else to say.

"What's this?" The old man pulled a dark hunk of something into the light. Blood flowed from the wound, and Faith helped the doctor staunch the flow.

"Oh, hell." Johnny grimaced. "An old man came in this afternoon." His eyes fluttered shut. "Said he forgot to give it to you earlier."

"Whatever it was, it saved his life. See? The bullet's stuck in it." Doc tossed it aside, more concerned with his patient now that the bullet was out.

Faith stared at the lump. Black stone. White flecks. A sliver frame. The brooch. She swallowed. It had saved Johnny from death and her from murder charges. She looked at Cord.

She'd never really understood what it meant when someone had their heart in their eyes until now. She scooted over to him, and he wrapped her in his arms.

"I love you, Faith."

She lifted her head, staring into those much-loved eyes. "Oh, Cord." Tears formed again. "I love you, too. I was too afraid to hope...for a future. We've only known each other a short time."

"No." His gaze sought and found hers. "We've known each other forever."

Cord startled her by running his finger down the side of her cheek where a tear left its track. He pulled his finger away and they both stared at the thin layer of soot covering it.

"I could have lost you forever," he whispered. "Marry me."

Several long, silent minutes passed as the world seemed to hold its breath. "Oh, Cord. Yes." Faith wanted to launch herself into his arms, but she hesitated, afraid of hurting him. He slipped his hand beneath her chin and pulled her face close. All of his love poured through in his kiss.

From out of the darkness where Delta had disappeared, another light seeped from the shadows. "Cord?" Faith didn't think she had it in her to fight anymore. She moved to his side.

His innate strength bolstered her.

The light grew brighter and closer with each passing second. They watched as it merged into a tiny figure. It didn't take but an instant for Faith to recognize him.

"Timmy?" She stood and went to stand before the form.

"Mama?" His tiny face looked up at her, and she knelt down to meet him eye to eye.

"I...I think so."

"I tried really hard to help you. But she was too strong."

More tears formed in Faith's eyes as Delta's revelation filled her mind. He looked so alone and tiny in that bubble of light. Her arms ached to reach out, to hold him, but she knew that wasn't possible. She'd find nothing to hold. "You did your best. It's easy for good to overshadow evil. We just have to let it." The words of her father's sermon reached out across the years to comfort her.

"Sid said you'd win."

"Sid?"

"My bear." He held out a bear glowing with the same light. Rafe's present to him that fateful night so long ago. A bear infinitely familiar to both she and Cord. "I got him for Christmas, remember?"

"I remember." She smiled at the stuffed animal, and the little boy's sweet face.

"I have to go. I just wanted to tell you and Pa, thank you."

Faith glanced over at Cord, wondering how he liked being referred to as Pa. Pride filled his eyes.

"Thank you for what?" Cord asked.

"For making my wish come true."

"Wish?"

"Yeah." Timmy turned as if hearing something behind him. "I gotta go. Doc?"

"Y...yes?" the old man's voice wavered.

"Buck was awfully glad you picked up that phone. Made him proud. 'Bye Mama, Pa. I love you." And with that, the bubble shrank, and Timmy's image faded away. The last glimmer flew upwards, bouncing joyously in the air and out through the window.

Faith rushed to watch as the light soared through the night sky like a shooting star. Through a hole in the clouds he found an empty spot in the heavens and filled it with the bright glow of a new star. She stood staring at it until a cloud slipped by, blocking her view.

"Doc?" Johnny called to the doctor who still sat where he was, staring. "Who's Buck?"

He was silent for a long minute, and they all wondered if he'd heard the questions. Tears of joy trickled from the old man's eyes. "My father."

"Faith?" Cord called her back to him.

"I'm dreaming again, aren't I?" Faith wiped her cheeks and watched him shake his head.

"Look over there." He extended his hand toward the spot where Timmy's image had been. A small, furry lump lay on the wooden floor.

"Sid." She scooped up the worn bear and pulled it tight against her heart.

Epilogue

"Come on, honey. Focus. You can do it," Cord's soothing voice spoke near her ear.

Faith turned to look at the stuffed bear—Timmy's bear—that they had chosen as their focal point during the Lamaze classes. She tried to focus, but the pains were coming closer together, and each was more intense than the one before.

"This is all your fault, Cord Burke," Faith growled after the contraction subsided.

"Guilty as charged." His smile spread as he looked at his wife, who was in the last stages of labor. It had been a long night, and as the hours passed, her temper had flared. "It'll be over soon, don't worry."

"And you're never touching me again, do you hear?"

"Uh, huh." He didn't believe it for a minute and he knew the sarcasm in his voice told her so. Another contraction saved him from her angry retort. They'd warned him she'd be difficult to deal with. This was definitely a different side of his lovely Faith.

Damp hair clung to her brow. Her skin was sweaty, and a bright flush filled her cheeks. Cord knew he'd never seen her look more beautiful. The death grip she had on his fingers made him realize he'd never loved her more.

"Okay, Mrs. Burke," the doctor said. "We're close. Come on. Push."

"How the hell does he know if I feel like pushing?" Faith grumbled to Cord. Cord shared an amused glance with the doctor.

"You're doing fine, honey," Cord crooned. His own exhaustion threatened his even temper. Just then another contraction gripped her. She bent upwards with Cord's strong arms to help. Several long, painful minutes later the doctor's voice rang out in the room.

"I've got the head. There you go. Push one more time."

With the next contraction the tiny body slipped into the doctor's arms.

"It's a boy."

Over the surgical mask he wore, Faith saw Cord's smile in his eyes. She felt her own smile, and the warm love blossoming in her heart for the tiny baby the doctor lifted to her waiting arms.

He was perfect. The doctor didn't spank the little guy to get his lungs breathing. He actually looked happy to be out in the world.

As the tiny body lay across her chest, Cord counted his fingers and toes while Faith looked into the little eyes so very much like Cord's, so much like...No, her mind was playing games on her.

"Timmy?" she whispered, looking deep into his eyes. She couldn't believe she heard a giggle come from the baby. She looked over at Cord to see if he'd heard. He was staring at the baby, but there was no recognition in his eyes.

"Cord?" she spoke urgently enough for him to tear his gaze from his son's fingers. "Look into his eyes."

"Hey, little guy." Cord shifted around to see his son's face. "Look up here at your Papa." He met the little blue stare. "Timmy?" Another giggle filled the room.

"You don't think?" He met Faith's tear filled gaze. "No, it's not possible."

"Anything's possible. It's Timmy. It's really Timmy. He's ours again." She pulled the baby close to her breast and cried tears of joy so deep they reached past her mind, past her heart, to her soul, cleansing away all the pain and loss of several lifetimes.

Cord gathered his wife and son close in his arms. Joy filled his heart as her tears dampened his surgical gown. Nothing could come between them again. They'd fought time, battled death and faced damnation—and they'd won.

Lightning Source Inc.
LaVergne, TN USA
14 August 2009

154819LV00001B/132/A